"Playing the role of your intended will help us both, right?"

Corliss's laughter seemed nervous now. "Wouldn't want you stuck with me in that way for longer than necessary."

"It'll be pure torture," Ryder agreed. "You should have given me some warning, though. What kind of fiancé am I that I haven't given you a ring?"

"Well, in your defense, this engagement was kind of sprung on you," Corliss teased as he untangled one of the strings used to tie up their sandwiches and reached for his pocket knife. "What are you doing?" Corliss asked.

"Improvising." Ryder grasped her hand and wound the string around her engagement ring finger, tied off the ends in a knot that mimicked a stone. He tried to ignore how his heart pounded, how his breath caught in his chest at the very idea of putting a ring on this woman's finger.

This was no doubt as close as he'd ever get...so he was sure going to enjoy every second of it.

D0053172

Dear Reader,

Sometimes writing a book is like coming home. The Blackwells are back, this time in Eagle Springs, Wyoming, where Big E's estranged sister, Denny, has been building her own legacy with the Flying Spur Ranch, a renowned facility for training cutting horses, without any help from her big brother. But times have gotten tough for Denny and her grandchildren, two of whom oversee ranch operations. Going against her grandmother isn't on any list for Corliss Blackwell, but with her family's future hanging by a thread, she's out of options. It's time for this family to mend fences.

From the moment us five authors began brainstorming this new collection of stories, I knew Corliss was mine. I could see her, fully formed in my mind. Despite her being a devoted single mother to a teenage son, I knew something was missing from her life: love. What better hero to fill that void than her childhood best friend, Ryder Talbot, a now-single father who is still recovering from a devastating event that's led him home to Eagle Springs? Ryder's loved Corliss all his life, so he's ready to take a chance. Convincing Corliss to do the same could be the biggest challenge Ryder's faced yet.

Welcome to Eagle Springs and the Flying Spur!

Anna J.

HEARTWARMING

Wyoming Promise

—

Anna J. Stewart

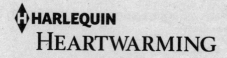

HARLEQUIN
HEARTWARMING

If you purchased this book without a cover you should be aware
that this book is stolen property. It was reported as "unsold and
destroyed" to the publisher, and neither the author nor the
publisher has received any payment for this "stripped book."

HARLEQUIN®
HEARTWARMING™

ISBN-13: 978-1-335-58458-8

Wyoming Promise

Copyright © 2022 by Anna J. Stewart

Recycling programs
for this product may
not exist in your area.

All rights reserved. No part of this book may be used or reproduced in
any manner whatsoever without written permission except in the case of
brief quotations embodied in critical articles and reviews.

This is a work of fiction. Names, characters, places and incidents
are either the product of the author's imagination or are used fictitiously.
Any resemblance to actual persons, living or dead, businesses,
companies, events or locales is entirely coincidental.

For questions and comments about the quality of this book,
please contact us at CustomerService@Harlequin.com.

Harlequin Enterprises ULC
22 Adelaide St. West, 41st Floor
Toronto, Ontario M5H 4E3, Canada
www.Harlequin.com

Printed in U.S.A.

USA TODAY and nationally bestselling author **Anna J. Stewart** writes sweet to spicy romance for Harlequin's Heartwarming and Romantic Suspense lines. When she's not writing, she thrives on watching a certain British baking show, dreaming of her next trip to Disneyland and futilely psychoanalyzing her two cats, Rosie and Sherlock.

Books by Anna J. Stewart

Harlequin Heartwarming

Butterfly Harbor

The Bad Boy of Butterfly Harbor
Recipe for Redemption
A Dad for Charlie
Always the Hero
Holiday Kisses
Safe in His Arms
The Firefighter's Thanksgiving Wish
A Match Made Perfect
Bride on the Run
Building a Surprise Family
Worth the Risk

Visit the Author Profile page
at Harlequin.com for more titles.

As always, to my Blackwell sisters: Melinda, Cari, Amy and Carol.

And to our readers.

You're why we do this.

PROLOGUE

Fourth of July

"HEY, GRAN." CORLISS BLACKWELL dropped out of her beat-up red truck and circled around to help eighty-year-old Denny Blackwell out of the hospital wheelchair. "Happy Independence Day."

"In more ways than one," Denny announced as she motioned for Corliss to open the rusted passenger door. "Told the doctor to release me today or I'd make a break for it by sundown." Denny touched gentle, trembling fingers to Corliss's hand as she sat and pivoted into the seat.

Her gran's long silver braid that once upon a time had been the color of sable hung long over one shoulder. Tanned, weathered skin stretched over her lightly lined face, but the spark of light—the light that had kept the home fires of the Flying Spur Ranch of Eagle

Springs, Wyoming, burning for more than sixty years—was newly restoked. "Not even a bout of kidney disease is going to stop me celebrating the holiday with my kin. That's what I told them, isn't it, Raymond?"

"Yes, ma'am, Miss Denny, you did." The elderly orderly who had aided Denny's approved "escape" winked at Corliss. "To everyone within hearing distance. Miss Blackwell?" Ray handed over the travel bag Corliss had delivered to the hospital shortly after Denny's admission. "All your grandmother's medications and discharge instructions are in here along with the doctors' contact information. If you have any questions, just let us know."

"Thanks so much, Ray."

"Miss Denny?" Ray leaned over and gave Denny a wave. "You take care now, you hear? Drive safe," he added to Corliss before he wheeled the empty chair back inside.

"We're wasting daylight!" Denny called as she reached out to pull the door closed.

Corliss signaled to the truck pulling in behind her and, after tossing Denny's bag behind the driver's seat, quickly jumped behind the wheel to make room in the patient-pickup roundabout of the Wyoming Medical Center. The Center was one of the smaller hospitals in the state and more than thirty miles outside Eagle Springs. It had been a drive to get here. But the drive was worth it for the closest facility capable of treating Denny's chronic kidney condition. "How do you feel?"

"Fine. And I'm gonna tell you what I told those doctors," Denny said with obvious exaggerated patience. "I'll be less fine if I have to keep answering that question. I'm right as rain and plan to stay that way for a good long time. Understand?"

"Yes, ma'am." Corliss echoed the orderly's tone even as she tamped down on the worry that had locked around her chest ten days ago when she'd found Denny passed out on the bathroom floor. Worry she'd thankfully been able to share with her sister and two of her three brothers. Partially, at least. Denny's worsening health came on top of a devastating year for their business and town. But with Denny coming home, things looked promising once more. "Understood."

"Glad to hear it," Denny said with a firm nod. "Make sure you pass that information along to the rest of the family. I don't want any fretting and fussing."

Fat chance of that. Blackwells always took care of their own. It was just the way things were. Even when it came to stubborn, independent, elderly female Blackwells. But Corliss played along, nodded and said, "Understood."

"Hope that boy of yours has the barbecue stoked," Denny went on as she watched the open sky of Wyoming guide them home. "I've got me a mean appetite after all that hospital food."

"Mason put the brisket in the smoker last night," Corliss confirmed. Just the thought of her thirteen-year-old son brought a smile to her face. She might have struck out big-time in the relationship department, but she'd been gifted with an amazing kid. "I don't think Nash appreciated being ejected from the meat-and-fire process, so he dragged out the charcoal grill for ribs and steaks. Wouldn't be surprised if he turned tonight's dinner into a grilling competition."

Denny chuckled. "Your big brother's always had his way of doing things. Thankfully, he's magic with horses, otherwise he'd have driven both of us around the bend by now."

Corliss cleared her throat. "Speaking of horses—"

"Mason's fixing a batch of his baked beans, isn't he?" Denny asked. "And corn bread. Can't have a barbecue without corn bread. No sir, not on Blackwell property. And it best have jalapeños. Corn bread ain't corn bread without jalapeños."

Corliss's brows shot up. "You really are hungry." It had to be a good sign considering Denny's appetite had been dwindling for months. Given Denny's upbeat attitude, Corliss wasn't about to remind her grandmother about her new dietary restrictions: low sodium, high fiber, less meat. Little to no sugar. And no alcohol.

Corliss cringed. That last one was going to be fun to enforce. Denny Blackwell loved her evening shot of whiskey with a beer chaser. But they'd get to work on all of it. Starting tomorrow. Tonight? Tonight they were going to celebrate.

"In answer to your question," Corliss said, "yes to all of the above and more. Levi's picking dessert up at the Pie Place in town. Adele's bringing the salad. And the twins."

"Good." Denny's approving nod was firm. "I need some toddler time. Adele still doing that brokering thing?"

"If you mean is Adele still selling vintage antiques and farm equipment to online buyers, yes." Her younger sister had to do something to earn a living after the family auction-and-rodeo business shut down last year, thanks to a devastating blight of strangles. The respiratory infection had swept through their stables and wreaked havoc with both the Flying Spur Ranch and its connected businesses. The long-reaching effects had wrapped a stranglehold around the entire town of Eagle Springs, as Blackwell-sponsored events like the annual rodeo and livestock auctions came to a screeching halt.

The Flying Spur was only now, almost a year later, beginning to recover the business their cutting-horse training facility had lost. The rest was going to take more time.

Time they might not have.

Which was why Adele, a widow with two-year-old twin girls was making the best of things by putting her online skills into action.

While Adele loved the ranch, she was more of a social creature than the other Blackwell siblings. Living in town in the house she'd bought with her late husband gave Corliss's sister the chance to pick up extra jobs to supplement her income. Besides, living on the ranch was impractical for Adele as the only reliable thing about the ranch's internet connection was its constant unreliability.

"You're thinking awfully loud over there. Something on your mind, Little Miss?" Denny tapped a finger against the air vents. "Air conk out on you again?"

"I'm hoping Wyatt can fix it when he gets back to town." Her youngest brother was pretty handy with the mechanical side of things. Corliss stared into the distance, finding comfort in the deep violet and fire yellow streaking across the sky. She sighed. There was nothing like a Wyoming sunset.

"Don't go loading up your baby brother before he's even here," Denny warned.

"Wyatt might be *the* baby, but he's not *a* baby," Corliss reminded her grandmother.

"He's got jumpy feet," Denny said. "Doesn't like to be tied down to any one place."

"I am aware," Corliss said slowly. "But

he's twenty-seven. That's old enough to take on some of the family responsibility." The baby Blackwell had been flitting from ranch to ranch, hiring out his cowboy services long enough. Before the blight, she could let it slide; they'd had plenty of ranch hands on staff for Wyatt to sow whatever oats he wanted. Having to let all of their own help go had been devastating, but as they'd been left with very few horses and animals to care for, Nash, Corliss and their brother Levi, a rodeo rider, figured they'd be able to cover.

Then Levi had injured his back, which left him with physical limitations coupled with a massive reevaluation of his future. At least, as far as work was concerned. Since his divorce, Levi, who shared custody of his ten-year-old daughter, Isla, lived on the opposite side of town in the two-story money pit of a home he'd built for his family. With Levi down and no income for the ranch to hire a replacement, cornered Corliss called Wyatt to ask him to come home. It would be the opportunity she needed to also fill him in on the new bank-loan developments.

They needed his help, and not just with the ranch. It had taken some coaxing, but Wyatt was on his way back to the Flying Spur, and chances were, he'd be bringing a defiant attitude along with him. A concern for later, Corliss supposed.

"Gran, I need to talk to you about something."

"Thought as much." Denny sat back and sighed. "Always could tell when you were worrying. You and your daddy, you have that in common, you know."

"That's about all we have in common," Corliss muttered.

"Don't you go disrespecting your father, Little Miss," Denny said with more sadness than anger. "He wasn't meant for the ranch like I was." She turned her head and surprised Corliss by touching a gentle finger to Corliss's cheek. "Like you are. He stayed a lot longer than I had any right to expect. Him and your mama. He gave this town a caring doctor for a good long while."

"And now Dr. and Mrs. Hudson Blackwell are living in sunny Arizona off the money you gave them." It still irritated her that her parents literally took the cash and ran. She'd floated the idea of asking her parents to give the money back to help pay off some of their debt, but her in-town siblings had overruled her.

"It wasn't a *give*," Denny said. "I bought your dad out of his inheritance. Him and your uncle both. They've relinquished their claim on the Flying Spur. I don't hold it against them. I can't." Her matter-of-fact tone couldn't hide the sadness in her voice. "You don't stay where you don't belong, and neither of my boys ever felt as if this was home."

Corliss could only imagine how much it must hurt that Denny's only offspring had rejected everything Denny had built.

"If it makes you feel better, the Flying Spur is the only place I belong." Corliss swallowed the lump in her throat. Softening the blow, that's what she was doing. "I had a meeting at the bank last week, Gran." Better to dive in before she lost her nerve. "I went in to apply for another loan."

"Another loan? What happened to the—"

"Hospital bills, mainly." Some things she couldn't keep secret. Gran still looked over the books; she'd know exactly where each penny went soon enough. Best to prepare her for the financial reality now. "Then there were the settlements with clients over the horses we lost in the blight. The deductibles we had to pay on our insurance policy, a policy that's now nearly doubled. I figured that since the ranch is in the clear with the health department and we have clients back on the books—"

"We do? Since when?"

"Oh. Right. Surprise!" Corliss cleared her throat. "That was supposed to be a welcome-home announcement for you tonight at dinner." She flashed her grandmother a smile. "We have two clients willing to take another chance on us. Horses should arrive within a few weeks. We had to offer a severely discounted rate for the boarding and training, but Nash is over-the-moon excited to get back to work. Anyway, I figured we had some new collateral to apply for an additional loan to get us over the last few humps."

"I take it the bank turned you down." Denny's temper caught like a lit match. "I should go down and have a talk with that branch manager. I was one of the first investors in that bank. There wouldn't be a bank without my money."

"Something I did remind him of," Corliss admitted. "To make a long story short..."

Her pulse kicked up several beats. Better to just rip the bandage off the wound, right? "They didn't just turn us down for a new loan. They've also called in the others, supposedly on the say so of a new investor. All one hundred thousand dollars. We have until the end of December to pay it." Her hands tightened around the steering wheel as she braced for her grandmother's reaction.

"Supposedly...*on the say so*?"

"That's the rumor. Around the bank and around town."

"I see."

Corliss frowned. She'd expected anger. Prepared herself for it. She'd definitely expected a few choice descriptions for Brock Bedford, the current manager of Eagle Springs Treasury. Denny's subtle, subdued reaction definitely set warning bells clanging in Corliss's overwrought brain.

"We'll figure it out, right?" Once Corliss got over the initial hurdle of admission, the rest came out in a flood. "I've got some ideas, and Nash and I have been talking about investing in new cutting horses to train. Ones we can sell for a significant profit. We're going to... Well, we'll need a little investment cash, of course, but it'll work out. We'll be fine."

"Of course we will," Denny said as if it were a given. "We're Blackwells. We've had tougher times than this."

Corliss wasn't so sure. The bank was literally pounding on the ranch house door. It was only a matter of time before they nailed an eviction notice to the porch post. Corliss didn't want to lose her home, let alone the only way of life she'd ever known. The only life she wanted. The ranch had been destined to be hers from her very first breath.

But the desperation inside of her went far deeper than that.

Property, house and income aside, she wasn't going to let Denny lose what it had taken her six decades to build. And she had built it. By herself.

Post by post. Nail by nail. Horse by horse.

"We'll find an answer somehow," Denny said as if chanting a mantra. "We'll find an answer."

"I've been thinking…" Corliss slowed as they drove through downtown Eagle Springs. Downtown might have been a misnomer. It consisted of a solitary street of shops, businesses and offices. Side streets led to homes, the grammar-slash-high school and the sheriff's office, which was attached to the fire station. Everything a small town needed, nestled into one compact area. Eagle Springs's biggest attraction was the Cranky Crow, a family-friendly bar and grill that offered various games and options for entertainment. All in all, Eagle Springs was a blink-and-miss-it kind of place, and it didn't take long for Corliss to reach the other end of town and veer off toward the Flying Spur.

"You were thinking what?" Denny asked when Corliss didn't continue.

"I've been thinking about family. How important it's been to us. To you." The words were there, right on the tip of her tongue, but they didn't seem to want to emerge. At least, not without some effort. "I've been thinking about your brother. Elias," she added as if Denny had any other sibling. "I've been thinking Elias Blackwell could help."

"Stop the truck."

Even at thirty-two years of age, Corliss knew when to obey her grandmother's commands. Especially when uttered in *that* tone.

She pulled off to the side of the road and

slipped the truck into Park. She didn't dare turn the engine off for fear she might not get it started again. They sat there, in silence, while the engine idled and the sun settled into its fiery bed for the night. "They'll be wondering where we are, Gran."

"They aren't going anywhere." Denny took a deep breath and let it out in slow, loud increments. "I'm going to say this once and only once, Corliss. Because it will not bear repeating. And I want you not only to listen but to hear me." She shifted in her seat and waited for Corliss to meet her determined gaze. "For sixty years, I've gotten along just fine without any assistance from my big brother. He made it clear when I was nineteen years old that what I wanted out of this life was no matter to him. He and my parents, they turned their backs on me and wrote me off when I fell in love with your Grandpa Cal. They disowned me when I left with him. I vowed then and there I would never go back to Falcon Creek. And after Cal died, I started over here in Eagle Springs. I used the little money we had left and I bought this place. I built that house on my own. I started that ranch on my own. And I did so pregnant with twins I birthed on my own."

"I thought Miss Odette—" Corliss held up a hand at Denny's glare. "Sorry. You were going for dramatic effect. My bad."

"There will be no going to Elias Blackwell, do you hear me, Corliss?" It wasn't anger she saw in her grandmother's eyes, or even defiance. It was pain.

Plain, simple, heartbreaking pain.

But it was pain Corliss couldn't allow to sway her.

"Gran, I'm sorry, but I don't think I have a choice. Adele and Levi, they're already each working on raising a portion of the loan payment, but me and Nash? We don't have anything to barter or bargain with. I can go to Elias myself, on my own, ask for a loan. We still have Skyfire. I can offer him as collateral. With his pedigree and promise, it's a no-lose offer. And then I can use the money to buy enough cutting horses for Nash to train and sell for our portion. Gran, I'm telling you, it's the only way. If there was another, I'd have found it by now." She took a long breath. "No other bank will do business with us. We've gone to Billings and Cody and had every door slammed in our faces. No one will invest in the ranch. In us. And we're fast running out of collateral. We are officially out of options."

"I forbid it." Denny's voice trembled. "I forbid you to go to my brother."

Tears burned Corliss's throat and blurred her vision. She twisted her fingers together as the tears dropped onto her cheeks. "I love you, Gran. I've always done what you've asked, what you've demanded of me, even when I thought you were wrong." She shook her head, wishing there was another path to take. "But I can't do that now. I'm going to go. Because I won't let us lose what you've spent your entire life building."

"I'd rather lose the Flying Spur than go crawling back and begging to my brother." The detached chill in Denny's tone made Corliss shiver. But she couldn't back down.

She was Corliss Blackwell. Firstborn granddaughter of Denny Blackwell. Manager and primary operator of the Flying Spur Cutting Horse Training Ranch. She'd survived being ditched on her wedding day, single motherhood and thriving in a traditionally male-dominated business. Corliss Blackwell did not give up.

Even if it meant defying the person she admired most.

"Then I guess we've finally discovered the difference between us. I'm not willing to watch it disappear without a fight, Gran." Corliss put the car into Drive and gently pressed her foot on the gas. "It's going to take all the ammunition we've got to keep our home, and the only bullet I've got left is Elias Blackwell."

"He'll disappoint you," Denny warned and crossed her arms, defiant. "It's what he does best. Especially when it comes to his family. He'll send you packing the second you step foot on his land."

"Then I go forewarned." But she was going.

Once she and Nash got their two new clients' horses settled and a routine established, she was going to Falcon Creek, Montana.

With or without her grandmother's blessing.

CHAPTER ONE

August

RYDER TALBOT WAS officially home.

Not just for a visit, but to stay.

After ten tumultuous, life-changing years, he took the highway turnoff to Eagle Springs, Wyoming, and as he crossed into the city limits, felt his lungs expand as if breathing for the first time.

Home was a word he'd learned not to take for granted. How could he, after spending most of the past decade bouncing around the world as an oil rig firefighter? Granted, he'd set down some roots in Florida, gotten married, had a daughter, but those roots had always felt fragile. Temporary. But his heart? His soul? They were tied to this town—to the Flying Spur—in knots tight enough to trap a wild stallion.

Sure, he'd traveled all over the place, but

he'd never found somewhere that rivaled Wyoming, with its natural symphony of colorful landscapes and seasonal change. One could drive past wide, rolling, grassy hills one minute and find themselves in a dry, sage-brush accented prairie the next. Rock formations exploded out of the ground as if searching out the sun, but all of it—every single inch of this land felt like a huge welcoming hug. Now he was minutes away from another hug or two, from the people he called family.

Speaking of family, Ryder tapped the button on his steering wheel and connected to the incoming call from his eight-year-old daughter. "Hey, Sprout. How was swim camp today?"

"Oh my gosh, Dad, it was so awesome!" Olivia's voice was the perfect accompaniment to his drive. "This older boy was bugging Clara, like big-time, and I thought she was going to cry, but you know what happened next?"

"What happened next?"

"She stood up to him and he walked right off the edge of the high dive! Ker-splat. It was epic!"

"I hope the young man got a talking-to

after the fact," Ryder said more to himself than to Olivia.

"Oh, he did. They made him leave and he can't come back for the whole rest of the summer. Which is only a few weeks, but still. Clara's the new pool hero."

"Sounds as if you really like it there." Doubt crept in under his contentment. Since the death of his estranged wife eighteen months ago, Olivia had been living with his in-laws while Ryder served out his contract with Triton Roustabouts. It had been tougher than he'd expected being away from Olivia, especially after Nina died. But they'd found a way to talk most every night, made easier after Ryder sent Olivia her own cell phone. Her text messages had kept a smile on his face while the rest of his life was in shambles. "You're probably going to miss Florida and your friends a lot."

"I guess." He could hear the shrug in her voice. Eagle Springs was a far cry from the wealthy gated community in Florida his in-laws resided in. But just as Ryder anticipated the worst, that Olivia would change her mind and want to stay with her grandparents, she lowered her voice and whispered, "I'm still coming out to live with you, right, Daddy? You said once you got to Eagle Springs—"

"And I just did." Relief crashed through him, erasing the lingering doubts. If she'd truly wanted to stay, he'd bend over backward to make it work. But now he could push those worries aside and know his daughter would be with him again soon. "I'm about ten minutes from the ranch as we speak. This time next week, we'll be fitting you for your very own pair of cowboy boots. What do you think about that?"

"Cow*boy*?" Olivia said in that same disapproving tone her mother had excelled at. "Dad, that just won't do. I'm a girl, remember?"

"Right. Girl. I keep forgetting," he teased. "How about you put your grandpa on the phone now? Let me talk to him about your travel plans."

"Okay. I'll call you tomorrow night before bed so you can tell me everything that's going on with the ranch and Corliss and Miss Denny and all the animals."

"It's a deal." That his daughter had embraced the Blackwells already, remembered the countless stories he'd told her about growing up with Corliss and her siblings, warmed his heart. Those memories had saved his sanity these last ten years. Even more so the last few months. "I love you, Sprout."

"Love you, too, Dad. Grandpa! Dad wants to talk to you!" Olivia's voice echoed over the line, and Ryder kept his eyes on the road ahead, hoping, praying that transitioning Olivia into his care would go smoothly.

"Ryder." Whitlock Standish sounded officious as usual, which made sense, considering the older man had spent more than a decade on the bench of the Florida Supreme Court. "Olivia tells me you got to Eagle Springs in one piece. I take it you're still determined to make a go of things out there."

Ryder sighed. So much for hoping. "I do, sir."

"And what do you plan to do for employment? Not much call for oil rig firefighters around those parts, I'm guessing."

"I'm keeping my options open." After more than a decade of fighting some of the most dangerous fires on earth, Ryder couldn't quite conceive of another profession where he could use his skills and make an actual difference. He'd be lying if he said he'd found anything that was as satisfying to him as fighting fires. Despite what the last one had done to him.

His therapist in the hospital had advised him to continue to work his way through that. It would take time. Time and a lot of honest thought. But some things were just in your blood to stay. "I have an appointment at the school tomorrow morning to get Olivia registered for the new term. Shall I arrange for her flights or would you prefer to do it?"

The silence stretched. "Guess you've got this all planned out, then."

"Yes, sir, I do." He took a steeling breath and tried to tell himself he was just looking for problems.

"Her grandmother and I remain unconvinced this Eagle Springs place is appropriate for Olivia."

"Worked out just fine for me, sir." More silence. "I understand how difficult this will be for you and Vivian. I appreciate everything you've done for both of us since Nina died. But Olivia is my daughter." He kept his voice as calm and kind as possible. "I'm back and I plan to be a full-time father to her. It's time, sir." He hesitated before adding, "It's time for Olivia to come home."

"What about your financial status? Olivia has educational needs that need addressing. She's gifted. She needs to be challenged. Extra tutors, classes—"

Heat rose up Ryder's neck, despite knowing Whitlock was purposely pushing his buttons. "My finances are perfectly fine and the school here is top-notch. I plan on asking for a tutor referral tomorrow at my meeting. I can manage with Olivia even on my own. She will have everything she needs."

"Except a mother."

Considering Ryder had been thousands of miles away when Nina died, regret, grief and guilt crashed over him like black storm clouds tumbling across the sky. His and Nina's marriage had been over long before they'd separated. Olivia was the only thing holding them together. But Ryder choked that back.

Whitlock and Vivian Standish had lost their only daughter—their only child. Had Ryder been in Whitlock's place, he never would have recovered. It made sense his father-in-law needed someone to blame, and Ryder, who had never lived up to Whitlock's standards, was the easy target. It was, perhaps, the only thing he could give Whitlock at this point. "Olivia will have me," Ryder said carefully. "And she'll have the Blackwells. Despite our separation, Nina's will was very clear that should anything happen to her, Olivia would be left in my custody." It had cost him a pretty penny to have a lawyer confirm that with the state court. "There's nothing else to be discussed."

"I found you a steady security job here in Florida," Whitlock said. "If you took that, there'd be no need to move Olivia halfway across the country."

"Florida's not my home. Eagle Springs is." Ryder's hands tightened around the steering wheel as the Flying Spur Ranch came into sight.

Painted a rich blue, with its white trim and wide front porch, the Blackwell house sat like a beacon in the valley. Just the sight of the house, the barn, stables and corrals calmed the emotions swirling inside of him as he drew his conversation with Whitlock to a close. "You and Vivian are welcome to come and visit Olivia any time, and I'm more than happy to send her out your way for a few weeks every summer."

"That's hardly enough."

Ryder chose his words with precision. He needed to keep things civil and respectful. One wrong comment and Ryder could find himself in a custody battle he was half-convinced Whitlock was itching to start. "Fighting about this every time I call isn't going to get us anywhere, sir. I'm more than willing to make her travel arrangements myself, but I'd rather be respectful of yours and Vivian's schedules."

One thing Ryder had learned being married to Nina was how she dealt with her parents, who at times could be overbearing. It was something he and Nina had joked about once upon a time. He'd never imagined he'd have to implement her tactics because she wasn't there.

"All right," Olivia's grandfather finally said. "I'll take care of it."

"Thank you." He couldn't have hidden the relief in his voice if he'd tried. "Have a good evening, sir."

Whitlock hung up without returning the sentiment.

"One step closer," Ryder told himself as he focused on moving forward and pressed his foot down harder on the gas.

He'd expected the Flying Spur to look—and feel—different from his last visit. A lot had changed in four years. They'd repainted the house, redone the roof. A rustic log fence had been erected around a good portion of the outlying property that now had a significant garden exploding with summer color and bounty.

Remodeling aside, one thing that would never change was his friendship with Corliss. The bond they'd forged well before either of them hit puberty was unbreakable.

He knew about Denny's health issues and Nash's growing restlessness with no horses to train. He knew Adele had twin girls and that she'd lost her husband around the same time Ryder's wife had died. Levi had sent him endless photos of the barn-style home he'd built for his own family, and Ryder had even recommended the fire suppression system Levi had installed. At one time, he, Nash and Corliss's son, Mason, even had an ongoing, online, fantasy-world battle quest in play, but that had fallen by the wayside when Ryder didn't have easy access to a gaming system these past few months.

Most importantly, Ryder was aware that

Corliss was doing what she always did: juggling as much as she could in an attempt to keep the family, the ranch and everything in between under control.

Ryder slowed as he approached the main house. The usually boisterous activity was severely curtailed, with nary a hand to be found. He craned his neck one way and then the other for a good look. It was true. They needed help. Not that Corliss had been the one to admit it. He'd gotten that tidbit of information from Nash, and Levi as well. At least, there was one thing he could do to make himself useful, until he figured out what the future held in store for him.

To be honest, though, Ryder was not in peak physical condition at the moment. After more than a month in the hospital, then another six weeks in a burn unit and rehabilitation center, his energy level wasn't near where it should be, but there were fewer places more suited for physical training and recovery than a working ranch.

Dust plumed up from under the tires of his truck as Ryder drove along the path to the house. He pulled to a stop next to Corliss's ancient vehicle. Typical Corliss. She ran everything right into the ground until it had nothing left to give. He imagined the other, larger silver truck belonged to Nash. It felt odd not to see Denny's antique, restored two-seater truck parked next to the porch, but from what he'd heard, she was no longer driving. "I'd have hated to be part of that conversation."

With the engine off, he sat in the quiet, hands clasping the wheel as he stared at the familiar ivory curtains draping the living room window. He took a long, controlled breath. He was here. It seemed ages since he'd made the decision to accept the settlement offered by his company and walk away from the job he'd loved. Ages since he'd started to plan what he would do when he set foot again on the Flying Spur.

It was time to embrace the second chance he'd been given after making it out of that fire and do what he'd spent most of his life too terrified to consider doing.

Eagle Springs had given him a solid foundation for his adolescence.

He wanted the same thing for his daughter. Whatever he had to do to keep Olivia safe and happy, he'd do it. Starting over here, reconnecting with the best friend he'd ever had and her family, was the first block in his new foundation. It was that thought he clung to as he dropped out of the truck.

It took him more than a few minutes to stretch out the kinks, wincing as his body protested after far too many hours behind the wheel. His physical therapist would be beyond irritated he hadn't taken more breaks, but needs must.

He walked around Corliss's truck, his boots crunching in the gravel and dirt as he bypassed the front door and made his way along the side of the house. The second he caught sight of the training paddock, he stopped, a slow smile spreading across his face.

Nash Blackwell eased a young filly around the perimeter, with a gentle hold and even gentler voice. Two dogs—one a spitfire Jack Russell terrier, the other a gorgeous chocolate Lab—jumped to their feet, barking, and raced toward him.

"Hey, guys." Ryder stayed where he was as the dogs circled and yelped and got a good sniff. "You must be Arrow," he said to the little one. "Which makes you Bow." Because the dog demanded it by dropping to the ground and rolling onto her back, Ryder crouched and offered a solid belly scrub. "Well, you don't have any qualms about strangers, do you?" Arrow yipped and plopped his tail-wagging behind on the ground, wide dark eyes pleading for similar treatment.

"Well, well, well. Look what the cat coughed up." Nash's voice carried across the paddock. Ryder nodded as his friend approached the fence. Nash tipped his hat back against the late afternoon sun. "Wasn't expecting you until next week."

"Nowhere else to be," Ryder said by way of explanation. "Hope it's okay. Thought I'd surprise her."

Nash grinned. "Oh, you'll surprise her all right. She's in the stable with our other new arrival. Fair warning. She's in a mood."

"Corliss or the horse?" Ryder abandoned the dogs and walked over to Nash, who greeted him with a hearty handshake.

"Corliss, for sure." Nash slapped his other hand on Ryder's arm. "You look good. Better than I expected. You doing okay?"

"Doing fine." The last topic Ryder wanted to talk about was his injuries. "Don't go worrying over me."

"You sound like Denny. Speaking of worrying, storm warning where Gran's concerned, too." Nash cringed before glancing over his shoulder at the horse, who had nudged her nose against Nash's shoulder. "She's not speaking to Corliss. And no, it's not something that's going to pass anytime soon. Been going on for nearly a month now."

"I take it this has to do with Corliss's secret plan to raise a portion of the funds to pay back the loan? She hasn't filled me in on the details yet," Ryder said quickly. "I think she was waiting to spring them on me."

"No doubt. And yes, it definitely has to do with our plans." Nash inclined his head, reached back to run his hand down the horse's nose. "You're a good girl, aren't you, Fayette?" The horse whinnied softly as if in agreement. "They're trying to wear each other down. Denny responds in one syllables to twist the knife and Corliss does her best to pretend nothing's wrong."

"Sounds about right."

"Where are you staying?" Nash asked.

"Dozey's Boarding House." The local cowboy hotel in town offered short-term tenancy for seasonal ranch workers. "Figured I'd grab a room there until I find something better. I'm betting they have plenty available."

"Bunkhouse here is empty. Take your pick of beds. No need for you to go spending cash you don't have to when we have plenty of room."

"Yeah?" Ryder nodded. "Thanks."

"Heard a rumor in town that Fire Chief Bellingham is thinking about retiring?"

"Really?" Was that excitement pinging in his chest, or dread? "Well, if it becomes more than a rumor—"

"Ryder?" Corliss stood frozen in the doorway of the stables. She swiped a hand across her sweaty brow, tilting her hat up so that he could see her beautiful face break into one of the most incredible smiles Ryder had ever seen. She let out a loud whoop. "Oh my gosh, Ryder, is that you? You're really here?" She ran toward him, launching herself at him, her hat falling to the ground. "You're early!"

The air rushed out of him as she locked her arms around his neck and hung on.

"Hey, Corliss." He rubbed a hand up and down her denim-covered back. "Surprise."

"Best one I've had in a long time."

He heard the hitch in her voice and leaned back, just enough to get another look at her.

Tall, curvy, sturdy, stunning Corliss Blackwell. She was the exact image of how he always thought of her. That smile, the way her golden-brown hair caught the Wyoming breeze, that stance of hers with her thumbs hooked into the front pockets of worn, fitted jeans, one hip kicked out as if a swagger was a mere step away. The sight jolted his heart in an unexpected way.

"I can't believe you're really here. And that you're whole. Safe." Corliss hugged him again, harder this time, giving him the chance to slip his arms around her. "I've missed you, Ryder. So much."

He blinked back unexpected sentiment and rubbed her back. "I've missed you, too." When he moved to stand back, she clung, tightened her hold and let out a sob. The sound brought a flood of memories of one of the only days he ever recalled her crying.

"Hey." He tilted his head and put a gentle hand under her chin. Tears glistened in her eyes. "Hey, Corliss, what's this? You crying over me?"

That his teasing did nothing more than trigger a shuddering breath out of her unnerved him. Were things really that bad?

He glanced at Nash, who offered a simple nod before he moved off with the filly.

Ryder shifted and settled an arm around her waist, drawing her with him toward the back door of the kitchen. "What's going on? Is it Denny? Nash told me she's not happy with you at the moment."

"No, she's not." Corliss sniffled, and just like that, she slipped behind a mask of indifference. "But listen, that's not for now. I don't want to talk about it. Instead, we need to celebrate." She wrinkled her nose. "And I need a shower."

Ryder chuckled. "How about dinner at the Cranky Crow. My treat?"

"Oh wow, that sounds amazing." She sagged as if she'd just been offered an all-expense-paid, tropical vacation. "I haven't been off this ranch in weeks. Getting contracts in place, working with the new horses, one wall of the main stable needed replacing…never mind."

"On the contrary," Ryder assured her. "I want to hear everything. But over dinner. Hurry up and change. I'm starving."

"Okay." Corliss gave him another squeeze before she ran toward the back door, only to skid to a stop as it swung open. "Gran. Look who's back. It's Ryder." Bow and Arrow barked and raced toward the open door.

"I see him." Denny stepped back to let the dogs in but barely spared a glance at Corliss. After a frustrated huff, Corliss slid past her grandmother and disappeared into the house. "Well, don't just stand there, young man. Come on in and let's have a catch up."

"Yes, ma'am." Ryder detoured to pick up Corliss's hat, which he quickly brushed off. His boots landed heavy on the porch steps leading into the mudroom. He could practically hear his and Corliss's laughter from when they'd race in after a busy day hanging out on the ranch or Denny's threats to hose them off along with the dogs if they didn't get themselves cleaned up.

The washer and dryer were new, as was the paint on the walls and the additional hooks by the screen door. There was a small waist-high shower stall for the dogs beside the open pantry just off the kitchen. He hung up Corliss's hat with an amused shake of his head.

Ryder stood in the kitchen doorway as

Denny retrieved a pitcher of what he hoped was lemonade from the refrigerator. The once-dated and simple design of the room had been fixed up with carved cabinetry and pretty, pale yellow walls. They'd restored the scarred hardwood floors but kept the same large kitchen table and chairs that provided more than enough seating for the entire Blackwell clan. "Kitchen looks nice."

"We did some remodeling a couple years back," Denny said as she poured him a glass. "Mason's tweaked it, since he's taken over most of the cooking. Not all of it, mind you. I still lend a hand during the holidays."

"I should hope so," Ryder said. "It wouldn't be Thanksgiving or Christmas without your apple-cranberry stuffing."

Denny set his glass down, but before he took it, she held out her arms and motioned him in. "Ain't a proper welcome home without a hug."

Ryder smiled and stooped a bit to do as she asked, hugging her frail frame gently. "It's good to be home."

"Where're your things?" she asked when she patted his back and released him.

"I've got a duffel in the car." He lifted his

glass. "Most of my stuff's in storage, which I'll ship here once Olivia and I find a place. Nash said I could stay in the bunkhouse."

"Bunkhouse?" Denny's voice was as sharp as a shot. "Shame on both of you. Family doesn't sleep in the bunkhouse. You'll stay in Nash and Levi's old room. It's just collecting dust now that Levi's moved out and Nash has his mobile home out behind the barn."

Her kindness, while not surprising, touched him. "I don't want to be any trouble."

"You never were and you won't ever be." Denny touched a hand to his cheek. "It's settled." As if embarrassed at being caught showing affection, she quickly took a seat at the large table. "You'll stay here for as long as you need to. Now, sit and tell me what's going on with that girl of yours. I want to hear all about Olivia."

CHAPTER TWO

"MASON!" FRESH OUT of the shower, hair dripping down her T-shirt–clad back, Corliss hopped to her bedroom door, trying to pull on boots that didn't want to cooperate against still damp feet. Arrow, shot out of her room and skidded to a comical halt beside Bow, the beleaguered, smart-as-a-whip older dog, who was lying forlorn outside Mason's bedroom door.

The pulsating drumbeat echoed from down the hall and made her wish, not for the first time, she'd been able to afford those noise-cancelling headphones for him for Christmas last year. She grabbed the door frame, balanced and finally stomped her foot securely into the leather.

She reached Mason's room in a few long strides, knocked as loud as she could and pushed the door open.

"Hey, Mom. Hey!" Mason dropped his tablet computer onto his chest and glared up at her from his double bed. "Boundaries, remember?" He scooped Arrow toward him and gave him an affectionate scrub behind the ears.

"Volume level, remember?" Corliss tapped a finger to her ear and waited until he turned the music down with his universal remote. "Ryder's here."

"Yeah?" Mason shot up, eyes brightening. "That's great! He can help me figure out how to get to level sixty-seven of Warrior War Games."

"I thought Nash was helping you with that game?"

"Please." Mason rolled his eyes. "Uncle Nash can't get past the hobgoblins guarding Tantaurant Keep."

"Video games are going to have to wait until tomorrow," Corliss told him. "We're going to dinner."

"We are?" Mason asked.

She laughed. "Sorry, champ. Not this time. Ryder and I are going out to dinner. Besides, I bet you've got tonight's meal all planned out. Although, if you want to call the grocery store with an order, I can pick it up on my way home."

Mason's smile dipped. "I thought maybe I could drive into town and get the things myself."

"Nice try. You can't drive any vehicle off ranch land and you know it."

"Stupid law. I've been driving around this place for more than a year already. They should have special dispensations for ranch kids, you know? Fifteen is ages away!"

"Take it up with the town council." It wasn't a change she'd have any issue with. Even at his young age, he was a better driver than most grown adults she knew. But the last thing they could afford right now was a ticket, or worse, an arrest. "Come on downstairs and get your list together."

"Sure." Mason's go-along attitude had pride and a quick pang of longing hitting Corliss dead center of her heart.

Her little boy, the boy with a head of thick, dark curls and equally dark eyes was all grown up. The boy who had been too scared to swim in the lake but not too intimidated to light a barbecue. The boy who loved so hard and so fiercely he put any other person she knew to shame. She'd never not see him as the boy who had won the school science fair *and* shot the winning basket for his junior varsity basketball tournament. Even if he was looking at her now with a wise grin that exposed the dimple in his left cheek.

"So, dinner with Uncle Ryder." That dimple was on full display now as he stepped back and examined her head to toe. "And that's what you're wearing?"

"Yes." She tugged at the hem and looked down at her classic-country-rock T-shirt. "We're just going to the Cranky Crow. Why? What's wrong with it?"

"Nothing." That shrug of his spoke volumes.

"It's just—"

"There's nothing *just* about Ryder, Mom. He's your other."

"*My other*. What does that even mean? Is that some new TikTok thing?"

"You're so embarrassing sometimes," Mason said with a shake of his head. "It just means he's your person. The one who fits."

"Fits where? With what?"

He rolled his eyes. "Everything. He's your constant. Always has been. At least, as long as I've been around. It's okay, you know." He frowned, inclined his head as if trying to read her thoughts. "It's not a bad thing to want someone in your life. Someone other than me and Gran and the rest."

"Good heavens, you need to stop listening to your Uncle Nash." *Uncomfortable* didn't come close to describing how his observations made her feel. Her *other?* "Ryder and I have been friends since second grade. *Friends.* That's all." But her protests did nothing to stop the butterflies fluttering in her belly. It was just excitement that he was back, that he was home. "Don't you have dinner to cook and a list to make?"

"It's pasta night," Mason told her as she grabbed his shoulders and pivoted him to the door. "It won't take me more than… Hey! Uncle Ryder!"

"Mason." Ryder froze at the top of the stairs and dropped his oversize duffel on the floor.

Corliss stared, mesmerized. It was Ryder. The same Ryder she'd known most of her life. Same lush dark hair, same piercing eyes. Same solid form that both lifted her up and provided a shoulder—sometimes two—to cry on. It was Ryder. And yet...

And yet her fingers suddenly itched to dive into that hair of his. Her gaze snagged his and she remembered the moment of perfection of being held in his arms. *Stop it! You're being ridiculous.*

Ryder blinked but not fast enough that Corliss didn't see the shock in his eyes as she stared at him. "You neglected to tell me he's almost as tall as me." He held out a hand, and after Mason's grin widened, pulled him in for a quick hug. "I guess video chats don't tell me everything. Good to see you, kid."

"You, too." Mason looked between them. "Mom said you're going out to dinner. Can I come? I'll be good, I promise. I'll even order off the kids' menu."

"He's teasing," Corliss said before Ryder felt obligated and shoulder-nudged her son. "He has kitchen duty tonight."

"Tonight and every night." Mason sighed dramatically.

"Hey, it was your choice to take that on. Cooking or horses and fence fixing. Everyone's gotta pull their weight around here."

"Horses still hate you?" Ryder asked with a widening grin.

"More than ever," Mason admitted. "But the kitchen doesn't."

"I look forward to your culinary creations." Ryder pointed down the hall. "Denny said I could stay in Nash and Levi's old room. Last door on the right?"

"Uh-huh." Corliss blinked, her heart suddenly jumping into her throat. "Yeah, sure. Of course." She didn't sound remotely convincing. "I'll wait for you downstairs."

"It'll just take me a sec." He flashed them both a smile and disappeared into his room.

"What do you know?" Mason's eyes grew wide and innocent. "Your other's just moved in down the hall."

"One more word and I'll have you mucking out stalls in the boarding stable."

Mason backed off, but the playful grin remained. "Yes, ma'am."

Mother, son and dogs thundered down the ancient, creaky stairs in their typical fashion. Mason headed straight into the kitchen, humming on his way. "Pasta for dinner, Uncle Nash. Don't fill up on junk!"

A barefoot Nash growled something at her

son as he emerged from the kitchen, an over-size chip bag in hand. "You and Ryder going out then?"

"Yes. Won't be too late."

Nash shrugged. "Don't come back early on my account. I'll keep an eye on her."

"'Her' can still hear just fine, young man." Denny brought in one of the porch plants, scowling at its drooping buds. "Darn thing's trying to kill itself, I think."

"Probably all the negative energy vibrating through this place," Nash said before stuffing a handful of chips into his mouth. "It's not just affecting the plants."

"Comedy is not your forte," Corliss said when Denny silently walked past both of them. Corliss's heart twisted in her chest. "Darn it, why won't she understand?"

"She'll come around, sis." Nash elbowed her gently.

"It's been nearly a month. If she hasn't accepted this yet—"

"I wouldn't give up on her," Nash said. "You've got a secret weapon at your disposal now." He jerked his head toward the stairs. "She's always had a soft spot in her heart for Ryder."

Gratitude swept through her. She couldn't have made it through the last couple of years without Nash. Her older brother. Her sibling confidant. Her right hand on the ranch and her partner in so many things. "You might be underestimating his powers of persuasion."

"Oh, I really hope I'm not." The smirk Nash offered had her narrowing her eyes.

"Not you, too," she muttered and snatched her purse off the narrow table by the front door.

"Not me, too, what?"

"I just got Mason's he's-your-other lecture."

"Oh yeah. That." He laughed and slouched on the arm of the sofa. "The kid's maybe on to something. Makes a lot of sense if you ask me. He thinks we all have an 'other.'"

"Well, I didn't. Ask you," she added at his questioning expression.

"So that's what you're wearing, huh?"

"Stop it." Corliss scowled.

"It's not bad or anything." Nash shrugged. "It's a choice. Also looks like you're sneaking out your bedroom window to go to a concert. Didn't you and Ryder do that your junior year of high school? You got caught sneaking back in if I remember correctly."

"I snuck out multiple times." Corliss lowered her voice in case Mason was listening. "I only got caught once." She looked down at the faded image. "I actually got this shirt at one of those concerts, and it still fits, so back off."

"Whatever." The ways of the brother were strong with this one. "I'm sure Ryder will approve of whatever you're wearing."

She would not be baited. She would not...

Footsteps echoed down the stairs and Ryder joined them. "Hey, sorry I took so long. Nice makeover on the room up there. Thought for sure I'd find yours and Levi's Legos all over the carpet or your car models on the shelf."

"Don't be fooled by that. Not all of us have grown up," Corliss said, anxious to put some distance between herself and her brother. "You ready to go?"

"Absolutely." Ryder slapped his hands together. "I've been craving one of Harriet's onion stack burgers for weeks."

"Take your car, Ryder," Nash called after them. "You ride in hers and you might not make it back."

CHAPTER THREE

THE CRANKY CROW, owned and run by the Amspoker family for decades, was as eclectic and memorable as the name implied. Part bar, part restaurant, part entertainment venue with pool, dart boards and air hockey tables, it served as the social hot spot for most Eagle Springs residents and a good share of tourists. Under the current management of Harriet Amspoker, the joint was becoming well known for its custom-brewed beers and mile-high burgers topped with anything from onion rings to bacon jam to fried jalapeños.

It had been a while since Corliss visited the well-known eatery for more than takeout. The place always made her smile, though. The kitschy, over-the-top modern decor, accented with a mix of Old West couldn't be equaled or rivaled. From the barrel bar stools to the Most Wanted posters depicting past and present employees, the place embraced a Western flair.

Stuffed bison, deer and pronghorn antelope heads hung on the paneled walls while various stuffed bird species dangled from fishing wire across the ceiling. And of course, front and center over the bar was Waldo the Wolverine, who, after invading the Crow's original owner's shed late one summer evening, now doubled as the unofficial mascot for the local high school. Town legend had it that Waldo left his wall perch every night after closing to patrol the place once the lights were out.

It was Waldo that Corliss found herself eyeing after she'd finished deluging Ryder with everything she hadn't told him in their emails. Town legend aside, Corliss swore Waldo was some kind of surveillance device, always watching, always listening. Probably always judging, Corliss added with a twist of her mouth.

Seconds after she'd gone silent, Ryder took a slow drink of his beer and tossed a handful of the Cranky Crow's infamous spicy popcorn-and-pretzel mix into his mouth.

"Well?" Tired of waiting, she twisted her

hands on top of the table. They were sitting across from each other in the back corner booth. "What do you think?"

"I'm thinking if I hadn't put most of my settlement money from Roustabouts into Olivia's college fund, I could help solve a lot of your problems."

Corliss swallowed hard, emotion clogging her throat. Of course Ryder would think that. It illustrated the kind of man he was and she loved him for it. "I appreciate that. But I meant, what do you think about my plan?"

"That if you're expecting me to talk you out of going to Montana, I won't." Ryder dusted his hands against his thighs.

"Yeah?" She sighed in relief. "Thank goodness you agree with me."

Ryder inclined his head. "That's not what I said."

As fast as the calm settled, new panic set in. "So I'm wrong to overrule Gran and go to Elias Blackwell?"

"Didn't say that, either. I just know better than to try to change your mind when it's already made up."

"So…what? You aren't going to help me?"

"Sure I am." Ryder was suddenly all business. Having spent an hour or so together, she couldn't help but notice he seemed to have lost a little of his shine, which was understandable, considering the events surrounding his homecoming.

He'd nearly died in that last fire he'd fought. The level of terror she'd felt when he'd told her what happened had nearly driven her to her knees. She was grateful that he'd gotten firefighting out of his system and was taking a less risky step into the future. She was on the verge of losing everything else in her life; she couldn't imagine losing him, too.

"If you've told me everything—"

"I haven't paused for breath for fifteen minutes." Corliss lifted her beer. "You really think I left something out?"

"I do not." He leaned his arms on the table and met her gaze. "Let's cut to the chase. From where I sit, yeah. You're out of options. You want to save the ranch and raise your payment to cover a portion of the loan. You've only got one choice left. Doesn't matter whether I agree with your tactics. The situation is what it is."

"Right." This conversation really wasn't making her feel better.

"I do have questions."

"Okay." Corliss shrugged. "Shoot."

"What's your plan of action?"

She suddenly found herself fascinated by her beer. "Plan of action?"

"Corliss, you plan when you're going to wake up in the morning, down to the second. No way you're heading north to Montana without at least the inkling of an idea of how to approach Big E. That's right, isn't it?"

"It is." Corliss took a long drink. "And yes, I have a plan. I can't just turn up and say, 'Hey, I'm a long-lost relative who needs a ton of money.' That would go over great, I'm sure." She was, for the first time in her life, attempting to be inconspicuous. Until she couldn't be.

"Probably not the first time it's happened to them."

"No," Corliss replied as dread pooled anew in her stomach. "I'm sure it wouldn't be."

"Question two. What are you going to do if Elias Blackwell turns you down?"

"I can't think that way." She pulled the wooden bowl closer and picked out the spiced peanuts to nibble. Now wasn't the time to tell him the role she planned to cast him in for her venture north. "I can't think failure."

"Then that should erase any doubts you have about whether you're doing the right thing." He kicked Corliss under the table. She glared at him, but he turned and said, "Oh, hey, Harry. Long time no see."

Corliss sat up straight and pinned a smile on her face.

"Well, look who's back in Eagle Springs." Harriet Amspoker's husky voice carried the hint of age that was displayed on her face. Her wrinkles had wrinkles, and each one, Corliss was certain, had a story. She was taller than most and wore her now stark-gray hair in two braids that reached nearly to her waist. "Ryder Talbot. Denny tells me you're back for good." She shot Corliss a look that let Corliss know Harriet was up to date on all the Blackwell drama.

Corliss gave a curt nod acknowledging the fact.

"She's right," Ryder said. "Got myself settled in at the Flying Spur while I wait for my daughter to arrive."

"That'd be Olivia," Harriet said before Ryder could explain.

"Yes," Ryder said. "And this is one of the first places she wants to see. I've told her all about you and your critters, and she's already smitten with Waldo over there."

"You be sure to bring her by for a welcome–to–Eagle Springs milkshake special once she's settled." Harriet shoved her hands into the front pockets of her jeans and rocked back on her black booted heels. "You doing okay, Corliss?"

"I'm fine."

"If you're as fine as Denny, then you aren't at all. She's heartsick over this situation you've proposed about Falcon Creek."

Corliss nearly choked on a peanut. "Figured she'd filled you in." She coughed as her eyes watered. "You going to tell me to forget about it, too?"

"No," Harriet said slowly. "I'm not."

"You're not?" Corliss and Ryder spoke at the same time, turned surprised eyes on each other.

"Your grandmother is one of the most stubborn people on the planet. From what I hear about Elias Blackwell, that's a genetic trait." Harriet looked at Corliss. "I know what you want to do comes from a place of caring and devotion to your ranch. Denny will see it, too. Eventually."

"In my lifetime?" Corliss asked hopefully.

"Remains to be seen," Harriet said. "Just know that I didn't take her side in this. Not saying Elias's betrayal didn't cut her heart in two. It did. And that wound won't heal anytime soon. But stubbornness and anger aren't reasons to walk away from an opportunity to protect what's yours."

"That—" Ryder pointed at Harriet with an overbright smile on his lips "—is what I was trying to say."

"It's good to see you two back in here together," Harriet said with an approving nod. "Friendships like yours, they're built to last a lifetime. Glad to see you both realize it." She stepped aside as their orders arrived.

"Hey, guys."

"Adele!" Corliss's sister slid their plates onto the table. "What are you doing here? Where are the twins?"

"Honestly, I've heard those two questions so often tonight that I'm thinking of legally changing my name. Hey, Ryder." She bent down, kissed his cheek and gave his arm a squeeze. "Glad to have you home."

"Thanks."

"And to answer your nosy-big-sister question, Corliss, Nikki had an emergency." Adele cast a quick, uneasy glance at Harriet as she pulled utensil packets out of her apron pocket and handed them over. "I was already here, grabbing a burger, so I said I could fill in for the rest of her shift. It's no big deal. I was taking a 'me night,' anyway."

A "me night" for Adele usually consisted of monitoring the deals she brokered between online buyers and sellers of ranch equipment and, well, anything else she thought someone would value. "And Quinn and Ivy?"

"Betsy's watching them for me." Adele referenced one of her teenage neighbors who was also one of Mason's best friends. "She needed some tutoring in math, so we're trading services. The girls are fine," she added quickly. "This isn't a big deal, Cor."

Since her younger sister had difficulty saying no to anyone in trouble, it was a very big deal, but arguing the point in front of Harriet, of all people, would only create a scene. That didn't mean Corliss planned to stay completely silent, however. "Hopefully you'll keep your tips this time."

Harriet's spine went steel straight. "Now what kind of nincompoop would work a six-hour shift in my place and not keep what she earns?" Harriet demanded.

Adele glared at Corliss, who merely grinned and popped a garlic-seasoned fry into her mouth.

"I'm just helping a friend," Adele said. "She needs the money and the job just as much as anyone."

"Then she can stop taking phone calls from that whiny boyfriend of hers," Harriet announced. "You and I are going to have a talk before you leave tonight, Buttercup. About owning your worth."

"Yes, ma'am." Adele reached over and snagged one of Corliss's fries before she muttered, "tattletale," and moved off.

"That sister of yours." Harriet shook her head and waited until Adele was out of earshot. "Sweetest girl that ever was but always afraid of disappointing. Don't you worry about her getting paid," she added before Corliss could comment. "And don't think I won't be giving Nikki a talking-to when she picks up her next check. Taking advantage of kind people is a character flaw that needs adjusting. You two want refills on your beers?"

"No thank you, ma'am." Ryder shook his head. "Could do with some water, though."

"Water?" Harry's brow creased. "You been away too long, boy. We'll get you reacclimated soon enough. Been working on a new whiskey in the distillery, next building over. Don't suppose I could tempt either of you? Abel over there's calling it Mule because it's got one serious kick."

"Not this time," Ryder said. "I'm driving."

Corliss indicated her agreement. "Harriet?" She called when the older woman began to walk away. "Keep Mule from Gran, please? I'd like to avoid another trip to the hospital for as long as possible."

Harriet grinned. "Don't you worry, Corliss. I've got my own special Denny Brew on tap. No alcohol."

"At all?" Corliss's eyes went wide. "But she said last time she was in—"

"You think I told her? Young lady, I thought you were smart." She flicked a sly smile at Corliss and nodded to their overfilled plates. "I'm not in any rush to see my best friend kicking the bucket anytime soon. You two eat up before it gets cold. And don't you worry about your gran, Little Miss. I'll keep an eye on her and your boy while you're gone."

Feeling surprisingly better, Corliss took a big bite of her burger. "This should fuel me enough to kick your butt at pool before the evening is over."

"Keep dreaming." Ryder grinned and gathered up his double barbecue burger in both hands. One bite, and the melted Jack cheese oozed all over his fingers. "The day hasn't been created where you beat me at pool."

"We'll see, fire boy. We'll see."

"WHAT'S THE WORD on brother Wyatt?" Ryder asked as Corliss lined up an impossible shot. "Last I heard, he was in New Mexico."

"That was a few jobs ago." She stuck her tongue out between her lips, narrowed her eyes as she examined her lineup and missed. "He's finishing up working on a ranch in Nevada. Said he'll be home by the end of the month."

"You don't sound convinced."

"When was the last time you appreciated anyone ordering you around?"

"Don't mind it at all as long as I'm getting paid for it." He chuckled at her questioning look. "I suppose in his position, I wouldn't like it one bit. But he's a Blackwell. He'll show."

"With attitude in check, I'm sure." She shook her head. "I'm being too hard on him, I know. It's easy to do when he hasn't been around. But I can't blame him. It's not like he's ever stayed still long enough to grow anything resembling roots. He is who he is. Once we're over this hump and we've got things settled, he can go back to whatever it is he wants to do wherever he wants to do it. So." Corliss held her pool cue in one hand and planted her other hand on a kicked-out hip. "What are your plans?"

"Right now?" He leaned over and lined up his shot. "I'm going to finish this game and continue my decades-long winning streak."

Ryder grinned at her snort. He wished he could say she wasn't a distraction, but the truth was she'd been distracting him ever since second grade. Back then, he hadn't known what those squishy, uncomfortable feelings were churning around his insides. But when he'd hit puberty?

He hadn't needed any high school health class telling him exactly what he was dealing with. There was a reason that things like this were called crushes.

He pulled the cue back, shifted ever so slightly and aimed not for the easy shot, which would sink the four ball in the right corner pocket, but one that sent the cue ball hopping over two others to knock the striped six straight down. The resounding clack had him biting back a gloat as Corliss frowned.

"Obviously you've not lost your touch," she muttered as he set up another shot. "I meant, what are your plans for work? You know what kind of job you want?"

"Preferably one that pays, but I'm good helping with whatever you need doing on the ranch for now. Why?" He narrowed his gaze, but this time he missed. She did an excited shimmy as she scooted in front of him. "You know of something?"

"Spurs and Saddles is hiring." She nudged him aside with a swing of her hips. "Not sure how much you'd enjoy fitting locals and weekend cowboys for new boots and hats."

"Not much," he said, carefully easing into the other idea he was considering. "Nash mentioned Chief Bellingham's getting ready to retire."

It wasn't easy to shock Corliss Blackwell, but that statement got her attention. "Fire chief? I thought you were done fighting fires."

"Hard to be done with the only thing I've ever been good at."

"That's not true," Corliss said. "It's also not the best choice to do something that almost cost you your life, especially since Olivia's joining you soon."

"True enough." He shrugged. "But it's what I know, Corliss. Me and horses, we do okay together, but that's an arrangement of mutual tolerance. At some point we're both going to get irritated and bored."

"Horses won't kill you," Corliss reminded him.

"I can think of a few rodeo riders who might disagree. And remind me again, how did Levi get hurt recently?"

"You know what I mean. After the last few months, how can you even think about walking back into that life?"

"That's all I am doing, Cor. Thinking." After all these years, he knew when she wasn't going to understand something, especially when it was something he didn't understand himself. There wasn't any doubt his connection to the job was emotional. His father had been fire chief of Eagle Springs when he was a boy. He'd made that station house his second home. Having a love-hate relationship with something he was talented at was beyond difficult. It was impossible to untangle himself from it. "Don't go working yourself up into a tizzy. Nothing's set in stone."

"A tizzy? Really?" The concern and worry faded behind the triggered challenge. "I'll show you a tizzy."

"Please do," he teased.

"Men." Corliss shook her head, but there was worry in her eyes. "I bet growing up you had some kind of dream about me beating you at pool."

"I had a lot of dreams about you growing up," Ryder said before he thought better of it. He saw her hesitate, saw her blink away the creases of confusion on her forehead. Confusion, he had to admit, he shared. He straightened against the sudden tightness in his back where the burn scars were still healing. And they would heal. He hoped the scars no one could see would also heal one day.

Corliss missed her shot, but rather than moving aside, she stepped closer and laid a hand on his shoulder. "I know you haven't wanted to talk about the accident—"

"No," he said in a tone he hoped she'd understand. "I haven't. And I don't." He didn't owe anyone an explanation as to how he was dealing with the trauma of the rig fire that had nearly ended everything. But Corliss was—and always would be—different, and thus she deserved a better answer. "It won't help, Cor. I did the mandatory therapy while I was in the hospital. I did the group thing and the one-on-one thing. There are just some issues that can't easily be worked out with words. I'm dealing. I'm fine," he added despite the doubt. What he kept bottled up during the day found its way into his dreams.

Into his nightmares. One reason why sleeping wasn't his favorite activity these days.

Disappointment flashed in those amazing green eyes of hers. Eyes he used to wish could see him in the way he saw her. "All right." Her fingers curled in against his shirt. She inclined her head to the table. "It's your shot."

He didn't respond, but the tension and memories he'd been trying so hard to keep locked away surged free. The sound of the fire ripping through the steel hull of the rig. The echoes of slamming doors and air being sucked out of sealed compartments. The muted banging of fists against unbreakable glass as the oxygen slowly evaporated beneath the voracious flames.

He took his shot and not only missed, he sent the cue ball soaring halfway across the bar. With a sigh, he walked over to retrieve it.

As painful as the last few months had been, it wasn't the fear of going back into the flames that had him worried. It was wondering if he'd be whole again if he never did.

"Maybe you should consider professional pool player for your next career." Her joke pulled a laugh out of him when he set the ball back on the table. She took her next shot without much thought and sank, not one, but two balls. "Huh. Clearly, I've been playing this game wrong all these years. What do you think about coming to Montana with me to talk to Elias?"

"Is that your way of saying you don't want my help on the ranch?"

"It's my way of saying I don't want to go alone."

"That why you haven't already gone and come back?"

"I haven't left yet because Gran keeps finding stuff for me to do that can't wait. She's probably hoping I'll get past the idea and focus on something else."

"It's like she doesn't know you at all. When do you want to leave?"

"I'm going to call tomorrow morning to make a reservation."

"Montana, huh?" Ryder had to admit, the idea held appeal. And the timing fit in with his appointment to enroll Olivia in school. "Been a while since the two of us went on a road trip alone."

She missed her next shot. "And Skyfire."

"Ah, our chaperone." Ryder laughed as he thought about the Flying Spur's last remaining breeding stallion. "I don't know. From what I remember, that horse can get pretty chatty on car rides."

Corliss said with that appealing yet dangerous glint in her eye, "He might have developed an affinity to singing show tunes."

"Heaven help me." Still. A road trip with his best friend definitely appealed. "Well, if

Nash can hold down the ranch on his own, and since you need me and all."

"That's not what I said," she warned.

Wasn't it? He slammed the last ball into the right side pocket and set his cue stick down. "When do we leave?"

CHAPTER FOUR

BOW LET OUT a low woof as Corliss wound the hose up and dropped it on the ground by the stable door. Her road trip with Ryder was happening sooner than expected. The night before last, she'd tossed the idea to him over the pool table, then yesterday she'd snagged an unexpected reservation at the Blackwell Family Ranch for the weekend. Considering the risk she was taking with this trip, best she get it over with as quickly as possible.

She'd already packed up a cooler with water and snacks—she didn't want to stop any more than necessary on the long drive to Falcon Creek, Montana. After a fitful night's sleep, she'd made an early start cleaning out the travel trailer and getting it ready to go.

She'd checked all the fuses and tires, made sure the brake lights were working when connected to her truck. By the time she was finished with that, Nash and Ryder were both up and helping her fill the trailer with fresh hay and supplies from an emergency vet kit they kept on hand.

They'd been tempted back into the house for breakfast, while she topped up the water tank and added a good amount of woodchips to the floor of the trailer.

She'd also gathered up the necessary paperwork and vet records to present to Elias Blackwell if—*when* she corrected herself—*when* Elias Blackwell asked to see them. Because they were taking Skyfire across state lines, she wanted to be prepared for any eventuality.

With the trailer windows open, and a perfect summer day stretching before them, Skyfire was going to have a royal five-hour ride to Montana.

Anything more than eight hours and Corliss would have to plan for rest stops for the horse to get out and walk around. With the trailer and supplies waiting for them, all that was left was to check her truck's oil level, hitch up the trailer and load in Skyfire.

She rounded the back of the trailer and skidded to a shortened halt in front of Denny. "Gran." She pressed a hand to her racing heart. "You scared the life out of me. What are you doing out here? Are you all right?"

"The boy said you need to eat something." She shoved a foil-wrapped parcel at Corliss. "Nash and Ryder made themselves scarce, so it's on me. Go on." She stepped closer. "It's your favorite. Bacon and egg on an English muffin."

"With hot sauce?" Corliss asked hopefully as she accepted the offering and unwrapped it. The spices wafted up with the steam and hit her right in the face. "Oh yeah, extra-hot sauce." She bit in, nodded. "Thanks, Gran."

Denny looked at her for a long moment, then nodded and headed back to the house.

"Gran." Corliss hated the desperation in her own voice as she hurried after her grandmother, the sandwich all but forgotten. "Gran, please. This has gone on long enough. It's been a month—"

"There's no time limit on betrayal." Denny spoke with her back to Corliss, inched her chin up when the kitchen door opened and Ryder stepped out. "Don't think you're getting off easy. You may be disappointed with my decision, but I'm disappointed in you, too." She pushed past him and slammed the door behind her.

"Ouch." Ryder winced as Corliss looked down at the breakfast that no longer held any appeal.

"It'll be just my luck if we manage to save this place and she disowns me." She raised blurry eyes to the sky and squeezed them shut. If tears were going to do her any good, they'd have helped weeks ago. "I need to finish with the truck."

"Corliss—"

"Don't." Corliss waved him off as she headed around to the front of the house. "Please don't try. There's nothing you can do, Ryder. I'll meet you at the truck when you're ready to leave."

"Brrr." Nash shivered and rubbed his arms when Ryder returned to the kitchen. "Given the way Gran blew through here, I think we're headed for a long frost."

"Wouldn't be surprised," Ryder agreed. "She go upstairs?"

"In the living room, I think." Nash said. "I heard the TV."

"Thanks." The past two nights he'd spent

in the Blackwell house were nothing like he remembered. The tension between Denny and Corliss was so thick he couldn't have burned through it with a blowtorch, which made Nash and Mason walk around on tiptoe.

The fact the three of them had stayed up until after midnight playing video games without a complaint from either woman was enough to make Ryder wonder if he'd somehow entered an alternate universe.

Ryder eyed his repacked bag that sat by the door, expecting to find Denny where Nash had said, but instead the room was empty. One of the hall doors that had been closed previously now stood open and sunlight streamed into the hall.

He kept his steps light, hands in his pockets as he approached and found Denny sitting spine-stiff on the edge of one of the twin beds.

"I remember this room." Stepping into Corliss and Adele's childhood bedroom was like stepping through a time portal into the past. "Doesn't feel quite the same without the countless horse pictures all over the wall," he added, then chuckled at the elbow-sized hole in the drywall that served as testament to Corliss trying to teach him to dance before the eighth-grade winter ball.

The room was and continued to be, a contrast in personalities. One of the twin beds, Corliss's, was simple, practical and covered with a handmade wedding-circle-scrap quilt while the other beneath the window had more frills and lace and a whole lot of pink.

Instead of teenage-crush-inspired, high school decor, there were piles of boxes and various household junk that had turned the space into a bit of a dumping ground.

"I'll be forever grateful Adele outgrew her pink phase." Denny pushed a stack of books back before they tumbled to the floor. "'Course, now that she has those twins of hers, it could come roaring back. I'm thinking this space would do well for Olivia."

"I don't want you going to any trouble for us, Ms. Bl—Gran," he said when she sent him a look of warning.

"Until you find where you belong, it'll do. If this works for your girl, then I'll get Nash and Mason to work on it and focus on you next. It'll be nice to have some youth in this house. Mason doesn't count on that front anymore. Place has felt empty ever since Levi,

Wyatt and Adele moved out. I'll aim to have it ready by the time you and Corliss get back."

"Thank you. It'll be nice to give Olivia her own space until we find a home of our own." One thing the Blackwells had always extended in his—and a lot of people's—direction was welcome and kindness. Didn't matter how hard times might get, there was always an open door and a seat at their table. "You can't stay mad at her forever, Gran. She doesn't deserve it."

"Should have known you'd take her side."

"If she can help save this ranch—"

"I don't want or need his help."

"Gran." He crouched down in front of her, rested a hand on her knobby knee. "If she found another solution, she'd have used it by now. She might be wrong. But she could be right."

Denny's eyes glistened. "She's stubborn. Been like that ever since she was a baby. Only person more stubborn than Corliss Blackwell is me, and that's saying something."

"No argument there."

"I guess if she's roped you in—"

"No one ropes me into anything. Not even

Corliss." If that wasn't one of the biggest whoppers he'd ever told.

Knees protesting, he straightened and reached for a high-back chair under one of the small desks in the corner and flipped it around. He straddled it and sat directly in front of Delaney Blackwell. She was not a woman who showed any sign of weakness or fear, even when the tightrope she was walking on was as thin as a spider's web.

"Here's what I do know." He reached out, took hold of one of her trembling hands and squeezed. "When Corliss loves, she loves so fiercely nothing else matters. And she loves you so much. That's at the bottom of everything she does. Deep down, you know that."

Denny's jaw worked overtime, stemming tears Ryder was convinced she hadn't let herself shed in six decades. A lifetime of hurt was an awful lot to attempt to break through, but he was willing to give it a shot.

"Do you remember the night my father died?" Ryder asked.

"Hard to forget," Denny said. "The whole town of Eagle Springs loved your daddy. Best fire chief we've ever had round here. We all mourned him. Mourned him hard. Good man."

Ryder cleared his throat as a band of grief cinched his heart. It hadn't been a fire that stole his father from him, but a heart attack at the tender age of forty-two. Glancing at the small window near Adele's bed, he said, "I was absolutely lost and my mother—"

"Your mother did the best she could," Denny said. "Evelyn, she was never particularly grounded in reality."

"No," Ryder agreed. Last he'd heard, she still wasn't. She'd done everything she could to put Eagle Springs behind her and move on. "I remember going out to the stable and saddling up Dad's favorite horse, rode it all the way out here in the pitch-black. I swear that horse could read my mind." He shook his head, nostalgia knocking against his brain. "He knew just where to come. I snuck in that window right over there, after midnight. I thought if I wasn't home in the morning that there couldn't be a funeral. I thought if I didn't go back home, then my father wouldn't really be gone."

"I remember." Denny sniffed and her lips twitched. "And just so you know, you didn't sneak anywhere. You were ten years old and clumsier than a donkey in rain boots. Made enough of a racket to wake the…" She trailed off. "I remember."

"Corliss and Adele tried so hard to keep me a secret, yet in you came, first thing in the morning, acting as if you expected to find me sleeping under Corliss's bed."

"Always said you and Corliss weren't attached at the hip, you were attached at the heart. Made sense you'd come here, especially when you were grieving so."

Ryder smiled. Corliss had been right there when he'd cried about his father for the first time. "After breakfast, you sent Corliss and the rest out to do their chores and you kept me behind. You sat me down, and while you fed me more pancakes, you said that ignoring something doesn't mean it didn't happen. Acceptance was the first step on the new path that's been carved out. My mother…" He struggled for the right words. "My mother's entire life was wrapped around my father. I was an added responsibility she didn't know what to do with.

"You stepped up and you gave me a base, Denny. You gave me a place to be me, someone, a family to be accountable to. A fresh start and a new perspective. My address was with her, but my home? That was the Flying Spur. But you also made certain that I knew how to face what life doled out. That's what I'm telling you needs doing now, Denny. You need to trust Corliss. You need to trust me and your other grandchildren. You need to trust in their love and devotion for you because that's the only thing that's going to give you shelter in the coming storm. And there is a coming storm," he said more firmly. "Pretending there isn't will only increase the damage it's going to do."

"I've spent my life giving lectures, not taking them, Ryder Talbot." Denny's grip on his hand tightened as her eyes shined with still-unshed tears.

"And yet here we are. Trust, Gran. If you can't quite trust Corliss, or even forgive her, trust me. For a little while at least."

"I'm trusting you with the greatest gift I've ever gotten. I'm trusting you with my girl."

He smiled. "I will always have your granddaughter's back."

"Even when she's too stubborn to see you for who and what you really are?" She touched his face, sympathy radiating on hers. "Someday you're going to have to tell her, Ryder."

That odd confusion that struck the other night when they were playing pool descended once again. "I don't know what you mean." Even as he said the words, he could hear the doubt.

"Yes, you do. Deep down? You know," Denny told him. "We don't know how much time we've been given. Mine's running out, and Corliss's? Hers is ticking by. Yours is, too. Make the most out of what you have, Ryder. Make the most of every single second."

It was, Ryder thought, as Denny tugged her hand free and patted his shoulder before she walked out of the room, very sage advice.

Whether he'd ever have the courage to take it? Now, that was the real question.

CHAPTER FIVE

"I DON'T BELIEVE THIS." Corliss turned to one side and stretched her arm as far and deep as she could into the engine of her truck. "I bet Gran did this, didn't she?" She flexed her fingers in an attempt to catch the end of the fan belt she suspected had popped off. "She's got that kind of power over people and things."

"Problems?" Ryder's amused voice had her grinding her molars. "You ever give up ranching, you might have a second career as a contortionist." Ryder grinned at the scathing look she shot him. "You're eating up daylight, trying to fix this thing. Let's just take my truck. I've got a trailer hitch on it."

"I don't want to take your truck, I want to take mine. Ow!" She snatched her hand back and shook out the effects of an electrical shock. Well, that wasn't good.

"I have two words for you." Ryder sauntered around the front of the truck to face her. He was, Corliss thought, a pulse-kicking example of male perfection. From his toned, tanned arms that strained against the fabric of his gray T-shirt, to the perfectly molded jeans right down to his scuffed, pointed boots. A Remington portrait come to life. Minus the horse, of course. Although, if memory served, the sight of Ryder Talbot on horseback did its own special number on every female pulse in Eagle Springs.

"Two words?" She gulped. He was looking at her with those…those blue eyes of his that rivaled the ocean waters he'd battled on more than one occasion. Eyes that seemed particularly determined today "What two words?"

"The two most important words ever spoken." He moved closer, so close she could sense the heat drifting off his skin. He bent down, his breath hot against her ear. She held her breath, tried to remember how to breathe even as her brain fogged. *"Air. Conditioning."*

She jerked her head back, looked up at him and saw that ridiculous grin of his spread across full, tempting lips. She couldn't help but laugh. "You think that's the way to my heart?"

"Today?" He glanced up at the still climbing sun. "You bet. Let Nash play with this piece of ju—" He stopped at her arched brow. "Classic machinery," he shifted smoothly. "We can take a good thirty minutes off our trip just by changing vehicles."

"How do I know you didn't sabotage my truck so we'd have to take yours?"

"Now, why would I have done that?" His overly innocent blinking had her wondering if perhaps he'd somehow managed to kill her truck after all.

"You wouldn't have put up with my driving, anyway." Surrendering, she reached up, unhooked the support rod and closed the hood. "You've always hated how I drive."

"*Hate* is a strong word." Ryder was already pulling out her bag and cooler from the back seat of the cab. "I like to think of it more like a preference for survival. You have anything else you're bringing?" He headed for his shiny, perfect and far-too-clean truck. Personally, Corliss didn't consider a truck functional until it had at least three inches of mud and dirt permanently caked into its tires and grills.

"I'll get the rest." She dragged out her all-weather jacket, the lunch bag Mason had put together for them, and at the last second, re-membered her cell phone and charger in her bedroom. Having collected the last items, she headed for the front door and found her grandmother waiting for her. Denny's arms were folded across her chest and her jaw was set, but there was softening in her eyes. Cor-liss had spent the past few weeks longing to see that.

"We're heading out," she said as if it was news. "Nash and Mason'll be around to help with whatever you need."

"I don't agree with what you're doing." Gran's tone held a gentleness that brushed against Corliss's heart.

Corliss nodded. "I know."

"All the money in the world doesn't make Elias Blackwell a good man." She angled a warning look at her. "You don't forget that, you hear me? This thing between me and my brother, it goes both ways."

Corliss nodded again. "Okay."

Denny frowned, as if deciding to say some-thing else. But she didn't continue. Instead, she stepped forward and reached up to clasp Corliss's shoulders. "The days of me tell-ing you not to touch the hot stove are over.

You've got lessons to learn for yourself. This is one of them. You get this fool idea of Elias Blackwell saving us out of your system, you hear? When he says no, you skedaddle back here and we'll figure things out. Together. No more of this running-to-him-for-help nonsense."

"Yes, ma'am."

"All right, then." She shifted her hold, drew Corliss against her and patted her back, much like she had when Corliss had been a child. "I love you, Little Miss. Attitude, misguided notions and all. You be careful with yourself and with Ryder. I'll see you when you get back."

"Okay." Corliss was smiling when Denny released her. Whatever waited for her in Falcon Creek, she could handle it now, without this weight on her heart. "I love you, Gran."

"Love you, too, Little Miss. Now get. Sooner you go, sooner you come back."

"Everything okay?" Ryder asked, leaning on the fender, when she returned to his truck.

"It is now." She handed him her charger and tucked her phone into her pocket.

"One thing about you, you travel light." Ryder opened the passenger door for her "Ahhh, feel that?" he asked with a grin.

"No."

"That's comfort, baby. Pure unadulterated comfort." He stood back as she hoisted herself up into the cab.

"It looks like NASA central control in here," Corliss grumbled. Bells and whistles and a variety of knobs and buttons. Where was the dinged-up tape player? The broken air vent? The jumble of rainbow poker tokens tossed onto the top of her dashboard. This looked nothing like her truck. "What about music?"

"What about it?"

"Where's the CD player? Or is there a tiny orchestra in the glove box?"

"Oh, there's music. It comes from this thing called the internet. Trust me, you'll love it." He slammed her door shut, and she grudgingly admitted this was a pretty cool vehicle. If the Blackwell Family Ranch lost their reservation, they could easily sleep in here.

"Let me guess," she said when he climbed in behind the wheel. "Driver picks the music. Shotgun hums along."

"You remember our mantra." He patted a hand against his heart.

"Hard to forget," she mumbled. "We still have to pick up Skyfire in the trailer."

"On it." He started up the engine, which was nearly as quiet as a Wyoming sunset. "Let Operation Save Flying Spur commence."

NEARLY THREE HOURS and enough classic country rock music to leave him questioning his devotion to the genre later, Ryder pulled off the highway. He brought the truck to a stop at the side of the road, opened the windows and turned off the engine.

One thing about Wyoming was the amount of quiet. Just pure wind-whipping-through-the-thigh-high-grass-clouds-kissed-by-the-sun quiet.

"What's going on?" Corliss blinked awake, looking slightly confused and slightly irritated. "Are we there?" She sat up straight, almost at attention, as if she expected to find Elias Blackwell standing beside her window.

"I don't know about you." Ryder unbuckled his belt and shoved open his door. "But that lunch Mason fixed us is calling my name. Come on."

She unbuckled her seat belt but stayed in the cab. "A truck like this can't come cheap."

A shiver raced down his spine as he pulled a wool blanket out of one of the storage compartments in the truck bed. "It didn't."

"You hit the lottery or something?" She finally jumped down, peeked over at him.

"No." He pulled open the back door and tugged out the bag and cooler. "This was Mac's truck."

"Mac," she said as if trying to place the name.

"Mac Corbitt. My training supervisor at Roustabouts." Arms loaded, he kicked the door closed, probably with more force than was necessary. The grief washed over him. "His wife gave it to me when I got out of the hospital."

"Oh. Mac, of course. I'm sorry." Corliss shook her head, shoved her hands in her pockets as he walked past her. "I didn't mean to tease. Not about that."

"It's okay." He should have lied about where he'd gotten the truck. About anything relating to the last few months of his life. But the one thing he'd never been able to do was not tell Corliss Blackwell the truth.

He led her across a small field to a patch of a dozen or so trees. She took the blue-

and-green plaid blanket and tossed it open to drape across the somewhat-even, grassy space. "I didn't want to take the truck at first. I told Lorna, Mac's wife, I told her she should sell it, use the money for the kids' college or help pay the mortgage, but she wouldn't do it. She said Mac would want me to have it. And that she liked the idea of something of Mac's taking someone home."

Once she was settled on the blanket, they unpacked and dug into their lunch.

"It is a beautiful truck," Corliss said, looking back at the vehicle. "Needs a little breaking in, of course. I'm sorry about your friend. I'm sorry about all your friends."

Ryder swallowed hard. He couldn't be upset about the topic of conversation when he was the one who hadn't been able to divert it. "It's hard, knowing they were with me one minute and then gone the next." Three of his best friends—Mac included—passed away in a literal flash. He should have been with them, should have died in that fire beside them, but he hadn't.

And that, even more than the burn treatments, more than the recovery, more than the fear he may have lost his mettle for the job he loved, had been the most difficult thing to deal with. If it hadn't been for Olivia, he very well may have surrendered to the grief. Olivia and Corliss.

The one certainty he'd clung to was that if he left this world without saying goodbye to Corliss Blackwell, she'd follow him into the afterlife and chew him out.

He looked down at the parchment-wrapped bundle Mason had carefully tied with string. "You weren't exaggerating about Mason's kitchen wizardry."

"Like he said—" Corliss shrugged "—he likes to eat. And by eat, I mean he can empty a fridge in two days flat. But he's taught himself to cook like a dream." She hefted half the roast beef sandwich in one hand in a kind of toast. "I'm never going to complain about that, plus it's given him a purpose on the ranch. He's also proof that not all talent is necessarily genetic."

Ryder smirked. "Well, I know he didn't get it from you. Must have been Jesse."

"Mason didn't get his cooking ability from his father, either." Corliss bit into her sandwich with a lot of vigor.

"That was my roundabout way of asking if you've heard from him at all."

"Nope." She examined the French bread–and–meat construction a little too closely. "Mason added some of his famous horseradish sauce. I keep telling him he should bottle it. I bet that would make us a fortune."

"Corliss…"

"Do you really think if I'd heard from Mason's father I wouldn't have told you? Come on, Ryder. The man dumped me on my wedding day." She dug into the bag for the chips and popped that container open. "You couldn't have forgotten that."

"I did not." He'd been forced to stand in the shadows and watch sixteen-year-old Corliss fall head-over-teakettle in love with Jesse Remington, a guy who exemplified the bad-boy stereotype right down to the leather jacket, swagger and devil-may-care attitude. For two years, Ryder kept his opinions to himself, offering a much-used shoulder to cry on every time Jesse broke her heart. But he'd kept his thoughts and doubts to himself because at the time he thought that that's what friends did.

Their planned wedding was the stuff of

Eagle Springs' legend now—Denny, despite her reservations, had gone all out for the big church do and invited the entire town. They'd planned a barbecue reception, only to have Jesse take off an hour before the ceremony, belongings in his motorcycle saddlebags and former backup-cheerleader-turned-hairdresser Sally Jennings along for the ride.

It had been Ryder who found Corliss sitting on the back porch in her sparkling gown, a wilting bouquet of daisies in one hand, a positive pregnancy test in the other.

It had been Ryder who held her as she cried, as she processed the anger and changed herself into the determined, independent woman seated on the blanket near him now. It was Ryder who had held her hand in the labor room when Mason was born and pressed a kiss on her forehead as she'd held her son for the first time.

Now, here he was, at her side, once again diving into whatever zaniness she got into.

"So Jesse's never even asked about Mason? Not after all these years? I thought maybe now that Mason's older—"

"Again, I would have told you, and besides, Mason's not interested in him." Corliss popped a chip in her mouth. And for a moment, much like Denny a few hours before, controlled tears glistened in her eyes. "I don't give a flying rattrap about what Jesse did to me. Not anymore. But I will never forgive him for wanting nothing to do with his son. I'm just grateful Mason's had Nash and Wyatt and Levi as surrogate fathers. And you," she added as her eyes cleared. "I can't even think about how hard those first couple of years would have been without you holding both our hands."

"That's what friends do," Ryder said and glanced away before she saw too much. Denny's advice echoed in his ears, but he silenced it. For now. He wasn't ready. And neither was she. "I told Denny and I'll tell you. I will always have your back, Corliss. Always."

She swallowed visibly, wincing. "Don't be so sure about that." She set her sandwich down, curled her legs under her. "There's something about our trip to Montana that I haven't told you."

"Oh?" Interest piqued, Ryder glanced over at the trailer as Skyfire whinnied and clomped. "He okay in there?"

"He'll be fine. Not sure I'd get him back in there once he got a look at this view. The, um—" she wiped her mouth "—the Blackwell Family Ranch has a lot of extracurricular activities for guests. And it's a great destination for, um, well, for family reunions. Birthday parties. Weddings." She offered him a far-too-wide smile. "When I made the reservation, they asked if there was anything in particular I had some interest in and I, without thinking, might have mentioned I was interested in the place as a wedding venue."

"I see."

"It's crazy, I know, but it made sense at the time. I mean, one of Elias Blackwell's grandsons runs the touristy part of the business, along with his wife, Hadley—she's the one I was talking to, and well, it just kind of came out, you know?"

"So." Ryder did his best to keep his voice even as his heart did this odd, unfamiliar jig. "I assume I'm the fiancé?"

"I know, I know." She covered her face with her hands. "This puts you in a weird position—"

"It's fine," Ryder said, reassuring her. "Glad you told me so I can start to prepare.

That's what actors do for a role, right? They prepare?" He chuckled at the way her brow furrowed. "Honestly, it's okay, Corliss. I can play along."

"Oh, thank goodness." She sagged and put a hand over her heart. "I couldn't quite figure out how to bring it up. And with your history with Nina, I wasn't sure how you'd feel about the whole marriage thing. I know that was hard on you."

"Nina's and my marriage was harder on Nina than it ever was on me." Another of those layers of guilt he couldn't quite seem to peel away permanently. "The only reason we stayed together as long as we did was because of Olivia. We tried, but in the end, we didn't…fit." He'd lost hope of finding someone who did fit, especially with Olivia being back in his life full-time. He'd like to give marriage another go, this time with his full attention and affection. But he couldn't imagine any woman ever understanding him the way Corliss did.

"Great. I guess I can stop worrying then," Corliss said. "You're good with playing the role of my intended? I've said we'll be traveling back home with a new horse, which will explain Skyfire. At least, until the truth comes out." Her laughter seemed nervous now. Nervous, forced and not at all like Corliss. "Wouldn't want you stuck with me in that way for longer than necessary."

"You should have given me more of a warning, though. What kind of fiancé am I that I haven't given you a ring?"

"Well, in your defense, this engagement was kind of sprung on you," Corliss teased as he untangled one of the strings used to tie up their sandwiches and reached for his pocket knife. "What are you doing?" she asked.

"Improvising." Ryder grasped her hand and wound the string around her engagement-ring finger, tied off the ends in a knot that mimicked a stone. His heart pounded so hard in his chest it felt as though he'd lost his breath. "There." He used his knife to cut away the remaining string, then offered her an easygoing grin. "Now you have an actual story to tell. We got engaged over your son's roast beef sandwiches and…" He dug into the bag for the last container. "Brownies."

Corliss blinked, staring down at her hand as if she couldn't quite process what had happened. "Wow." She twisted her hand around as if showing off a ten-carat sparkler rather than some limp and discolored twine. "It certainly makes a statement, doesn't it?" She fanned her face. "Sorry. I don't know why I'm so emotional. You ready to get back on the road? Check-in is at four." She hopped to her feet and gathered up their trash, seemingly looking anywhere but at him. "On the way, you can bring me up to date on what's going on with Olivia and your in-laws."

"Forgive me if my former in-laws aren't something I like to talk about." He followed her lead, plucked up the blanket and shook it out before folding it to store in the truck.

"But you're going to have to. I need to be prepared for anything once Olivia gets to the Flying Spur. I assume her grandparents will continue to be part of her life, right?" She flashed him a smile and headed to the trailer to check on Skyfire. When she was out of sight, Ryder let out a pent-up breath.

Pretend engagement or not, of all the ways he dreamed of how this day might turn out, putting a "ring" on Corliss's finger hadn't come close to being on his list. The thought put a smile on his lips and lightened his heart, almost as much as the idea of seeing his daughter again.

Pretend-engaged to Corliss Blackwell.

Maybe hope wasn't so lost after all.

CHAPTER SIX

"According to the GPS, we're almost there."

"Good. Great. Thanks." Corliss wasn't entirely sure what she heard in Ryder's voice—irritation, assurance, regret—all of which would be perfectly reasonable, considering she hadn't been able to sit still for the past half hour. She finally had to sit on her hands to stop herself from twisting them into knots. "I just keep thinking what if this doesn't work? What if—"

"*What if* your uncle says yes and you can set some of this worry aside?" Ryder clicked off the sound system—finally—and kept his speed steady along the rather barren yet picturesque landscape of Montana. "How about you focus on that possibility?"

"Because that's not the way the Blackwell luck has been running these days."

"You and Denny called a truce. And I'm

back. I'd say both those things are positive shifts in the wind."

She forced a smile at his teasing, but the memory of him wrapping a simple piece of string around her finger caused a new kind of anxiety to slide through her. Being around Ryder today, heck, being around him at all since he'd come home felt…different. She felt different around him.

She rubbed her hand against her stomach in an attempt to calm herself. She didn't like different where anything was concerned, but especially not with Ryder. She couldn't shake the suspicion that their relationship was shifting like slippery mud under her feet. Not only couldn't she get her balance, she wasn't entirely sure she wanted to.

"So, Denny and Elias. What's the story there?"

"I only know what little my father told me years ago. When Gran was nineteen, she ran off with a man named Cal Wesson."

"Go, Denny." Ryder sounded impressed.

"The way Dad tells it, Granddad Cal was what some might call a scoundrel."

"I don't think I've ever heard that word used outside of old movies."

"Yeah, well, it fits. Cal had his share of vices. Drinking, gambling, but Gran was crazy about him. The idea was for them to get married immediately, but Cal gambled their savings away more than once. By then, Gran was pregnant with my dad and uncle—"

"I always forget your dad's a twin," Ryder said.

"Yet another branch of the family tree that's been pruned," Corliss said. "After Cal was killed wrangling wild horses, Gran, significantly pregnant at the time, moved to Eagle Springs, not only to get a fresh start but also to get out from under Cal's debt and toxic reputation."

"So that's why she still has the Blackwell name?"

Corliss smirked. "Dad always said she did it as part defiance, part revenge. She was determined to make the Flying Spur as successful, if not more successful, than the ranch of the family that disowned her." Up until last year, Denny had come pretty close. The Flying Spur had been on the cusp of breaking into the big leagues when it came to training horses, especially the difficult, emotionally damaged cases. And then, in the blink of an eye, everything that could go wrong, did.

"You've never heard anything about her past from Denny herself?"

"Nope." Corliss shook her head. "I tried a few times over the years. You know, played the I-want-to-know-more-about-who-and-where-I-come-from card, but Gran reminded me in very plain terms that the family I have is the only one that matters. On the one hand, she isn't wrong. On the other..."

"On the other, it would be nice to see just how deep those Blackwell roots go." Ryder flashed that smile of understanding her way.

"All this is why I need you to let me take the lead with what information I share with these folks," Corliss told him. "I'm not sure about much other than the fact that Big E—"

"Big who?"

"Big E. That's what everyone calls Elias."

"O-kay." Ryder chuckled. "Sounds like a real character already."

"I only know what I read on the internet. There's no telling how much resentment's built up since Denny left. But we need his help. Whether Gran can bring herself to admit that or not."

"You do what's necessary to protect your family. It's what you've always done, Corliss. It's what makes you the strong woman you are. I wouldn't hesitate to do the same for Olivia, or you, for that matter, so mark any concerns about me off your list and move on."

"So this doesn't feel… I don't know…weird to you?"

"What part? That you're staying at your great-uncle's family-vacation ranch under false pretenses in the hopes you can convince him to help his long-lost sister? Or that we're pretending to be engaged?"

"Yes." Any other answer got caught someplace between her heart and her throat. She touched the string he'd tied around her finger. "Ryder, I have enough weirdness and uncertainty in my life right now. I don't want this to change things between us."

"Nothing's going to change, Corliss. We won't let it. We're best friends. Now and forever."

Corliss pressed her lips together. Clearly, he wasn't as hesitant about the situation as she was, which meant he was probably right. She needed to set her discomfort aside and go with the flow. Reassured, she sat back in her seat, only to sit forward again when she saw the overhead sign indicating they'd arrived at the Blackwell Family Ranch.

"Okay, here we go." She blew out a breath and gripped the top of her seat belt as Ryder made the turn onto the winding road. "I can see why Gran's heart broke at the thought of never coming back here," Corliss murmured as she took in the endless blue sky filling the landscape and the vast, lush green hills. "It's beautiful."

"It's a close second to Eagle Springs," Ryder assured her with an appraising nod. "Definitely a stunner but doesn't have quite the same feel of home, does it?"

"No." Corliss turned her head and watched the landscape whip by. "But I bet it wouldn't take much for it to." Ryder slowed the car, dragging her attention back to the front window as he climbed up the last hill. "What's happening here?"

"Looks like some kind of end-of-summer party. I think maybe now we know why the town seemed so empty when we drove through."

"Looks like half the state's here," Corliss agreed.

Cars and trucks were parked on both sides of the road, leading the rest of the way, as they followed signs to the main lodge. People flooded in and out of the area; balloons and thin, colored ribbons were being whipped around on sticks. Children carried popcorn buckets and novelty drink holders, along with stuffed animals and other carnival-inspired toys. Corliss rolled down her window, and music drifted into the car, fun, danceable, bringing a smile to her face.

Ryder drove slowly until stopped by a tall man in jeans, T-shirt and a brown cowboy hat pulled low over his eyes. "Afternoon," the man greeted them as Ryder lowered his window. He inclined his chin to the trailer. "You must be Corliss Mills. Hadley told me to keep a lookout for you. I'm Ty Blackwell." He tipped his hat at Corliss, shifted his gaze back to Ryder. "Glad we didn't spook you away from your stay, with all the activity."

"What's going on?" Corliss asked.

"Other than a wedding last night, the school's end-of-summer carnival. Normally, they hold it at the school in town, but a pipe in the basement burst and flooded the gym last week. Easier and cheaper to just move it here to a wide-open space than pushing the repair job into overtime. There's a small utility road to the left of the main lodge." Ty pointed to the two-story structure that looked like a fancy bed-and-breakfast. "Follow that around and I'll meet you at the stables. We've got a stall already set up for your horse."

"Thanks." Corliss watched Ty move off and jump on an ATV that he drove slowly around the other side of the lodge.

"Mills?" Ryder asked.

"My mother's maiden name," Corliss said. "I guess that's my cousin. Well, one of them." She hadn't come in completely cold. She had done enough research to know Big E had ten adult grandchildren, including Chance Blackwell, one of her all-time favorite country singers. Her estranged family was definitely a sprawling one.

"They were waiting for us. For you," Ryder corrected as he waved at a pair of teenagers who stopped to let him turn onto the side road Ty had indicated. The second they were on the other side of the lodge, the noise from the festival faded. A few minutes later, Ryder pulled to a stop between a stable and barn large enough to house a substantial number of livestock. "You ready?"

"As ready as I'm going to be." She blew out a breath and dropped down out of the truck as Ty headed toward them. Only he wasn't alone. An adorable—and cheeky—redheaded little girl, wearing the brightest pink cowgirl boots Corliss had ever seen, gave Corliss an enthusiastic wave.

"Well, hello." Corliss couldn't stop the smile from spreading across her face. She judged the little girl to be around seven or eight with personality to spare. If she ever grew into that twinkle in her eye, her parents were going to have their hands full. "Are you part of the welcoming committee?"

"Uh-huh. I'm Rosie Blackwell. Uncle Ty said I could come meet your horse."

"Uncle Ty said to ask first, remember?" Ty came up behind her and rested a hand on her shoulder. "Rosie and her sister are staying with me and my wife at the lodge while her parents are in Bozeman for a few days."

"Holly's still little," Rosie announced. "She's only two. You can meet her if you want."

"I'd like that very much, thank you, Rosie.

How about you stay right there and I'll get Skyfire? He's pretty friendly normally, but it's been a long drive."

Corliss walked around to the back of the trailer and dropped the ramp while Ryder joined Ty and the little girl. She heard them exchange pleasantries, talking about the drive. She stepped inside and unlatched the butt bar keeping Skyfire secure.

Walking up the other side, she ran her hand over the horse's flank. "Long day for you, huh, fella?" She curled her fingers under and felt the horse's pulse pounding beneath her touch. "We're counting on you to make a good impression." She moved closer to his head, touched her hand to his face. "I hate to put so much pressure on you, but Gran needs this. We all do." She leaned in, rested her forehead against his cheek. He was their last chance.

He was also the animal that held the biggest chunk of her heart. Nash might have trained him to be one of the best cutting horses in the rodeo business, but from the moment they'd brought him on to the Flying Spur, he'd been hers.

Skyfire gave a gentle snort and eased some

of the tension tightening in Corliss's chest. "There's someone hoping to meet you outside. I know you're anxious to stretch your legs, but let's make a friend first, all right?" She untied the two ropes and slowly backed the horse down the ramp.

As soon as Skyfire got his first free breath of Montana air, the horse let out a whinny before raising his head up and down as if in approval. "Yeah, you'll like it here," Corliss whispered and, catching the leads, brought him over to where Rosie waited with Ty and Ryder. "But don't like it too much. I'm not going to part with you easily."

"Ooooh, he's so pretty!" Rosie said in a mock whisper. She held her clenched fists up close to her chest, bounced on her toes. "What's his name again?"

"Skyfire."

"Is he a quarter horse?" Rosie scrunched up her nose in concentration.

"Good guess," Corliss said. "You know your horses."

"I'm trying to learn. Uncle Ethan lets me go with him to treat the animals sometimes, and I ask lots of questions."

"Rosie excels at questions." Ty stayed close as Corliss held out her hand to Rosie.

"Skyfire's friendly," Corliss told the little girl whose eyes were growing wider by the second. "He's used to my nieces and they're your sister's age. Here." She took Rosie's hand and pressed it against the horse's neck. Skyfire turned his head slightly and sighed as Rosie petted him. "There you go. Sky, this is Rosie. I have a feeling she's pretty important around here, so mind your manners."

"He likes me!" Rosie grinned. "My daddy said I got all kinds of horse sense he didn't, right, Uncle Ty?"

"Chance is gifted in other ways," Ty confirmed and Corliss nodded, thinking of her favorite country music artist. "I was thinking we could give Skyfire some time in the east pasture. Let him run off that drive while we get you two checked in and settled."

"Can I take him over?" Rosie asked. "I can unlock the paddock myself. Mama K showed me how."

"Take Felix with you." Over Rosie's head, Ty motioned to one of the stable hands. "There's feed and water aplenty available. I also need to photocopy his paperwork before we put him in the stable with other animals. We just like all our *T*s crossed."

"Sure, of course." Even a year past the blight, she found herself growing nervous. The paperwork included info on the outbreak as well as a copy of the certification that the Flying Spur was in the clear. But strangles was nothing to take for granted. "You okay, Sky? To go with Rosie? She's got a pretty place for you to get some running in."

"It is pretty," Rosie told Skyfire as she accepted the leads and walked him away. She continued chatting with him as if he were her new best friend. Skyfire looked back at Corliss with an expression that said he might just have found a new mistress as they disappeared from sight.

"Girl's a handful but brings a smile to everyone's face," Ty said as Corliss stared after them.

"Family trait no doubt," Ryder muttered under his breath and earned an elbow in the ribs from Corliss.

"You two have kids?" Ty asked.

"Ah, no. Not together. I have a teenager. A son." Corliss found herself taking that first uncertain step into the story she'd concocted.

A story she planned to keep as close to the truth as possible. "Ryder has an eight-year-old daughter. Olivia."

"She's visiting my in-laws," Ryder explained as Corliss retrieved the paperwork she brought.

"Well, any questions about blending a family, you'll have plenty of people to ask around here." Ty shuffled through the documents, made some notations on his phone before handing them back. "I suggest you leave your truck and trailer here for now until you're checked in, especially since I don't think Hadley's decided which cabin she's putting you in. I'll have one of the hands unhitch the trailer and store it on the other side of the stable. And we'll also make sure we clean it out and set it up fresh the evening before you're due to check out."

Ty led them to the front of the main lodge that boasted a long, wide covered porch filled with rocking chairs and flowers blooming into their last gasp at summer. "Quick rundown of the place, which will be back to normal by tomorrow," Ty explained as he climbed the steps. "This is the main lodge. We've got a dining hall for meals and also a small office area with printers and internet access. Speaking of which, Wi-Fi can be spotty at times, especially during storms. Sometimes, you can't win against Mother Nature. Guest rooms are on the second floor, with separate guest cabins scattered around the property. We've tried to give every window a view of some kind. So, you two are from Wyoming? Whereabouts?"

"Oh, I'm sure you've never heard of it," Corliss said. "It barely registers as a dot on the map."

They stepped out of the way of a young couple exiting the lodge, so wrapped up in each other—literally and figuratively—that they nearly collided with Ryder. Corliss and Ryder turned and watched the couple wander off into the carnival crowd.

"Bride and groom from last night," Ty explained. "They remind me of those old cartoon characters with pulsing hearts in their eyes."

"Young love," Corliss softened the edge in her voice at Ty's expression. "Long story," she added.

"You couldn't have planned your visit any better. Hadley's leaving up all the decorations in the chapel so you can get a feel for what you'd like your wedding to be." Once inside the lodge, Ty stopped in front of a beautifully polished oak desk. "Hadley!" he called out and held his hand over the desk bell but lowered it before striking it. "She hates this thing."

"Only because you always seem to hit it at nap time." A tall blonde woman emerged from the doorway behind the desk, her arms filled with a miniature replica of Ty, all dark eyes and thick dark hair. "You take strange pleasure in waking your daughter up."

"Oh, sure." Ty held out his arms and lifted the grinning little girl against his shoulder. "Aurora's my daughter when she's awake, but when she's sleeping like an angel, she's yours."

"Hey, I got the labor, remember?" Hadley said with a cheeky grin. "You must be Corliss. And Ryder." She stretched out her hand. "Welcome to the Blackwell Family Ranch. It's not normally this hectic."

"Thanks for fitting us into your reservations at the last minute," Corliss said, then caught sight of a stack of binders and spreadsheets on the other side of the registration desk. "Looks like you're busy."

"Oh, these are about to be filed, thank goodness." Hadley motioned to the front door. "The Cunningham wedding is officially in the books. So to speak," she added with a grin.

"A few more like that and I'll be pushing harder to hire a dedicated wedding coordinator," Ty muttered as he tweaked his daughter's nose.

"Don't listen to him," Hadley said even as she shot her husband a look of warning. "Ty, since Holly's still asleep, why don't you take Aurora out to the carnival?"

"She thinks I can't take a hint." Ty tipped his hat up. "I'll be seeing you around."

"Bridezilla wedding?" Corliss asked Hadley.

"Oh, I wouldn't put her in that category. I can't complain, really. Her parents paid a small fortune to make their only child's dream wedding come true and filled up nearly every room we have. So what if she changed her mind two days ago about the cake she wanted. Or that she wanted steady rather than blinking fairy lights in the chapel." Hadley took a deep, calming breath. "I have run into a bit of an issue with your reservation."

"If it helps," Ryder said. "We're pretty easygoing."

"Oh, that's helpful, thanks," Hadley said on a sigh. "Considering a number of the wedding guests brought…additional family members, I'm afraid the only cabin I have left for tonight is a one-bedroom. It's also the cabin that's furthest away from the recreation area and lodge. Normally, I like to keep those guests who are boarding animals in the stable closer, but…"

"The one-bedroom's fine." Corliss had to clear the squeak out of her voice. Closer quarters with Ryder? Whoo-boy, this trip was getting more interesting by the moment. "And after being cooped up in the car today, the walk to and from the lodge while we're here will be nice."

"You are officially my favorite guests ever." Hadley laughed and tucked her hair behind her ear. "Between the wedding and taking care of Rosie and Holly, along with Aurora, these last few days, this is the silver lining I've been looking for. Let's get you guys registered."

Before Corliss could reach for her wallet, Ryder pulled his out and set his credit card on the counter. "We're in the process of merging our accounts," he explained. "Can you transfer her online deposit to this card? And use it for the balance?"

Corliss gnashed her teeth. This trip had been her idea. It was her responsibility to pay for it. As if sensing her mood, Ryder slipped an arm around her waist and squeezed, his too-wide grin telling her he knew exactly what she was thinking.

"Certainly." If Hadley picked up on Corliss's irritation, she didn't show it. "We've got dinner in the dining room this evening starting at six thirty. Most of the wedding guests are leaving in the morning after breakfast. Of course, we can always deliver your meals to you if you'd prefer."

"The dining room sounds great," Corliss said before Ryder could say otherwise. "Gives us a few hours to clean up and make ourselves presentable."

"We charge a boarding fee for horses," Hadley told them. "But I'm going to waive that because, well, let's call it a gratitude waiver. I love being reminded that people can be thoughtful and reasonable. I don't think you made mention in your reservation, Corliss. Are there any dates next year you're thinking of?"

"Dates?" She couldn't fathom what Hadley meant.

"Wedding dates, honey," Ryder said with a laugh and roll of his eyes. "She's still getting used to the idea of being engaged."

"Oh right. Dates." How were people good at lying? She couldn't keep anything straight! "Um, we're open, I think. Spring maybe? Or summer?" She beamed up at Ryder. "What do you think, honey?"

"I think it's entirely up to you."

Corliss narrowed her eyes. He was having entirely too much fun with this ruse.

"A couple after my own heart," Hadley said. "I've got time set aside tomorrow morning and we'll come up with options. Will that work for you? Say about ten?"

"Sounds great," Corliss squeaked out and earned a muffled chuckle from Ryder as he signed the invoice.

Hadley handed over two keys along with

a map of the property and a list of activities and meal times. "As far as the carnival, normalcy shall return to the ranch tomorrow." Hadley marked a path for them to follow to their cabin. "You have any questions or concerns, the front desk is open until eight tonight."

"Long days for you," Corliss said.

"Some days are longer than others," Hadley confirmed. "But not everyone gets their dream job. And now that I've met you two, I get to play with new wedding ideas."

Corliss waited until they were almost to the truck before some of the guilt slipped out. "I didn't expect keeping up this pretense would be so hard."

"Not easy lying to people as likable as Hadley and Ty," Ryder agreed. "How about we take a walk before we head to the cabin? Maybe check on Skyfire?"

How did the man always know the right thing to say? She needed a reminder of the real reason why they'd come here, and what was at stake. "Sounds good to me."

They walked in the direction they'd seen Rosie and the ranch hand go. Even from a distance, as they continued east, it was clear

Skyfire had found his place in Montana. The cutting horse was racing around with two other horses, as if playing an equine version of tag. Corliss's chest tightened.

Could a horse look…happy?

Rosie and two other slightly older girls were standing on the bottom fence rung, cheering them on. "Hi, Corliss! Hi, Ryder." Rosie jumped down and raced over. "Skyfire is having so much fun! He's even made friends."

Corliss nodded. This time last year, Skyfire had an entire stable of friends, but the outbreak had left him isolated and alone and, in a lot of ways, heartbroken. Horses might be majestic creatures, but their hearts were easily hurt.

She, Gran and Nash had managed to inoculate Skyfire with antibiotics fast enough that he hadn't gotten sick, but so many others weren't as lucky. Most, including their last two major-investment horses had to be put down. She'd lost count of the number of nights she'd hunkered down in the stall with Skyfire so he wouldn't be alone.

Corliss raised her chin and looked out over the fence. The good days were coming back, she told herself. She could feel it. All she had to do was make it through the next few days and convince long-lost Uncle Elias that she was worth taking a chance on.

Rosie grabbed Corliss's hand and dragged her forward. "These are my cousins, Abbey and Gen. They live with Uncle Jon and Aunt Lydia and their baby brothers over at their ranch."

"Hi," the girls said in tandem.

"She's Gen." The slightly taller girl pointed a thumb at her sister. "I'm Abbey."

"Nice to meet you." Corliss was going to have to start taking notes. "We thought we'd come check on him before heading to our cabin."

"We came to the festival," Gen, in a softer voice than her sister's, said. "But we prefer the animals."

"Smart girl," Ryder said and earned a smile. "Animals are more fun than people sometimes."

"So much for you winning me a teddy bear at one of those game booths," Corliss said with an exaggerated sigh.

"Goat," Abbey said. "They don't have any bears, but you can win a stuffed goat."

"Or a horse," Rosie added. "Those are really cute. One even has a white bow on one ear."

"How about we go try to win one for Olivia?" Corliss suggested.

"Maybe Mason would like one?" Ryder teased.

"Bow or Arrow might, maybe." Laughter accompanied her and Ryder as they said goodbye to the girls and strolled toward the crowd.

For a last minute shift of location, Corliss had to admit the carnival looked as if it belonged here. A variety of colorfully painted wood booths boasted various games of chance, food offerings and activities. Signs said they were raising money for upcoming school events: the football team, the 4-H club and the computer science department.

The Goldfish Ping-Pong Ball challenge, always a favorite of Corliss's, offered the chance to bring home a water-dependent friend. Hitting three balloons with darts could win them free tickets to the upcoming fall crab feed. "Oh, let's try the beanbag toss." She grabbed Ryder's arm and brought him over to the booth. "I want one of those horses for Olivia."

"Olivia doesn't know much about horses."

"Trust me," Corliss assured him as she forked over cash and was handed three palm-sized beanbags. "If she doesn't love them now, she soon will. Moving to Wyoming will see to that. Come on." She arched a brow in challenge. "Unless you don't think you can win. Your pool game was a little shaky. Maybe your pitching arm is too."

"Shaky…and yet I still beat you." He gave her a stony glare. "Watch and learn." He hefted one of the bags, and, after the vendor took a step back, sent it soaring straight into the twenty-point target. The second and third one followed suit before Ryder turned appraising eyes on Corliss. "Want to beat that?"

"Stand back." Corliss elbowed Ryder aside, handed off more cash, and hefted one of the beanbags in her hand. She was about to throw when she spotted an older man standing kitty-corner to the booth, watching her.

He was a big man. Well over six feet and wore his jeans, boots and belt buckle almost like a uniform. The clothes make the man, Corliss thought, as she took in the dark denim shirt and dark gray cowboy hat perched on top of his head. He was, from head to toe and despite his years, the quintessential cowboy. She could practically hear his spurs jangling.

Regret clanged against her heart, regret that Denny had never shared anything about her brother with her children or grandchildren—at least, nothing Corliss and her siblings could cling to or embrace. There was history here, on this land, with this man. Her great-uncle.

So much history. And so much hope.

Excitement and fear raced down her spine. "Elias." She whispered his name as if afraid that, even hundreds of miles away, Denny would hear her.

"Where?" Ryder moved up behind her as Big E inclined his head, his brow furrowing for a long moment before he turned around and walked away.

"He's gone." Corliss tried to refocus on her beanbags. She missed all three shots, but rather than teasing her about it, Ryder accepted his stuffed horse with a lacy white bow on its ear and handed it to Corliss. "Consolation prize," he said as they backed away from the booth. "You okay?"

"I don't know." She'd been so preoccupied

with what she hoped to get out of meeting her long-lost relation that she hadn't let herself dwell on the significant can of worms she'd be opening by bridging the family divide. "You ever feel like you've just stepped in something that's going to stick with you for a long time?"

"You having second thoughts?" Ryder took her by the elbow and led her away. "If you are, we can leave right now."

"I can't afford to." Was she trying to convince Ryder? Or herself? "I'm probably overthinking things. Let's—"

"Head over to the cabin and settle in," Ryder said and guided her over to the truck. "That's a good idea."

CHAPTER SEVEN

RYDER WOULD HAVE had to be unconscious not to have noticed Corliss's surge of nerves when they were given a one-bedroom cabin. She'd covered her reaction, at least as far as anyone who didn't know her was concerned. Those nerves of hers, however, seemed to have disappeared while she processed her unexpected run-in with Elias Blackwell.

Once they'd gotten to the surprisingly spacious cabin, she'd argued with him about the bedroom, as if she was offended that he planned to take the couch. He understood her coping mechanisms and her propensity to overthink everything. She'd pushed back because it gave her something else to think about, something she could safely attack while she reasoned out other things in her life—ones she couldn't control.

Truth be told, he wanted his own room in case the nightmares hit.

Ryder had deposited her belongings by the door and unloaded his own from the truck while she paced, muttered, and finally acquiesced and headed into the bedroom.

Minutes later, as he explored the galley-style kitchen, dining area and living room, sounds of the shower starting had him breathing a sigh of relief. Showers—water of any kind, actually—had always been Corliss's escape. When she couldn't cope with something or when her mind wouldn't stop whirring, she always took a long shower or, on more desperate occasions, headed down to the river along the north edge of the Flying Spur or the lake at the east end of the property.

He'd spent some of the best days of his childhood alongside that river and lake, not only with Corliss but her brothers and sister as well. The contests they had with one another over who could stay underwater the longest. The countless hours spent dangling lured lines for fish far too intelligent to bite. For such a ranch-focused woman, she thrived around the water, and in this arena, he was happy to see her where she felt safest.

"Woman's part fish," Ryder reminded himself as he took an inventory of the surprisingly well-stocked pantry and supplies in the cabinets. Basic cookware, plates, flatware, all the necessities of home. A lovely selection of offerings they could have delivered to the room, from a simple continental breakfast to a more elaborate, dare he say it, romantic dinner.

The cabin was simple but up-to-date. The rustic construction and decor fit in perfectly with the atmosphere of a guest and working ranch. The kitchen window, under which a square table and chairs sat, was accented with café curtains in the same green as the main lodge was painted. Hardwood floors boasted weathered knots and were a testament to some things getting better with age.

As entertaining as this fake engagement to Corliss may prove to be, he wasn't so foolish as to believe it was anything but a convenience. It was clear she didn't want to think about him in terms other than what she was used to—them being just friends. Why he found that disappointing, he couldn't quite decide.

Their relationship had always been safe. The trust between them was undeniable and the secrets, if there were any, few. The fact he found himself wondering if there was more lurking beneath the life-long friendship… That seemed to him to be asking for trouble.

His propensity to overthink things came in handy in some instances; planning for every eventual outcome was a requirement when fighting oil rig fires. When it came to relationships? That was a whole other thing.

"No wonder your marriage to Nina tanked," he muttered as the water was turned off and the cabin went silent. He'd been unfair to his late wife on so many fronts. He could count on two hands, with fingers left over, just how many months he'd spent at home. Even after Olivia was born, Nina had been the one steering the marriage ship while Rider, and his endless contracts, had plowed it straight into the ground.

In the end, despite every intention of not doing so, he'd broken Nina's heart. Now that Nina was gone, that was something he'd never be able to forgive himself for.

He unpacked what belongings he'd brought with him and then grabbed his phone to wait for Corliss. He was just reading through his latest text messages from Olivia, where she was regaling him with the antics of her fellow summer camp classmates, when the bedroom door popped open.

Corliss emerged wearing clean jeans, her hair damp against a T-shirt depicting a rudimentary illustration of Waldo and the Cranky Crow logo. Her bare feet told him she was feeling more at home than she was probably willing to admit, something that was proven true when she threw herself into the corner of the couch and curled up.

"Feel better?" He texted Olivia a few smiley-face emojis before setting his phone down.

"That shower is amazing." Corliss leaned her cheek on her hand and sighed. "I think it managed to wash a good couple of years off me. That Olivia?" She motioned to the phone.

"Yeah. She's supposed to send me her flight information, but her grandfather hasn't given it to her yet."

Corliss cringed. "Your in-laws aren't making this easy, are they?"

"No. He, they, believe Olivia should stay with them, where she's settled. Where they can pay for her education and keep her close." With Corliss he could let the frustration eke out. "They think I can just fall into any job and that'll be that."

"Whatever they believe doesn't really mean much. She's your daughter. And we both know you won't be happy with just any job."

No, Ryder thought. He wouldn't be. But this was one topic he knew he couldn't discuss with Corliss. Not yet. "I'm the one part of the equation they'd like to subtract. They probably think if they push me hard enough, I'll back down and let Olivia stay with them. No," he added at Corliss's questioning expression. "That will not be happening. But I have no doubt if Nina hadn't specifically stated in her will that I would be sole guardian if anything happened, they'd be suing me for custody."

"They can't blame you for her death," Corliss said in dismay. "You weren't even in the country when it happened."

"No, I wasn't, was I?"

"It was a freak accident, Ryder. No one's to blame."

"Depends on what you're being blamed for," Ryder said. "Nina wasn't happy in our marriage. Her father is of the mind that if she had been, she wouldn't have been on that boat in the first place. That's on me evidently." He hesitated before admitting one of the many things that kept him awake nights. "He's not entirely wrong."

"I'm sure that's not true."

"Nina was miserable those last few years, and me being away most of that time didn't help. The last conversation we had, she told me we needed to face the truth. That things were over and she was going to file for divorce. We were supposed to work out the details and custody arrangement for Olivia the next time I came home. It was all very civilized. Amicable." Cold, even. How could it be anything else when it was clear from the start that Nina's love alone had not been enough to sustain their relationship? "It was like closing the chapter of a book you aren't enjoying."

"Ryder." Corliss sat up and rested her hand on his arm. "You never told me any of this."

He shrugged. "There wasn't any point. The weekend after she and I spoke, Nina went boating with friends—her father's friends, primarily. They got caught in a storm, and Nina was just…gone. Olivia…" He closed his eyes for a moment, let the terror wash over him. "Olivia was supposed to be with her, but she came down with a stomach bug that morning. Nina's parents insisted she go and have a good time."

"And they blame you for that?"

"I get it. I understand why," Ryder said. "As horrible as losing Nina was, I can't begin to imagine what any of us would have done if we'd lost Olivia, too."

Corliss snuggled closer and rested her head on his shoulder, clasped his hand in hers. Feeling her warmth, her comfort, her very being just a heartbeat away from his...

Ryder tightened his hold on her hand. "Nina deserved better," he murmured. Deserved better than him: a man who, no matter how hard he tried, couldn't bring himself to love her the way she should have been loved. "She was a good woman. A good friend." And she'd spent more than eight years trying desperately to convince Ryder she could love him enough for both of them. "Her parents were right. I wasn't up to scratch for their daughter, and they're equally convinced I'm not up to scratch for their only grandchild."

"They're wrong," Corliss said in a defiant tone. "I've heard you with her on the phone. Your love for her is whole and unconditional. There's nothing more a parent can give to their child than that. You can come through anything if there's love."

"You say that as if you think your parents don't love you." Ryder kept his gaze glued to their entwined fingers and embraced the warm feelings from having her so close.

"Oh, I know they love me. I know they love all of us." He could hear the shrug in her voice. "But my father certainly never felt the connection to the Flying Spur that Gran does. Neither did his brother."

"Your mom and dad are happy in Arizona, then?"

"Happier living in their retirement community than they ever were in Wyoming. Maybe I wish my father hadn't expected to receive a lump sum in place of his inheritance. If Gran hadn't paid that out, chances are the two of us wouldn't be sitting here trying to figure out how to convince Big E to invest in my and Nash's plan. But that's water under the bridge."

"Personally, I'm glad to be here to witness whatever's coming next for you Blackwells." Ryder smiled. "I just wish I could do more to help."

"You *are* helping me. By going along with

this plan, even though—even though the more I think about it, it's over-the-top ridiculous." She forced a laugh that had him shifting to face her. "I mean, the two of us, engaged? After all these years who could possibly believe we—"

The impulse struck so hard and so fast Ryder didn't have the time or the inclination to resist. His hand caught the back of her neck as he leaned forward and, before another word fell from her lips, he covered her mouth with his.

There are moments in life, pure, picture-perfect moments that settle in a person's heart and stay there forever. This was one of those special moments. After all the years that Ryder had dreamed about kissing Corliss, in this one idyllic fraction of time, reality exceeded every expectation. He could feel her shock at first, but then just as quickly, her lips softened and she deepened the kiss.

Knowing he may never have another chance, he held her close and her grip on his shoulders tightened.

Just when he was hoping the moment wouldn't end, she pulled back, her quickened breaths warm against his face. It was a confirmation of everything he'd ever felt about her. And left him teetering on a precipice only she could save him from.

"Maybe you need to reevaluate your definition of *ridiculous*." He pressed his mouth to hers again, briefly this time, just long enough to have hers curving into a surprised, if not befuddled, smile. "I can't believe we've never tried that before." He couldn't explain it. Not to her. Not to himself. He stroked her flushed cheek and caught her gaze. "I wonder what took us so long?" He got to his feet, went over to the dresser to retrieve a fresh set of clothes.

"You've been thinking about kissing me?" she called as he headed into the bedroom. "For how long?"

He froze, debating only a moment before responding. With the truth. "Long enough for me to want to do it again."

CORLISS PRESSED HER fingers against her lips, which were still warm from his. Still tingling from his touch. This shouldn't be possible. This couldn't be happening.

But it was. It had.

Ryder Talbot had kissed her.

She stared blankly at the closed bedroom door.

One kiss, one single kiss had managed to tilt her already spinning world completely off its axis and left her with one stunning, mind-numbing question.

How could she make that happen again?

"Ooooh boy." She fanned her face, blew out a breath. "This can't be right." It was just her overwrought brain playing with her, making her feel things that weren't truly there, but... She drew in a slow, hitched breath. But they were.

She had enough to think about on her over-loaded plate. Ryder was her rock. Her one constant. Her...other.

Whether he was halfway across the world or sitting across the table, he was someone to count on. Someone to confide in. Some-one to...

The one person she never had to question what to expect. Yet here she sat, in a cabin in Montana, wondering if these last few minutes had catapulted her life in an unexpected yet potentially exciting direction.

Or maybe had left her clinging to a past that no longer existed.

She jumped to her feet, began to pace in front of the sofa, nibbling on her already nonexistent thumbnail as she debated calling her sister. Adele was better at these kinds of things than she was. Corliss didn't date. She didn't…well, she didn't do much of anything outside the ranch, not since her almost wedding fourteen years ago. Maybe that was why she was so surprised. And not just about the kiss but who had been doing the kissing. This was Ryder! Her best friend, her confidant, her…

"It's Ryder." She stopped stomping back and forth and let out a frustrated grunt. She'd never felt more unlike herself; it only added to her confusion. She lifted her hand, to run it through her hair, but didn't when she saw the string tied around her finger.

The string she'd watched him tie. The string that acted as an engagement ring and had made her laugh even as her once-hard heart began to thaw. At the time, she'd seen friendship in his gaze, but now…had she been seeing more? Had it been love? Ryder was her friend. Her *friend*, she reminded herself over and over even as the excitement of something new and good surged through her. Every teasing word her family had ever uttered about the two of them came flooding back, bringing with them the worst doubts.

This was wrong. Testing these waters, it wasn't worth potentially ruining their friendship over. Was it?

She was still standing when Ryder came out of the bedroom, tucking in a dark blue shirt into the back of his jeans. When he lifted his gaze to hers, she saw the question, the uncertainty behind his normal easygoing expression. "I thought maybe we could take a walk before dinner. Get some fresh air. Clear our minds."

"Sounds good." She headed for the door and had it open before Ryder reached for her hand. She spun and looked up at him. "What?"

"Shoes." His smile was slow but oh-so-tempting. "You might want to put some on."

"Shoes, right." She let out a laugh so completely forced and hollow she cringed. "One kiss from you and my brain's stopped working." She pressed her hands to her face as if that would prevent her cheeks from flaming. "Why now?"

"I shouldn't have made it out of that fire, Corliss." He shrugged, as if his kissing her hadn't thrown her for an absolute loop. "An event like that, it changes a man's perspective. Makes those chances that seemed too big to take seem not quite so big anymore. If I crossed a line—"

"Oh, you crossed a line." She rested a hand on his shoulder, shook her head. Reason battled against confusion. She should be more worried about this, but even while it felt strange, it also felt oddly…right. "I'll be back. Shoes," she added with a grin and hurried into the bedroom. As she was about to return to Ryder, she paused to stare at herself in front of the full-length mirror, a pair of socks in one hand, boots in the other, her heart beating in an entirely unfamiliar, unsteady rhythm. What was she thinking? Taking a solid friendship and throwing it into the unknown? Love, in her experience, only brought heartache. Ryder knew this as well. At least he'd made it down the aisle, and yet his marriage hadn't lasted.

Love simply wasn't worth the risk.

But what was the alternative? Trying to go back to something that might not exist any longer? "Start by putting on your socks," she reminded herself. She'd worry about the rest later.

As BEAUTIFUL AS she found the Blackwell Family Ranch, Corliss had never wanted to go home so desperately in her life. She wanted to be in the familiar, where everything made sense and nothing was at risk. Well, nothing beyond the things that already were. What she wouldn't give for her daily routine that had been pulled out from under her almost a year ago.

Instead, she was here in Montana on a wing and a prayer, hoping the only solution she'd come up with to save her family's business and home would pay off.

"That shower didn't do a thing to help you relax, did it?"

"It helped some," Corliss said. And then he'd kissed her and thrown her into a tizzy. The other night he'd accused her of having one. Until now she'd wondered how to define it exactly. Now she could. And she didn't like the sensation. Not one little bit. "I guess it's just that everything feels so up in the air. Like I don't have control." Over anything, it seemed. "Let's check out more of the carnival, huh?"

"Okay."

It was clear Ryder was going to do his best to shift things back into her comfort zone; the trouble was her comfort zone was about five hours southeast from here. Embracing what she could, she gladly lost herself in the noise of the dwindling crowd, despite the giant metaphorical elephant that had been dropped between her and Ryder. He tried to tempt her with caramel popcorn, one of her favorite treats, but her stomach was tied in so many knots it would have no place to go.

Across the way, the last bit of fresh lemonade was being served while the final pie and cakes were won in the silent auction. Signs were coming down, booths were being disassembled, and parents lugged small children over their tired shoulders and headed out.

"Looks like our first Montana sunset's coming up." Ryder inclined his chin toward the horizon as they wandered down between the main lodge and the stable. "Let's go check on Skyfire."

"Yeah? You don't think that's a bit mother hen-ish?"

"Oh, it totally is." She hadn't realized she'd been twisting her hands together until he stopped her, the silent concern shining in his eyes. "But he's the main reason why we're here, isn't he? Worst-case scenario, this could become his new home."

"I don't plan on that happening." As she said it, she realized he'd made that statement to get her to stop sulking and push forward. "Don't get me wrong," she added. "As nice as the Blackwell Ranch is, the Flying Spur is his home. And by the way, *this* is ridiculous."

"What is?" Ryder asked.

"This. Us. This…thing that's happened. So we kissed." She grabbed his arm, spun him to face her. "Like you said, it's kind of odd to think we haven't kissed before. I mean, right? We grew up together. How have we not tried that before now?"

"If you're waiting for me to argue with you, I won't."

It was the way he said it that gave her chills—the same kind of chills she'd felt the instant his mouth had touched hers. But she wasn't giving in. Not to something that would shove her already shaky world further off course. "We don't have to let it change anything. Not really," she insisted, as if he was arguing with her. "I'm still who I am and you're still who you are and—"

"I'm not the one worrying this into the grave." Ryder caught a strand of her hair lifted by the late summer breeze. "Maybe we should give it another go. Make sure that first kiss wasn't some kind of fluke." He reached for her, that darned charming smile of his sliding into the once-closed corners of her heart. "It would be tough, kissing you again, but I think I could give it—"

"You are not helping the situation." She tried to snap at him, but found herself laughing instead. He'd always been able to do that. Make her laugh even when she was at her most stressed. It was one of the things she loved about him.

Loved. Corliss's breath hitched. Loved. About. Ryder. Her mind spun so fast she couldn't think straight.

"Never said I was trying to help." Ryder locked his arms around her before she could wiggle away. She came up against him toe to shoulder, parts of her perfectly fitting parts of him. He ducked his head, sent her pulse rocketing into the stratosphere only to stop short and look over her shoulder. "Uh-oh."

"Uh-oh what?" She fought against the disappointment crashing through her. Despite her reservations, she wanted to test the waters again. Wanted to prove herself wrong. Or right.

"We aren't alone," Ryder whispered in her ear.

"We aren't?" She turned her head and spotted an older man standing at the fence line a ways away.

"That's him, isn't it?" Ryder asked. "Elias Blackwell. Looks like he's an extra in one of those old Westerns that Denny loves watching."

Corliss nodded, recalling her earlier observations about the man. There was only one horse in the pasture for him to admire—and he was watching Skyfire with admiration. It was written on his face as he tilted up his hat with a solitary finger as if in greeting. As if beckoning them closer.

"This is it," Corliss whispered as the knots in her belly tightened. What she wouldn't give to be able to breathe freely once more.

"Guess I should take this as a sign, right?" She smoothed a hand down her hair, tugged her shirt straight to make herself more presentable. "You think I should just come right out and introduce myself as a Blackwell?"

"Why don't you start with hello and see what happens?" Ryder dropped an arm around her waist, an action that quieted the loudest doubts ringing inside of her.

"Fine-looking horse you've got," Elias Blackwell called out to them without breaking his gaze from Skyfire as they approached. The horse was munching on what must have been a tasty bit of pasture grass. "Heard from my great-granddaughters he's called Skyfire. Fitting name with that coloring. When the sun hits him just right, it's like he's made of flame." He turned then, his focus shifting to Corliss for a long moment before he stretched out his hand. "You'd be Corliss Mills stopping in on her way down to Wyoming."

"Yes, sir." She hesitated only a moment before taking his hand and nodding to Ryder. "And this is Ryder Talbot."

"Ah, the fiancé," Elias said with a wide smile. He shook Ryder's hand, too. "Went in and had a bit of a chat with Hadley after seeing the two of you at the carnival. Welcome to the ranch. What do you think of it? Think it'll suit your wedding needs?"

Small talk, Corliss thought in relief. This she could do before easing herself into the harsh truth of her visit. "What's not to like?" Corliss said. "Actually, Mr. Blackwell—"

"Those grandsons of mine, they've whipped this place into some serious shape." Elias smiled with pride. "Got some considerable help from a few of my granddaughters, too, but what you see here? That's mostly my boys. Something on your mind, young lady? You're looking as jittery as a mare with a burr under her saddle."

"Yes, well." She tucked her hair behind her ear, rocked back on her heels. "In fact, Mr. Blackwell—"

"Now, we don't stand on ceremony around this place. Mr. Blackwell's far too formal."

"Oh." Corliss frowned. "All right. I understand most people call you Big E?"

"Almost there," Elias said with a wink. "How about we go with Uncle Elias." He leaned his elbow on the fence, and his smile went as wide as the horizon behind him. "You've got your grandmother's eyes, Corliss. For a minute there at the carnival, I could have sworn I'd stepped back in time." He shook his head, wonder and maybe a touch of regret mingling in his misty gaze. "Saw you standing there and thought maybe Delaney had finally come home."

"I—" Corliss found herself slipping an arm around Ryder's waist and holding on for dear life. "I don't know what to say. I've been trying to figure out the best way to introduce myself."

"She's been worried you'd chuck us both out onto the highway," Ryder added.

"Blackwells don't chuck out other Blackwells," Elias said. "No matter the issues or years between them."

"I believe that's a point my grandmother could argue." As nervous as she was, she wasn't about to stand here and listen to the old man rewrite family history.

But if she expected to trigger his anger, she saw regret instead flash across his face. "True enough." He slipped his hands onto his hips. "You've got your grandmother's spark, that's for sure. It's nice to see."

Corliss refused to look at Ryder. She could

only imagine what he must be thinking. "Big, er, Uncle Elias—"

"I'm always a bit rudderless when my Dorothy's away for a spell, so I'd be obliged if you two would join me for dinner later." He spoke as if Corliss hadn't. "I'm guessing we can find a thing or two to talk about over some chicken fried steak and the best darned mashed potatoes you've ever eaten."

"Oh, I don't know about that," Corliss argued, because he seemed to appreciate her forthrightness. "My son's amazing in the kitchen."

"Let's put that to the test, shall we?" Elias offered his arm to Corliss. "You don't mind, do you, Ryder?"

Ryder stepped back but stayed close enough to reassure her. A gesture that Corliss appreciated. She hesitated before linking her arm through her uncle's. "I am here for a reason."

"Never thought otherwise," Elias said. "Been sixty years since my sister or her kin have stepped foot on this ranch. Must be something mighty important to walk through all that."

Corliss nodded, only because her words still wouldn't form properly. "I hope Hadley and Ty understand why I used a different name. I didn't know—"

"Now you do. You've come to your kin for help. That means you're home, Corliss." He took hold of her hand and patted her fingers. "That means you're home."

CHAPTER EIGHT

"I GUESS IT'S too much to hope that you're here at Delaney's behest."

Ryder eyed Big E from across the small table by the window in the lodge's dining room, a dining room currently full of customers who were keeping half a dozen servers hopping. Whether Corliss heard the disappointment in her great-uncle's tone he couldn't be certain, but Ryder heard it. Loud and clear.

"If it had been up to her, I wouldn't be here at all." Corliss pushed the last of her onion-and-garlic sautéed green beans around on her plate before setting her fork down and sitting back in her chair. Ryder bit the inside of his cheek. Clearly, his fake fiancée had not outgrown her distaste of ingesting anything green. "As far as the banks are concerned, the only thing I can figure is that this rumored new investor has more pull than Gran has goodwill."

"Someone is definitely up to something." Big E signaled their server and pointed to his empty whiskey glass. "I take it Eagle Springs is a one-bank town."

"Yes, but we've done deals with other banks in surrounding cities before. This time? No one's biting." Corliss's mouth twisted. "It feels, I don't know. Deliberate. Gran being one of the initial stakeholders in Eagle Treasury isn't working in her favor. Coming to you was the only option left that I could see. I hope…" Corliss trailed off, looking far more uncertain than Ryder had ever seen her.

"Corliss is concerned Denny's continued animosity toward you could influence your decision as to whether to loan her the money or not."

She shot him an irritated look, then nodded in silent agreement.

"Let me ease your mind on that front," Big E said. "My decision about loaning you the money will be based on you and you alone, Corliss. That said, I've got some mulling to do about this."

"Okay." It was clear to Ryder that Corliss

had been hoping he'd jump at the chance to help his estranged sister. "Will your mulling take long? We're headed back to Eagle Springs day after tomorrow."

Translation, Ryder thought. She expected an answer before then. "Can we get coffee, please, Violet?" he asked when their server delivered Big E's drink.

"Of course." The young woman with a pixie cut and freckle-dusted nose beamed. "Big E?"

"Three slices of apple pie," Big E responded without losing a breath. "Ice cream on the side."

"I'm going to need another stomach," Corliss mumbled under her breath. "Since you aren't factoring Gran into this decision, can you tell me what happened between the two of you? Between her and your parents? Other than stubbornness being our shared family trait, I don't know very much about it beyond how you all disapproved of her choice in men."

"That's simplifying it," Big E confirmed. "Only one thing we Blackwells like less than being told we're wrong and that's actually being wrong. As for Delaney? I've made a lot of mistakes in my life. More than I care to admit and plenty of them have been thrown back in my face." His fingers tightened around the glass. "Took me a long time to admit my baby sister did the right thing. Following her heart to be with Cal Wesson might have felt like she was turning her back on her family, but in hindsight? She was better off. I'd say she broke our parents' hearts, but I'm not entirely sure my father had one. He wrote Delaney off as dead when she left with Cal. 'Course a lot of that was to save face. It was Cal's brother Frank who Delaney was supposed to marry, and my parents liked to keep their pristine reputation intact. Not an easy thing to do after an offer of marriage was accepted…and then rejected."

"Denny accepted the marriage proposal?" Ryder couldn't believe his ears.

"Our parents pushed and pushed until she agreed. Wrong, of course. But there it was." Elias toasted him. "The Wessons owned a substantial amount of property in this area, but they were also cash poor. Frank, who was Delaney's intended, was a good man. She probably would have run right over him had the marriage taken place, not that we were sharing that bit of information with the Wessons, mind you. The plan was to merge the two families and create a joint, multigenerational ranching empire. Delaney and Cal running off together destroyed any relationship our two families had. Bad blood set in, and resentment festered until there was no going back. The Blackwell name survived and thrived. The Wessons? They eventually moved on and away. I ended up buying their land years after my parents were gone. In the end, it turned out all right."

"And all it cost you was your sister." Ryder couldn't blame Corliss for the bitter note in her voice.

"As I said." Regret echoed in Big E's voice. "Mistakes were made. This is one I'd given up hope of ever being able to fix. You've now given me hope on that front, Corliss, so for that, I thank you."

Ryder spotted something else percolating behind those bright, knowing eyes of his.

"If Denny loses the Flying Spur, she'll die." Corliss couldn't have spoken any plainer.

Big E looked out the window as daylight faded beneath the rise of the moon. "I can understand where that would not be an exaggeration."

"Denny's not the only one whose heart is tied to the place." Beneath the table, Ryder rested his hand over Corliss's and gave the only kind of comfort he felt he could offer. "That ranch is more than their livelihood, Big E. It's their lives. Corliss has loved that place from the day her parents brought her home from the hospital. It wasn't an easy decision for her to come here and ask you for help. It's even damaged her relationship with her grandmother."

"Damaged," Corliss echoed. "Not destroyed."

Big E took a chest-expanding breath. "So, this forty thousand in cash you're asking to borrow, that only covers a part of the loan payment on the Flying Spur."

"Adele, Levi and Wyatt are each coming up with twenty to cover the rest."

"You plan to use my forty to buy four top-bred cutting horses for your brother Nash to train, then turn around and sell them off to pay me and your portion of the bank loan. In five months." He inclined his head. "That's a pretty steep mountain to climb. Takes time to properly train horses."

"Nash is the best cutting horse trainer in Wyoming. There isn't a horse he can't train or a challenge he can't meet." Pride echoed through Corliss's words. "He'll do what needs doing for the family."

"Spoken like a true Blackwell. You must have a lot of faith in your brother if you're willing to put up the only horse you've got left as collateral," Big E said.

"Skyfire's the best one we've ever trained. Given the competitions he's won, as an investment, you could potentially sell him for two, maybe even three times what I'm asking for with the loan."

Ryder squeezed her hand, silently willing her to ease back. Antagonizing Big E when the conversation was going better than Ryder anticipated wasn't going to win them any points.

"It's not the horse this all comes down to," Big E said. "As convincing as you are, Corliss, you're betting everything on your brother's abilities to train four horses in a short period of time. That won't be easy."

"Nothing worthwhile ever is. And Nash won't be working alone," Corliss said. "I'm his partner in this venture. The five of—"

"Six," Ryder interrupted. "I might not have the cash to invest, but I'm in this, too."

"Right." Corliss blinked at him, maybe realizing for the first time that he wasn't abandoning her or Denny or any of them. "Six. The six of us are in this together."

Big E eyed them. "As I said, I'll be taking a little time to mull this over." He sat back when their desserts were delivered. Before plunging his fork into the thick slice of homemade apple pie, he held it up, examined it closely. "The accelerated pace of your proposed deal makes me think there's more to this story than you've told me. You want me to take this offer seriously, I need all the cards on the table. Faceup. What aren't you telling me?"

Ryder glanced at Corliss in time to see her swallow. Hard. "There's nothing else—"

"Corliss." Ryder squeezed her hand again, before she yanked herself free and glared at him. "He has a right to know."

"She wouldn't want him to." Her statement showed once again how torn she was between Denny's wants and the opportunity Big E presented.

"Denny's sick." Ryder cut through Corliss's hedging. "Kidney disease. Stage three."

Corliss hissed out a breath through clenched teeth.

"Corliss also has a point," Ryder said without hope Corliss would forgive him. "If Denny knew we were telling you—"

"She'd change the locks on the house." Corliss sighed. "I'll have to move into your truck."

"You don't have locks on the house," Ryder reminded her and earned another fiery glare. "Be angry all you want at me. It's done now. He knows."

"Yeah, well, it wasn't your secret to tell," she muttered. "You're supposed to be here to support me."

"I'm not going to support something I don't agree with." Clearly, they needed to have a discussion about blind loyalty and the fact that it had no place in Ryder's life at least. He might be here to support her, but he wasn't going to aid in any kind of self-sabotage. "Keeping Denny's health issues a secret from her brother is a step too far. She's getting treatment." Ryder shifted his attention to Big E. "There's no reversing it, but its progression can be slowed, hopefully, with the experimental treatment and medication she's taking. Experimental means it isn't covered by insurance, so it's cost them almost everything."

"And that's why you all took out the second loan on the Flying Spur." Big E nodded as if the pieces were falling into place for him. He was looking at his plate more than he looked at the two of them. "For the record, kidney disease runs in the family. My—Delaney's and my—father developed kidney issues after he turned fifty. It was a struggle for a lot of years, right up until he died. I always counted my blessings it bypassed me. Seems like Delaney wasn't so lucky."

"On the bright side," Corliss said, stabbing at her piece of pie, "she's in pretty good shape otherwise. Ha, her blood pressure's better than mine. It's age that's mostly working against her."

"It's certainly not attitude," Ryder added with a sly smile. "I think that's partially responsible for her continued survival."

"Blackwell women are strong, lots of pride, too," Big E stated. "My sister's a fighter. I've no doubt about that, Corliss."

"I agree," Corliss assured him. "Does any of this aid with your mulling?"

"It will indeed." Big E wiped his mouth and set his napkin on top of his empty dessert plate. "Don't worry. I'll let you know by the time you leave Sunday morning where I am with things. In the meantime, I look forward to what details you and Hadley come up with for that wedding of yours." He eyed the string around Corliss's finger. "Nothing I like better than seeing my kin find their—"

"Please don't say 'other,'" Corliss groaned as Big E brightened.

"That's a right nice way of saying it. Now, if you'll excuse me, I have calls to make, questions to ask and a grandson whose equine opinion I need before I agree to anything regarding using Skyfire as collateral." Big E stood slowly and gave them a sly grin. "Consider the next couple of days a forced vacation," Big E suggested. "Good night, Corliss. Ryder." He retrieved his hat and carried it with him as he left the dining room.

"Well," Ryder said in a way he hoped broke the ice that had formed between himself and his fake fiancée. "He didn't say no."

Corliss looked at her dessert that had

turned into soup. "I really just want to get this settled and things moving forward. I feel stuck. I don't like feeling stuck."

"I know."

"You shouldn't have told him."

He shrugged. "It's done."

"I'm in enough trouble at home, so when Denny finds out he knows—and she will find out—I won't hesitate to throw you under one very big bus."

"Understood." He lifted his coffee, drank and dived into his dessert. "Don't worry. I'm prepared for anything. Isn't that the Blackwell family motto?"

"I can't speak to the Blackwells of Falcon Creek, but as for the Blackwells of Eagle Springs?" She smiled and let out a sharp laugh. "Absolutely."

STARING AT THE ceiling at two in the morning, bathed in a cold sweat, meant Ryder was awake when the light clicked on in the bedroom and shined under the door.

Despite his determination to put the past firmly where it belonged, the dreams had come with him to Montana. Thankfully, he hadn't woken up screaming, struggling to put out the flames that had scorched his body.

Anxious to leave the haunting sensation behind, he climbed out of the surprisingly comfortable sofa bed, tugged a shirt on over his pajama bottoms and, barefoot, padded over to the bedroom and knocked.

"Corliss?"

"Yeah?" She didn't say come in, probably because a second later she was at the door to open it. "How'd you know I was awake?" She shoved her mane of hair back from her face in that one-handed swoop she'd perfected. She wore bright pink shorts that accentuated her long, toned legs and a matching tank.

"I can hear the wheels grinding in your head through the door." He lounged against the door frame, tried to ignore that she was wearing what he now considered his favorite outfit. A rumble of thunder echoed in the distance. "Lightning storm," he said. "Since neither of us can sleep, how about we watch the show?"

"Now, that sounds like a plan." She grabbed a sweatshirt from her suitcase and walked past him to the front door. Minutes later, they'd each taken a porch chair situated at the perfect vantage point as the first flashes of light streaked across the horizon. She tucked her feet up on the edge of the chair and rested her chin on her knees and sighed. "How do people live in the city? All those tall buildings eating up the sky when there's this to watch."

With the solitary porch light burning behind her, Ryder watched the play of emotion and wonder cross her face. She had absolutely no idea how beautiful she was. And how perfectly suited she was for the life she lived.

"One of the first things I plan to do once Olivia gets to Wyoming is to take her out to look at the stars. She thinks she's seen them," he explained at Corliss's curious glance. "She likes to go into her grandparents' backyard and count them every night. I've told her there's no comparison, but she doesn't believe me."

"She will soon enough," Corliss murmured. "Remember that old tent we used to throw into the back of Nash's truck for campouts? We've still got it."

"You are kidding me."

"Some things you don't get rid of." Her smile was soft, almost gentle. "I guess you do remember."

"I'd never forget the first night we ever spent together." He didn't mean it the way it sounded and wondered what she was thinking when her lips curved upward.

"Wasn't that also the time Nash invited Susie Plaskin along? They dated for almost two years after that."

It took all of Ryder's self-control not to confess that he'd been the one to invite Susie in the hopes she'd distract Nash and give Ryder and Corliss some alone time. But given Ryder had already pushed her off-balance by kissing her earlier, he didn't think now was the time to admit his crush went back longer than she realized. "What happened to Susie, anyway?"

"She married Buck Winslow a few years back. Very happy, last I heard. They have kidlet number four on the way." She shook her head. "Good thing they inherited his parents' property. They'll need a lot of space."

Since she'd brought it up... "You ever think about having more kids?"

"Sure." Corliss shrugged. "I wouldn't mind giving it a shot now that I'd have a better idea of what I'm doing. What about you?" Her expression when she looked at him was shy of expectant. "Do you want more?"

"I do." He leaned back, kicked his bare feet up onto the porch railing. "I wasn't around a lot after Olivia was born. Two or three weeks here and there, then I was off on another job." Regret passed through him as the lights in the sky continued to flash and the rumbling echoed overhead. "I missed her first steps. Her first word. It was *no*, by the way, in case you were wondering."

"That seems to be a favorite," Corliss said with a soft laugh.

"And then there was Olivia's first trip to the emergency room because she took a tumble down the basement stairs," Ryder recalled. "She was three. Nina was terrified. In the end, Olivia was fine, but Nina had spent over a day trying to get in touch with me out on a rig."

"That had to have been rough. For all of you." Corliss said. "Being away isn't any easier than being left behind."

He wasn't so sure about that. "Olivia has a scar, right here." He rubbed his index finger across the top of his nose. "My daughter has a scar and I wasn't there when she got it, so yes." He nodded. "I'd really like to do the father thing some more. I feel like I've missed so much of what's made her into the interesting person she is."

"You did the best you could at the time, Ryder. Living with your in-laws couldn't have been easy."

"Nina moved in with them because I was never home, so it comes back to the decisions I made." For himself. And, in the end, for his family.

"I know it isn't the same, but you did well by Mason and me," Corliss reminded him. "You were there for his first steps. And his first word."

"Cookie." Ryder laughed. "I still remember the look on his face when he said it."

"And he hasn't been quiet since," Corliss agreed. "You're a good father, Ryder. Don't let your mother and father-in-law ever convince you otherwise. We do the best we can at the time and move on."

"Do I get to remind you of that if things don't go well with Big E?"

"Big E." Corliss sighed. "Boy, I pegged him completely wrong. In my head, I expected a cross between Ben Cartwright and Attila the Hun. Instead, he's like a big, squishy, grumpy teddy bear."

"I'm not entirely sure you were wrong on either front. Is that why you can't sleep? Wondering what you're going to do if he says no?"

"I don't think he's going to say no." Corliss's brow furrowed. "All the more reason to wonder why he doesn't just say yes now and be done with it. He's more like Gran than I expected. But I also get the feeling there's more going on in that mind than he's letting on. The way he reacted when we were talking about Denny's health issues, he was really bothered by that. He has a chance to make things right for both of them. He won't walk away from that, but he'll do it on his terms. I just need to be ready for whatever those terms might be. Denny won't make it easy. Or comfortable." She frowned at him in warning. "For any of us."

"She sort of gave you her blessing. That has to count for something," Ryder reminded her.

"Whatever you said to her must have gotten through. Yes." She turned her head and smiled at him. "I know you talked to her before we left. Nash said you'd work your magic on her and he wasn't wrong."

"It wasn't magic. I just assured her you had

her best interests at heart and that you were fighting for the greater good."

"And she believed you?"

"I caught her at a weak moment." As if there was any such thing. Denny's weak moments still came with a steel spine and locked jaw. "And in case you're wondering, she's planning on redoing yours and Adele's bedroom for Olivia. Hope that's okay."

"More than." That seemed to ease some of Corliss's worry. "It'll be nice having a little girl in that room again. We always meant to turn it into a playroom for Adele's twins but just never got around to it. I'm looking forward to meeting your Olivia, Ryder."

"Hopefully by tomorrow, I'll have a better idea of when that's happening."

"Speaking of tomorrow." She stifled a yawn, her eyes drooping. "As much as I'm enjoying the light show, I think maybe I've purged enough worry to actually get some sleep. You coming inside?"

"Not yet, no." He was enjoying the cool night too much. Enjoying the continued strikes of light dotting the skyline was far more peaceful than the images that ran through his dreams. "I'll see you in the...

I'll see you later this morning. Breakfast is served until nine thirty."

"Breakfast. Ugh." Corliss stood and pressed a hand against her stomach. "I might need to do some running before then. Or at least take a walk. Good night, Ryder." She trailed a hand across his shoulder as she passed, and he caught the look of uncertainty on her face before she stepped inside.

He wanted to think her confusion was because of him. Because she was still thinking about that kiss they'd shared. That kiss that had blown all his expectations out of the water and left him determined to reach for more. As up in the air as so many aspects of his life might be at the moment, his new relationship with Corliss was one thing he could actually feel positive about. Not only because she'd kissed him back.

But because she hadn't told him not to do it again.

CHAPTER NINE

RYDER NEVER DID get back to sleep. As the sun peeked up over the horizon, he felt the walls of the cabin closing in. He got dressed, brewed a pot of coffee so it was waiting for Corliss when she woke up, and made his way toward the stable and main lodge.

It was too early for breakfast, even on a ranch. He spotted several cowboys saddling up horses and hosing down stalls.

"Morning, Mr. Talbot!" One of the younger ranch hands who barely reached a grown stallion's haunches gave him a wave.

"Morning." Curious, he detoured inside and found Skyfire happily ensconced in a nice stall near the front door. "Good morning, Sky." He plucked a carrot out of one of the nearby buckets and gave the horse a snack. "You enjoying your vacation? Did you have a good night?"

Sky nodded his head, probably to aid in

finishing the crunchy carrot, then shoved his nose hard under Ryder's outstretched hand. "Nice and quiet around here, huh?" It was funny. Corliss had said something about this not feeling like home, but he'd bet that was more a protest against her heart's leanings. Eagle Springs may be where her roots were, but she fit in here just as easily with her extended family.

"It's all going to work out okay, Sky." Ryder rested his forehead against the horse's nose, closed his eyes. He wished he could do something tangible to make what Corliss was dealing with easier. He wished he could just snap his fingers and take all her worries away. "Somehow, it will."

"You looking for an early morning ride?"

Ryder jerked his head up and spotted Big E sauntering into the stable. Today's belt buckle was a brass eagle. And the attitude of the man who wore it? Pure patriarch.

"No, sir." Ryder straightened. "Skyfire's not mine to ride. Besides, it's been a while since I've been in the saddle."

"That's something we can remedy. No time like the present. Give me a few minutes."

Before Ryder could object—not that he

would have—Big E and two of the ranch hands saddled two horses—one tan, one black—and led them outside. The black-and-white Australian shepherd nipping at Big E's heels looked on with an approving eye.

"This here's Hip. She's Katie's. Katie is my grandson Chance's wife. And she's Rosie's," Big E added with a grin. "Hip's staying with me while Katie and Chance are away. Figured Hadley and Ty had enough to cope with the young'uns without an animal under foot."

Ryder, always unable to resist a dog, crouched and held out his hand, which was eagerly sniffed. Hip pushed forward for a good pet. "You're a beauty, aren't you, Hip?"

"And she knows it." Big E cinched the stirrups on the tan horse. "Your horse is named Wanderlust. Seemed fitting given your previous profession. He's easy going. A good choice to get you back into the riding habit."

"What do you think, Hip?" Ryder stood, looked from the horse to the dog. "You agree?"

Hip barked once, her tail wagging. "I'll take that as approval."

"Not often I get a chance to show this place off to family," Big E announced as he tightened the buckle on his own saddle and hefted himself up as easily as most people rolled out of bed. He clicked his tongue as Ryder grabbed hold of the saddle horn and, surprising himself, swung right up. "There now," Big E teased. "Not as rusty as you thought. Let's say you and I go chase the sun."

It became a chase, Ryder realized, shortly after the ranch faded into the distance behind him. Memories of his years in the saddle came back almost immediately. His concerns and worries dropped away beneath the sound of horse hooves and the wind rushing by. There was a streak of black-and-white as Hip raced out in front of him. He'd missed this, seeing the land stretched out before him, embracing him in its silent power. Spending weeks, sometimes months at a time landlocked and then caught in a battle between fire and water had left him starved for the wonder of the element that had always kept him grounded.

The wide-open space, while reminiscent of Wyoming, felt even larger here, where the clouds had miles of sky before them to fill. The Blackwell ranch seemed to go on forever, crossing over streams, arcing near riverbeds and stretching out to far beyond where Big E had stopped, just at the top of a hill. It took some maneuvering for Ryder to join him, but when he did, the air in his lungs emptied. "Now, that's a view."

"Best one in the world," Big E confirmed. "I've done my share of wandering, but nothing compares to coming home and seeing this." He looked at Ryder. "Well, almost nothing. Family comes first. Took me a long time to figure that out. Some might say too long."

"Is that related to those mistakes you mentioned last night?" Ryder asked.

"And then some. So you and my great-niece." Big E was clearly done pretending to play coy. "You plan on replacing that string with a pretty ring at some point?"

Ryder kept his face passive. It was the one lie they'd told he and Corliss hadn't been able to extricate themselves from. "Is that your way of asking me what my intentions are?"

"Ha! Son, your intentions are written all over your face. She's the only person on the planet for you. Sooner you close the deal, the better."

"That sounds so romantic," Ryder said on a laugh, even as his mind raced. How could his feelings be displayed on his face when he hadn't been able to decide what they were?

"Things aren't quite that simple. We've got a lot of things up in the air. She has her son, Mason, to consider. There's my daughter, Olivia. There's the Flying Spur and Denny…"

"Nothing a good dose of stability and love can't fix. Families merge and meld easier than you think. Sometimes, it's just easier to jump into the lake and then find out how deep it is." He turned his horse so he could face Ryder. "You love her."

"Corliss?" Ryder blinked against the one thing he didn't ever want to lie about. "I have ever since we were kids." That was the truth, but what that love may be transforming into was another question. "It's difficult though. Risking ruining a great friendship." Though what if the something new was something even better?

"Great friendships are what marriages should be built on. You know what I think?" Big E leaned forward and gave Ryder a look that had Ryder wondering if the old man could see straight through him. "I think you and my great-grandniece belong together."

"Like I said, lots of moving pieces and things to consider. Corliss'll let me know when she's ready." He needed to shift Big E off this topic of conversation before Ryder's ability to lie ran dry. "Tell me something."

"What?"

"Just how much of all this has the Blackwell stamp on it?"

Big E straightened, pride pushing his chest out as he shifted his gaze back to the horizon. "Son, as far as your eyes take you. You want to see more?"

"I do," Ryder said with a nod. "I want to see it all."

CORLISS COULDN'T RECALL the last time she'd slept past eight, but the fact that she didn't open her eyes until it was nearly nine had her almost jumping out of the bed. She'd never get back those lost hours.

The second her feet hit the floor she froze. There were no lost hours in Montana. This was supposed to be a vacation.

"Oh man." She pushed her hands into her hair, squeezed her eyes shut as her fuzzy brain gradually woke up with the rest of her. She didn't feel on solid ground with anything at the moment.

She wandered into the living room, grumpily noticed that Ryder had had a far more productive start to his day than she had. He'd already pushed the sofa bed back together, and left a small pot of coffee for her. It was stone cold, but she caught enough of a whiff that she dumped some into a mug and zapped it in the microwave.

The second she took a sip she felt the day tip into normalcy even as her stomach growled. "How can I possibly be hungry after that dinner?" Out of the blue, someone knocked on the door.

When she found Hadley on the threshold, Corliss blinked. "We have a meeting." It had skipped right out of her mind. "I'm sorry. Running late. I had trouble sleeping last night."

A tablet computer tucked under her arm, Hadley, looking even more cheery than she had yesterday, gave a shrug and hefted a paper sack in one hand. "I figured you had a bit of family overload from yesterday. Ryder took off on a ride this morning with Big E, so I snagged you a breakfast sandwich before Francie shut the kitchen down for the morning. Ryder said they're your favorite."

That man, Corliss thought. He never ceased to surprise her. "That is so nice of you." She accepted the bag and waved Hadley in, closed the door behind her. "It'll just take me a few minutes to get ready." She'd be dressing jack-rabbit fast after getting a whiff of smoky, crispy bacon emanating from the bag in her hand. And was that…? She lifted the bag, sniffed. "Is it on a fresh-baked biscuit?"

"Of course," Hadley said with a grin. "We specialize in carb loading for our active guests. Go on, take your time. I'll pull up wedding ideas for us to get started on."

"Right. Wedding plans." Corliss waited until her back was turned before she cringed. She really, really hated lying to Hadley about hers and Ryder's engagement. True to her word, in a flash Corliss pulled on jeans and a T-shirt, shoved her feet into her boots and ran a brush through her hair. She grabbed the sandwich bag and joined Hadley after setting a new pot of coffee on to brew. "I really don't want you going to a lot of trouble over the wedding." Better to lay the groundwork now for cancelling whatever plans Hadley had in mind. "Not yet, anyway."

"It's no trouble," Hadley assured her and spun her tablet on the table, tapped a couple of photos. "This is the fun part of the job.

You and Ryder strike me as a low-key kind of couple. That's code for drama-free," Hadley added as Corliss unwrapped the foil around her sandwich.

The melty cheese had oozed a bit, coating the egg and bacon in its greasy goodness. The biscuit was perfectly crisp on top and fluffy in the middle and had Corliss nearly humming in pleasure as she ate. "Comfort food," she mumbled and covered her mouth. "My son makes something similar, but I'll have to tell him to give it a little extra kick with the spicy cheese and up his biscuit game. That's amazing."

"Hard to believe you have a son old enough to cook," Hadley said as Corliss pointed to her mug in silent question. Hadley nodded. "Coffee? That would be great, thanks. What's your son's name?"

"Mason. Wise beyond his years," Corliss said with a smile. "But then, I guess most kids are these days."

"You must have been pretty young when you had him."

"I guess twenty's considered young?" She hadn't felt young at the time. "Having Mason's definitely the smartest thing I've ever done." She sipped her coffee. "Even if falling for his father was one of my dumbest. Funny how those two things tend to go hand in hand."

Hadley chuckled. "You've moved up the men ladder with Ryder. He seems great."

"Best friend I've ever had," Corliss admitted without a hint of guilt. Some things didn't need fibbing about. "Best man I've ever known."

"Mmm." Hadley nodded and scribbled something in a small notebook she had on the table. "How long have you two known each other?"

"Since we were seven. Ryder and his folks moved to Eagle Springs right before I started second grade. We met on the first day of school and pretty much hit it off." She grinned behind her mug. Hadley glanced up and, after looking at Corliss, leaned her chin into her hand.

"Looks like there's an interesting story lurking behind that smile."

Corliss shrugged, her grin widening. "At recess, Shelly Himmelfarb—"

"Poor kid," Hadley murmured. "She sounds doomed with that name."

"Right?" Corliss laughed. "Anyway, Shelly decided she was going to be queen of the playground and announced who got to play on what. When I took exception to this, she attempted to lay me out flat in the dirt."

"Someone should have warned her Blackwells don't get bullied."

"We do not," Corliss agreed. "Anyway, suffice it to say, Shelly was the one who ended up with a snoot full of mud. But not because of me. Ryder jumped in just as she was about to pounce and sent her flying."

"That's so sweet." Hadley tilted her head as her eyes softened.

"Seven-year-old me didn't think so," Corliss said. "I was plenty capable of fighting my own battles, and so I told him. It wasn't until later that day, after he'd been taken to the principal's office that I found out a teacher had been watching the entire thing. Ryder didn't think I should get in trouble for standing up to a bully, so he stepped in and took the hit." He'd been riding to her rescue ever since, whether she wanted him to or not. She patted a hand against her heart. "And so a lifelong friendship was born."

"What happened to Shelly Himmelfarb?" Hadley asked.

Corliss sniffed. "Her parents bought her a cosmetics company for her eighteenth birthday. Cornflower Beauty. Heard of it?"

"Sure." Hadley nodded. "Weren't they being sued by former employees for creating a hostile work environment?"

"Twice," Corliss confirmed. "Suffice it to say Shelly didn't eat enough mud on the playground." She noticed the decoration ideas Hadley had printed out. One featured a black silhouette of a horse with a simple smattering of flowers cascading over its mane and tail. "I like that. Simple. A little rustic. Nothing froufrou or fancy. Daisies. Peonies. Practical flowers."

"Yeah?" Hadley beamed. "I don't know why it called out to me when I was looking for ideas, but I'm not losing my touch. How about we take a walk over to the chapel and you can see what we did for this last wedding. Most of it is still in place. Then we can start talking about dates."

"Oh, sure." Corliss finished the rest of her breakfast. She needed to pull her mask of deception back on. One that was feeling more false with every passing minute.

"I hope you don't mind me saying." Hadley closed up her tablet and notebook. "You seem pretty subdued about this whole wedding thing."

"I'm pretty subdued about most things," Corliss admitted. "I did the whole excited thing last time, with Mason's father. All that wide-eyed, innocent bride stuff most girls dream about having." The money Denny had shelled out had been almost obscene. "Getting left at the altar leaves a bit of a sour taste." The only bright spot in that entire event had been Ryder, who didn't leave her side for a second. "Maybe secretly a part of me is thinking this one won't happen, either."

Across the room, Corliss's cell phone rang. Considering she and her family typically texted and only called when it was an emergency, she hurried over for it. An unfamiliar number was displayed on the screen. Her finger hovered over the decline button, but at the last second, she answered it. "Hello?"

"Is this Corliss?"

The tear-filled, little-girl voice had Corliss stiffening. "It is. Is this… Olivia?"

"Yes." Sniff, sniff. "My Dad gave me this number to use for an emergency if I couldn't talk to him. Is that okay?"

"Hi, Olivia, yes, of course it's okay." She gripped the phone tighter, tamping down her unease. "What's going on? Why are you crying?"

"I've been trying to call my dad all morning and he's not answering and I really, really need to talk to him."

"Okay. Cell phone reception's kind of crazy out here. Tell me what's happening."

Olivia choked back a sob. "Grandpa and Grandma's changed their minds. They won't let me come to Wyoming. Didn't get me my ticket like they said they would and now I can't come live with Daddy and can you get him for me?" It took Corliss a second to process all the information flying at her. "I need to talk to my dad so he can fix everything."

Corliss's heart broke. "Oh, sweetie." Why didn't adults ever see how much damage long-held resentment did to kids? "I'm so sorry you're caught in the middle of this. Do you know how to switch over to a video call?"

More sniffling. "Yes."

"Okay, do that now, and I will, too."

"Can I help?" Hadley touched her arm.

"It's Ryder's daughter. And a long story. Give me a minute?"

"Sure, of course." She returned to the table and picked up the mugs and trash.

Corliss hit the video chat icon and waited for Olivia's face to fill the screen. When it did, Corliss breathed a sigh of relief. She looked so sweet, with long, wavy brown hair and her eyes...oh, those beautiful big eyes of hers were all her father, even though tear-filled. "Hey, Olivia." She smiled and tried to keep her voice even. "I thought it would be better if we could see each other while we talked."

"Hi." Olivia's smile was shaky. "Can you get my dad?"

"I'm going to have him call you as soon as I can, I promise." She didn't have the first clue where to find Ryder. "Did your grandpa tell you why he won't let you come?"

"He wants Dad to take a job out here so I don't have to move away. And he says Dad is just being stubborn because there's nothing for him in Wyoming. He just wants to keep me from seeing Grandma and Grandpa."

Corliss had to bite her tongue to stop herself from calling Olivia's grandfather a liar. There was everything in Wyoming for Ryder. And for Olivia. But how could she judge a man who had lost his only child and was maybe trying to hold on to the last piece of her? "I'm sure your grandparents just want to make sure you're being well cared for, and Wyoming's a long way away from Florida."

"I guess." Olivia swiped her hand across her cheek. "It's just really mean. Dad's told me about you and your grandma and your horses and dogs. I've always wanted a dog, but Grandma's allergic, just like my mom was."

It shouldn't have surprised Corliss that Ryder had told Olivia about her, but it did. "Your dad and I have been really good friends for a long time. I've known him since I was your age. And you know what?"

"What?"

"Your dad is so excited to have you come to Eagle Springs." She struggled for the right words. "He's going to take care of this, Olivia. I promise."

"I'll still be able to come to Wyoming and meet you and the dogs?"

"And my brothers and sister and my son,

Mason, and my nieces. And my grandma Denny. She's going to adore you. We're all looking forward to having you and your dad stay with us for a while. We're even getting a room ready for you."

"On your ranch?" Olivia's eyes cleared. "You mean it? Like a real home and everything?"

A real home. Anger and concern rose up inside of her. Corliss ached to ask more questions, but she didn't want to take the chance of upsetting Olivia further. "I do. Olivia, you did the right thing by calling me."

She sniffed, blinked and smiled. "You're pretty. My mom was pretty, too. You're nice like she was. I miss her a lot."

"You're family, Olivia," Corliss said around a too-tight throat. "Just like your father is. Are you going to be okay for a little while? It's going to take me some time to get to your dad."

"I'll be okay." Olivia squared her shoulders like a little soldier. "I didn't tell Grandpa I was calling you. That's not lying, is it? I don't like lying."

"It's not lying," Corliss assured her. "But if he asks, you tell him the truth, okay? Your dad would always want you to tell the truth." Corliss found herself flinching at the thought of Hadley being on the receiving end of one of Corliss's whoppers of an untruth. "You keep your phone close, Olivia. If I can't find him in an hour, I'll call you back myself. All right?"

Olivia nodded, wiped her other cheek. "Thank you."

After the call ended, Corliss sank onto the arm of the sofa and dropped her chin into her chest. "What a little heartbreaker," she whispered.

"You did great with her." Hadley came over and wrapped an arm around Corliss's shoulders, gave her a squeeze. "I'm sure Ryder will be back soon. When I saw Ty earlier at the stables, he said he and Big E went out to ride. Not even Big E can stay out there all day."

"Just sitting around waiting, knowing Olivia's upset doesn't sit right." Corliss looked up at her new friend. "I don't suppose I could borrow a horse—"

"With the size of this property, you'd be out there searching all day. Best to wait until they get back."

"I guess you're right." How could those

grandparents not see what all this fighting with Ryder was doing to Olivia?

Hadley smiled. "Come on. You need distracting. Let's head over to the chapel. I'll leave word with Ty to send Ryder over when he returns."

Corliss nodded, and pocketing her cell, she followed Hadley out of the cabin.

IF RYDER HAD known a morning-long trek across Blackwell land was all it would take to reconnect him to the life he'd walked away from a decade ago, he'd have jumped on a horse the second he'd arrived here.

He'd loved his job as an oil rig firefighter. It was important work. Rewarding. Until it wasn't. He'd been good at it, and it had been good for his bank account, especially when he'd signed on to the more dangerous jobs. But now, as he and Big E headed back to the stables, he began to feel at peace for the first time in months, as if he'd finally accepted where he belonged.

While it was evident Big E was fond of talking, even he seemed humbled amid the beauty and serenity Montana had to offer. Ryder would continue to argue it took second place to Wyoming, especially when they moved into fall.

As they crested the final hill and the Blackwell Family Ranch came into view, Ryder found himself a bit disappointed his tour was ending. On the bright side, he had Corliss waiting for him not too far away, and that, he told himself, was even better.

"You've definitely got yourself a beautiful place. I'll return the favor if you ever turn up in Wyoming," Ryder couldn't help but needle the older man.

"I just might take you up on that." Big E chuckled in that deep, large-chested way he had. "Tell me about the Flying Spur," he added as if he'd been waiting for the opportunity to ask. "My sister do okay?"

Ryder cast him a wry look. "You already know she did. You said last night you'd been keeping an eye on all the branches of the family tree." And after all his bluster about needing to mull things over, Ryder had no doubt Big E had done plenty of research on his sister's family by now.

"Doesn't mean I've seen what she's built for myself." Big E shook his head. "I shouldn't have let the years pile on. As soon as I realized the mistake my family made, I should have headed right out there to make things right."

"No telling how that might have changed things," Ryder said. "Dwelling on the what-ifs and the should-haves only get you into holes you'll never dig out of." He shifted in the saddle, the still-healing scars along his back and shoulders tightening like rawhide left out in the sun too long. "You have the chance to help them now when they need you, Big E. I hope you'll take it."

"Been wondering when you were going to make your pitch."

"That's not what I'm doing." Ryder glanced over as they continued down the hill. "And you decided to accept Corliss's deal the second she offered it."

Big E smirked. "You sound pretty sure of yourself."

"She's family," Ryder said with confidence. "Distant or not, estranged or not, she came to you and that means something. To both of you. One thing I know about Blackwells," he added before Big E could attempt to argue. "You do whatever it takes to look out for your family. I'm sure you'll have your conditions—" Big E's snort confirmed another of Corliss's suspicions "—but when all is said and done, you'll do it because she needs you to."

Big E halted his horse a few yards from the stable. He turned in his saddle, pushed up the brim of his hat with one finger. "If I didn't know any better, I'd think you had Blackwell blood running through your veins. You and Corliss." He nodded as if finally seeing a completed picture. "You're a good match. You'll have a lasting marriage. Solid. Based on friendship and respect and more than a little passion."

Ryder tried not to cringe at the old man's observations, none of which made sense when factoring in the truth. "I understand her," Ryder finally said, refusing to feed into the lies anymore. "We'd do anything for each other. In the end, marriage or not, that's all that matters."

Ryder caught the flash of something behind Big E and he leaned over in his saddle, his brow furrowing as he watched Ty waving his arms in the air. Seconds later, the young Blackwell grabbed a horse, climbed on and headed quickly in their direction.

Concern tightened in Ryder's chest as Ty raced closer, sending up a plume of dust and gravel as he skidded his horse to a stop in front of them.

"You've been out of cell range," Ty said. "We didn't know which way you'd gone, otherwise we'd have—"

"What's wrong?" Ryder demanded. "Is it Corliss?"

"Everyone's fine. No one's hurt," Ty said quickly. "Your daughter called a couple of hours ago."

"Called? Called who?" Ryder yanked out his phone, but it still wasn't getting enough bars to receive messages.

"She called Corliss. Don't worry. Olivia's fine," Ty reassured him again. "Corliss and Hadley are over at the chapel. Come on." He clicked his tongue and steered his horse past them, kicking his heels and picking up speed. Ryder followed suit, as did Big E.

The small white chapel, located in a grassy grove with a pond, was visible after they crested another hill, transporting them into a perfect scene of wedding bliss. But he didn't focus on the details. His phone vibrated again and again, no doubt finally loading in the messages that had been stalled by the sporadic availability of cell service.

Corliss and Hadley must have heard them approaching, as the double doors at the top of the stairs popped open and the two women emerged, Corliss with her phone up to her ear.

Ryder launched himself off his horse and was already racing toward her before his feet hit the ground. "Is she okay?"

Corliss grabbed hold of his hand, gave him a quick nod of acknowledgement even as her lips split into a huge smile. "Hang on, Olivia. Are you telling me that a flea can move faster than the space shuttle?"

The panic building inside Ryder released as if a balloon had been popped. He bent over, braced his hands on his thighs and let out a long breath. If Olivia was offering her wild trivia facts, she was, indeed, fine.

"How is that even possible?" Corliss asked. "Seriously, Olivia, you have to be making that up."

"They've been talking for over an hour," Hadley said when Ty and Big E joined them. "She was worried about Olivia because you were taking so long to get back."

"My fault," Big E declared. "I got carried away with the tour."

Corliss let go of Ryder and held up a finger. "Uh-huh. Okay, well, you're just going to have to prove that to me when you get to the Flying Spur. And I'm still not convinced about the whole 'dolphins sleeping with one eye open' thing. I'll need video proof of that." She waited a beat, then laughed. "We'll make an evening of YouTube videos for sure. Hey, Olivia? Your dad just got here. You want to… Yeah. Okay. Here he is."

Ryder reached for the phone, but Corliss tucked it against her chest first. "She was crying and upset. She's not anymore. You're going to work it out with her grandparents so she can come out first thing Monday. This is the promise I've made her, the promise I know you've made as well, so kick the fear to the curb and act normal, okay? She just wants to hear her dad's voice."

Just like that, Ryder slipped into full-on Dad mode. He nodded, accepted the phone, breathing out the anxiety. "Hey, Sprout. Heard you were trying to call me. Sorry there's no cell service around here."

"Oh my gosh, Dad. Corliss is so cool! Do

you know she started riding horses when she was three?" The screech in her daughter's voice had Ryder holding the phone from his ear. He clicked on the speaker. "That's so amazing. I can't wait to learn, Dad, even though she says they're still rebuilding their stable stock. I've been reading up on ranches and riding already."

The four Blackwells surrounding him chuckled.

"So, you're okay now?" Ryder asked her.

"Uh-huh." As only an eight-year-old can, she seemed completely fine. "Corliss said you're going to work everything out with Grandpa and Grandma and I'll be there on Monday!"

"I'll talk to Grandpa in a few minutes," Ryder assured her, then, seeing the warning look from Corliss, softened his tone. "Did Corliss tell you about your new room?"

"Uh-huh. And the dogs! I'm going to get dogs. That is awesome. I hope they like me."

"I like her," Big E boasted. "I can't wait to meet her at the wedding."

"Wedding? What wedding?" Olivia's question had the panic resurging, and Ryder gaped at Corliss, whose eyes were as wide as a full Wyoming moon. "Who's getting married?"

"Um." Ryder swallowed hard.

"Well, go on." Big E slugged a gentle fist against Ryder's shoulder. "Tell her you and Corliss are getting hitched, Ryder."

"Does *hitched* mean getting married?" Ryder's ears roared even as Olivia's excited squeals erupted across the country. "You mean Corliss is going to be my new mom?"

"Um." Ryder couldn't seem to get anything else out.

"This means Grandpa was wrong!" Olivia cried. "I get a whole family when I come to Wyoming. A whole, new family."

"This'll go over well with her grandparents," Hadley murmured under her breath. She shot an irritated glare at Big E, who as far as Ryder could tell, knew exactly what he'd done and was very pleased with himself.

"Olivia, I'd better talk to your grandfather now," Ryder choked out.

"I'm giving him my phone right now so you can tell him. Grandpa!"

"This isn't awkward at all," Ty said with a forced smile. "Hadley, maybe you and I should—"

He didn't get a chance to finish that thought as Ryder's former father-in-law came on the line. "Ryder. What's this nonsense Olivia's telling me about you getting married?"

Corliss moved in, rested her hands on his arm and squeezed.

"It wasn't something Corliss and I were ready to share with everyone just yet," Ryder said, taking one word of the lie at a time. "We were hoping to surprise Olivia when she got here. This is why moving to Florida and taking that job is impossible. Corliss and her family have a working cutting horse ranch in Eagle Springs. It's where I'll be living. It's where *we'll* be living."

How could a stretch of silence be both terrifying and satisfying?

"I see." Whitlock finally spoke. "This Corliss—"

"Corliss Blackwell." The second he said her name, he wondered if Nina had ever mentioned Corliss before.

"Yes, well," Whitlock said. "Perhaps it would be better to wait and have Olivia join you after you and Ms. Blackwell are married and settled."

Ryder sagged in frustration. Whitlock was

always going to find an excuse to stop Olivia from leaving. "That's not your decision to make. Olivia's my daughter."

"And you should be setting a good example for her," Whitlock said in a tone that had no doubt sent shivers down the spines of many a convicted criminal waiting for sentencing. "We can discuss this again after you're married."

"Then we won't wait." Corliss's declaration shocked Ryder. She grabbed her cell phone, shifted so she could look at Hadley. "Mr. Standish, hi, this is Corliss Blackwell. I know it's very sudden and quick, but to tell the truth—"

Ryder nearly groaned at the irony.

"To tell you the truth, Mr. Standish." Corliss hesitated long enough to meet Ryder's gaze. "Ryder and I have decided to get married this weekend." Another look at Hadley, who was mouthing "tomorrow" at her. "Tomorrow in fact."

Ryder's heart skidded to a full stop. "We're what?"

"A Saturday wedding? Yep, I can make that happen," Hadley assured a stunned Ryder, and her husband Ty, given his pale expression.

"That's a perfect solution," Big E agreed in a booming voice and earned a shush from Ty. "Married tomorrow, drive home on Sunday, and Olivia will arrive Monday morning."

"Everything's all arranged." Corliss plunged ahead, dragging her and Ryder straight into the deep end of the deception pool. "It would have been nice if Olivia could have been here, but I suppose after the fact will have to do."

"I'm not sure I approve—"

"With all due respect, Mr. Standish, it's not up to you to approve." Corliss's eyes sparked, and Ryder suspected her obsession with winning had a lot to do with this knee-jerk, harebrained solution. "You're Olivia's grandfather. You always will be, and Nina will always, *always* be her mother, but Ryder and I are very happy and we are determined to get married. Olivia will have a good home in Wyoming. She will be safe and loved. I give you my word as a Blackwell. I know that doesn't mean anything to you, but it means everything in these parts. It's time, Mr. Standish. It's time for Olivia to be with her father."

More silence followed, and in those moments, Ryder's world stopped spinning.

"I'll make the flight arrangements for Olivia's Monday arrival and text Ryder the information," Whitlock said finally. "I... Good luck, Ms. Blackwell."

He hung up before Corliss, or Ryder, could respond. Was it possible it had been so... easy?

While Big E, Hadley and Ty started talking all at once, Ryder grabbed Corliss's arm and dragged her away and out of earshot. "What did you do?" he demanded as Corliss's smile faded and she slid her phone in her pocket.

"Did you want to head back to Florida for what I'm sure would be an extended custody battle?" Corliss asked in a tone that set Ryder's nerves on edge.

"Of course not," Ryder snapped. "That isn't what—"

"From what Olivia told me this morning, it sounded like that's exactly where things were headed. Us getting married gets you the one thing you need. Olivia. Home. Here with you. We can figure out the details when we're alone." Her voice dropped as she shot a glance at Elias, who looked far more interested in their conversation than Hadley's pre-wedding plans. "I know you don't like lying—"

"No," he confirmed. "I don't. Especially not to my daughter." What happens when she—when everyone—finds out this was just a ruse to get Olivia to Wyoming? What would Whitlock do when he discovered the scheme? He could only imagine the custody claim his former father-in-law would have then. By going along with this idea he could be making things worse in the long run. And yet...

"We needed to end the fight and not cause you or Olivia any more pain. The lie was already in place. I just..." She shrugged. "It's no big deal, Ryder. So we get married. You said it yourself, we aren't going to let anything change between us, but this can mean everything for you and Olivia. If we do this, your in-laws don't have any point left to fight you on. Let's do what we need to do to get your daughter a real home." She reached up and gave him a quick, albeit brain-frying, kiss. "What do you say? Wanna get hitched?" She stepped back and arched that challenging brow of hers.

For so much of his life, he'd been floundering, unable to find where he belonged and who he belonged to. Now, Corliss Blackwell, the best friend he ever had, was offering him a way to get his life back on track. Why was he hesitating?

"Well?" Corliss goaded him.

He reached out, pulled her close and, in front of her relations, kissed her in the way he hadn't allowed himself to dream of doing before now. After the embrace, he looked into her sweet, shell-shocked gaze and grinned. He didn't ever want this unexpected feeling of happiness to go away. However, they were both wrong about one very important point...

This was going to change everything between them.

"Okay," he said on a slow nod as he smiled down at her. "Let's get married."

BACK IN THEIR CABIN, Corliss tossed her suitcase on the bed and flipped it open. "We've got about fifteen minutes before Hadley comes to drag me to the main lodge to sleep tonight. Let's work out the details." She couldn't remember the last time her heart had beat this fast. Or she'd felt so out of breath.

"Fifteen minutes to figure out the rest of

our lives. Sure. What could go wrong?" He moved into the bedroom, stepped aside as she danced around him. "Corliss, this is bigger than just you and me. Getting married, it affects everyone we care about. Olivia, Mason, Denny, your family—"

"We'll make it work, Ryder. The way we've done everything. Together." She needed to keep moving, because when she stopped moving, she'd start thinking and that could very well lead to her realizing Ryder was right. This was one big mistake.

"Corliss, stop." He grabbed her arms. "I am not going to lie to my daughter. I know you think this is a harmless fib to get her here, but what happens next? What happens when Whitlock and Vivian come out here to check on her? Because they will. No doubt sooner than later. What happens when we get back to Wyoming and annul this thing?"

There it was. The buzzing in her brain she'd been trying to avoid listening to. "Okay, so we stay married." Even she winced at the casual statement. "I'm not saying we stay married forever, just long enough for things to settle down."

"And what happens when Olivia becomes

attached to you? To Mason and your family? What happens when we end the charade and disrupt her life? Again."

"You're acting as if this is going to take years to resolve, Ryder. It's a few months max. Between school and chores and everything else she'll have going on, there won't be time for her to—"

"She's already attached to you, Corliss. Or didn't you hear that in her voice? She's already lost one mother. I don't want her losing another."

Corliss swallowed her next words; the ones that admitted she already cared for his daughter more than he was clearly comfortable with. "She will never lose me as a friend. Look, I don't have all the answers," she said. "But if we don't get married and that stability your in-laws want for her isn't waiting for Olivia when she arrives, I may as well drive you to the airport now so you can take that security job Whitlock got you."

Ryder huffed out a breath, a sign she had almost convinced him.

"You, we are out of options, Ryder." She tugged free of his hold and sat on the edge of her bed. Was the idea of marrying her so concerning he was willing to jeopardize bringing his daughter home? "Marrying me, even for a while, is the price you pay for seeing your daughter again. Is that idea really so bad?"

"Of course, it isn't." The snap in his voice shocked her. "If anything, marrying you is the only thing about this wild plan that makes some sense. Getting married is the easy part. Staying married is the tricky part, but the worst is the idea of lying to everyone we know. And we'll have to lie, Corliss," he warned.

"I know." It was the one piece of the plan she didn't like. "But better the two of us lie to everyone than have everyone lie to Olivia. The stronger her support system is when we do put an end to this, the easier it'll be on her." How easy it would be on the two of them, however, was another question.

"So, what? We just tell them we had a sudden epiphany and embraced happily ever after?"

"It's not like we're strangers," Corliss argued. "Friends fall in love all the time. We can pretend to do the same." But even as she said it, she felt herself pitching into an arrangement that could leave her heart bruised and broken if she wasn't careful.

"But what do we tell people? I mean, Mason alone. How do I go from being the fun unrelated uncle he plays video games with to being his stepfather? And then there's Denny and Nash—"

"My family will always support the decisions I make for my life," Corliss assured him. "Even Mason. It'll take some getting used to, but it won't be for—"

"It won't be forever," Ryder finished for her. "Yeah. You keep saying that."

"Fair enough." She tossed the T-shirt she'd been clutching in her hands into her suitcase. "Six months. We'll lock this down. So you aren't stressing over lying to people indefinitely. We'll give this six months. That'll take us through paying off the loan, the horse training and the holidays. Ryder, wouldn't you like to see Olivia spend her first holiday season at the Flying Spur?" She reached up and touched his arm. "Let's do six months to get her settled and her grandparents off your back."

"And after that?"

"And after that?" She shrugged and ignored the lump of sadness that had already formed in her throat. "After that, we'll say we gave it a shot and it didn't work out. You're marrying me, remember," she attempted to joke. "Anyone who knows us won't find it difficult to believe that it didn't last."

"Corliss." Ryder exhaled and shook his head. "That's not funny."

No, it wasn't, she thought. But it was true. "You have been by my side for most of my life, Ryder. You've pulled me out of more scrapes and lent more shoulders than belong to an entire football team for me to cry on. This is something I can do for you. Let me do this."

"You really think you can? Lie to Denny and Mason and pretend we have a real marriage?"

"For you?" Corliss didn't hesitate. "I can do anything."

CHAPTER TEN

CORLISS'S IMPULSIVE MATRIMONIAL decision Friday evening left her holding on for dear life as the weekend pitched forward at high speed. Silly of her to assume a simple wedding, even one arranged in less than twenty-four hours, would be just that—simple. Hadley was happy to keep the details to a minimum and produce as little fuss as possible, but some traditions—like keeping the bride and groom separated the night before their ceremony, were firmly in place.

"You know the biggest difference between almost getting married at nineteen and actually getting married at thirty-two?" Corliss twisted and shimmied as Hadley attempted to straighten the pretty white summer dress the wedding organizer had insisted on driving Corliss into town to look for last night.

"Let me guess," Hadley mumbled around the safety pins in her mouth. Along with her other roles today, Hadley was also trying her hand at last-minute tailor. "You're less nervous this time?"

"No. Well, yes. But I was thinking about my family." Corliss frowned, touched her fingers against the scooped neckline.

"Hey, we're your family, too," Hadley managed to say.

"Thankfully, I don't really have anything to be nervous about this go around," she admitted. "It does help tamp down the nerves, knowing the groom won't be bolting town with the local hairdresser on the back of his motorcycle."

"If only we had the time for me to hear that whole story. Okay." Hadley stood back, grasped Corliss's shoulders and pivoted her so she could finally look in the mirror.

For some unfathomable reason, Corliss squeezed her eyes shut. She could feel the late Saturday afternoon sun's warmth radiating through the second-floor window, could smell the relaxing fragrance wafting off the lavender candles Hadley had lit a few hours before.

"You have to open your eyes to see," Hadley teased with a laugh and released her. Corliss took a long breath and, as she released it, did as Hadley said.

The rush of tears she felt was unexpected. The summery dress had clean lines and lacy cap sleeves that barely covered her upper arms. The now-cinched-in waist and tapered hemline offered a touch of elegance she hadn't anticipated, and the swept-up tumble of curls Hadley had somehow arranged on her head made Corliss appear both unrecognizable and yet…never more like herself. "Oh." Corliss lifted a hand to her perfectly subdued makeup. "Oh, Hadley."

Hadley, smiling, gave herself a little pat on the back. "Oh! One more thing. You're a size 8 shoe, right?" Hadley turned and dug into one of the boxes she'd brought earlier.

"I thought I could just go barefoot." Seeing as her other options were boots or sneakers.

"Or…" Hadley held out a pair of beautiful, sparkling high-heeled sandals that had every girly chromosome Corliss possessed leaping to attention. The subtle combination of rhinestones, gold and silver spoke of delicate, designer creations and far out of her price range. "What do you think? My cousin Peyton left these and a few other pairs after she and Matteo got married. She couldn't decide before the wedding, so she brought them all with her."

"Peyton is one of Big E's granddaughters? The one who works in big tech?" Corliss reached out and brushed her fingers against the straps, half-expecting them to disappear in a poof of smoke when she touched them. "She has wonderful taste."

"She really does," Hadley confirmed. "Go on. Try them." She pushed them into Corliss's hands and a knock sounded on the door. "Come on in!"

Corliss took a seat at the vanity as the door opened and Rosie, followed by a cavalcade of female Blackwells, flooded into the room.

"Oooh." Rosie, dressed in an adorable burgundy-colored swing dress headed right for Corliss. Abbey and Gen were on her heels, but had significantly less frills on their dresses. All three girls wore shiny, unscuffed boots. "You look so pretty, Miss Corliss."

"Don't touch!" Hadley ordered gently when Rosie reached out to grab one of Corliss's curls. "She's held together by sheer luck and a half can of hairspray."

Rosie giggled at Corliss's horrified expression.

"Okay, quick intros as we've got about a half hour before we get you down the aisle,"

Hadley said. "This is Lydia Blackwell. She's married to your cousin Jon."

"Hi, Corliss." Lydia offered a welcoming smile. "Welcome to Falcon Creek."

"She's our mom," Gen announced as she picked up one of the makeup brushes Hadley had used on Corliss.

"I'm glad we finally get to meet," Lydia continued. "Always nice to add another Blackwell to the flock."

"It's getting to be a pretty big flock," a younger, heavily pregnant woman said with a knowing smile. "I'm Lily Hannah. Blackwell by blood. My husband Conner and I live on a neighboring ranch. Congratulations on the wedding."

"Thanks. Congratulations on the almost baby," Corliss said with a laugh. Lily lowered herself into one of the nearby chairs. "I appreciate all of you coming to fill the chapel. It wasn't necessary." If there had been some way to fly Olivia out early to attend, she'd have moved heaven and earth, but between the logistics and the upheaval of a last-minute wedding, it hadn't made sense. Still. Corliss touched a hand to her heart. She already missed the little girl and they hadn't even met in person.

"It wasn't only necessary but required. Big E put out the call, and we were happy to respond," Lydia told her. "And, as I'm sure you've learned by now, you don't ignore the man."

"Ben and Rachel will be here soon," Hadley said.

Another woman stepped forward. "I'm Grace Blackwell. But I'm solo tonight. Ethan's out of town all week checking on some horses down south, and our son Eli is staying home with a sitter, sniffles." She hefted the box she was carrying and motioned at Hadley. "You've been waiting for these, yes?"

"Waiting for what?" Corliss asked as she stood up to test the shoes. She only wobbled for a second, long enough for Rosie to take hold of her hand and steady her. Given the shoe structure, they should have hurt six ways to Sunday, but they were surprisingly comfortable. By the time she reached Hadley, she was steady.

"Trixie at Pots and Petals owed me a favor." Hadley pulled beautiful flowers out of the box. "Not bad for a rush job."

"It's gorgeous," Corliss breathed. "Are those…dahlias?" She brushed her fingers over the rust, orange and burgundy flowers. "They're my favorite. I thought we talked about daisies and peonies? How on earth—"

"You're marrying a man who knows his flowers," Hadley said and earned exaggerated sighs from the other women in the room. "And his bride. Hang on. Girls, come here." She passed the bridal bouquet to Corliss, then produced three flower crowns that matched. "I know you didn't want any attendants," she murmured to Corliss as the girls squealed in excitement. "But I thought maybe you'd be okay with a few flower girls? I had a fourth one made and packaged for you to take back to Wyoming for Olivia."

"I love the idea." Corliss wouldn't have refused even if she'd wanted to. How could she, given the absolute glow on those kids' faces? She looked down at her bouquet and felt her heart surge. One offhand comment years ago to Ryder had resulted in him remembering her favorite flower on their wedding day. Did the man forget nothing?

It seemed he didn't. At least, not where she was concerned.

Something akin to fear prickled her skin. This was just a piece of paper, she told herself. They were getting married for a good reason. A just reason. So his daughter could finally come home without any further conflict. She and Ryder would still be friends; they always would be. But maybe…she tapped restless fingers against her chest. Maybe there was something more in the offing. Something that terrified her more than the idea of losing the Flying Spur. Something she wasn't going to let herself think about.

"Just got a text message from the minister," Hadley announced as Lydia and Grace settled the crowns on the girls' heads. "He'll be at the chapel in five minutes. Ty and Ryder are already there, and I've got the paperwork ready for you and the groom to sign after the ceremony but before the cake cutting."

"Cake?" Corliss asked. "Hadley, that wasn't necessary—"

"It absolutely was," Hadley said without hesitation. "No one gets married on this ranch without a cake."

"What kind of cake?" Rosie asked, a note of suspicion in her voice.

"Lemon with buttercream icing," Hadley

answered with a grin, and Corliss shook her head. "I heard you teasing Ryder about his dislike of chocolate last night after dinner."

"Sneaky," Corliss said. "But appreciated. Okay." She tried to quiet the fluttering in her stomach, but it was no use. The entire whirlwind of a day had left her spinning and there was no fighting it. "I'm ready to do this."

"Great!" Lily announced and held out both hands. "Happy to tag along as soon as someone hauls me up."

RYDER CLIMBED OUT of Ty's SUV and looked up at the shiny white spire of the chapel. Was it possible what he'd spent most of his life wanting, what he'd quit hoping for, was finally going to happen?

He shoved two fingers under his suddenly too-tight collar and forced himself to breathe. Yes, he told himself for the hundredth time since Corliss sprung this arrangement on him yesterday. He really was going to marry Corliss Blackwell.

The chapel, which according to Ty had been built less than a decade ago, reminded Ryder of one of Olivia's storybook settings. Bright white with a line of windows on either side of thick wooden stairs. Dark double doors that were currently adorned with two wreaths of the dahlias he'd mentioned to Hadley, along with burgundy and apricot roses, orchids, fern leaves and tiny, delicate baby's breath.

Why did he feel as nervous as a rookie fighting his first out-of-control fire? He tugged at his suit jacket as if it were too tight. He hadn't felt this way when he and Nina got married. Then again, he hadn't had any input into that ceremony. He'd told Nina she deserved the wedding of her dreams and she'd gotten it—frills and all. That day, he'd been calm, almost as if detached from what was happening. Hoping beyond hope his relationship with Nina would grow and last. Now he had to hope what he and Corliss were doing today wouldn't end up damaging their friendship or other relationships.

He stood at the base of the church steps as Ty headed up to prop open the doors.

"Ryder?" A voice called out to him.

Big E's tone snagged Ryder's attention right away and he turned. The late afternoon air was cool, but carried enough warmth to promise a pleasant evening. Trees at the sides of the chapel rustled in their pre-autumn dance, casting leaves into the rippling pond situated just beyond a path that stretched from chapel to shore.

Thick grass provided ample cushion for the ducks quacking and paddling in the water. Above them, all around them, stretched the pristine blue sky of Montana that maybe, if Ryder was pressed to admit, seemed a bit brighter than the Wyoming sky he'd missed so much these last years.

This was, Ryder realized, as far away from his former job as he possibly could have gotten.

Big E strode toward him, decked out in what Ryder could only assume was his best cowboy duds. Despite the opportunity to rent a tuxedo in town, Ryder had opted to buy a new pair of jeans at Brewster Ranch Supply, along with a new black hat. The white shirt, black suit jacket and bolero tie came courtesy of Ty. He'd spent a good hour polishing his boots to shine as brightly as possible, befitting his bride.

Still, watching Big E head straight for him added to the tension already streaming through his system.

"Son, you need to relax before you snap in two," Big E teased. "My Dorothy sends her regrets. She's not going to make it back in time for the ceremony."

"I'm sorry to hear that." Ryder had to admit he'd been looking forward to meeting the woman who had managed to lasso this ornery cowboy. "Not that any of us could have imagined this happening the way that it did." He eyed the old man. "Rumor has it you've had a hand in a number of your grandchildren's marriages over the years."

Big E grinned the grin of the guilty. "No rumor about it. I'll take full credit and enjoy every single great-grandbaby that's arrived as a result. Tell me something. You planning on doing something about that ring you gave my grandniece?"

"Ah." Ryder flinched. He'd taken a walk through the antique store in town but hadn't come across anything he considered Corliss appropriate. She was as practical and down-to-earth as they came and didn't particularly gravitate toward things that sparkled. "I'm afraid not."

"Well, then, perhaps this might work for you." Big E reached into his pocket, pulled out a box and handed it over. "This was my grandmother's. My mother, she never wore it, probably because she chose her own wedding set, but she kept this for Denny. Since she never had a chance to give it to her..." Big E shrugged as Ryder opened the box and admired the rings. "I thought maybe these might suit Corliss."

The thin bands of gold were dainty; one had a small diamond while the other band was a circle of the stones, all elegant and beautifully crafted. Just like Corliss.

"I would have thought one of your granddaughters—"

"That ring was meant to be Denny's," Big E said. "I might not know a lot about my sister these days, but I think she'd approve."

"She would." Ryder nodded, touched the older man had thought this through. "Thank you. I appreciate this. And the vote of confidence."

"Corliss loves you. A woman doesn't do what she did yesterday without love. Whatever else is going on with the two of you, there's love." Big E rested a hand on his shoulder. "You keep faith in that, you'll be fine. Ah, there's the minister." He took a step back as a red truck stopped nearby. "You ready to get this show on the road?"

"I'm ready." Ryder glanced down at the ring as Big E moved off to greet the minister. The tiny diamonds glinted at him as if winking in encouragement. "I'm ready."

CORLISS WAS A woman who prided herself on going with the flow. Of being able to keep herself in the saddle of the bucking bronco called life. She wasn't easily thrown, but when she was, she quickly got back up and climbed right back on.

But that was before her great-uncle Elias Blackwell walked her down the aisle of the quaint chapel on the Blackwell Family Ranch. Before she saw the pretty decorations accenting the highly polished pews, the pops of color outlining arched windows, and stunning stained glass that reflected every beam of the late afternoon sun.

That was before she stepped up in front of the minister, with Gen, Abbey and Rosie flanking her, and new friends and family surrounding her.

And it was before she laid eyes on Ryder Talbot, standing tall and proud at the base of the altar, hands clasped together as his eyes met hers. Her breath caught, trapped somewhere between fear and excitement as her blood raced through her veins.

They were really doing this.

Clutching her bouquet in one hand, Corliss slipped the other into Ryder's even as the doubt and anticipation she'd been tamping down since this morning surged. The minister began to speak. The words didn't penetrate, only the unexpected emotions of the moment. She squeezed Ryder's hand and dared to turn her head to look at him.

His eyes didn't reflect any of the uncertainty and concern she felt. That content, bordering on joyful, excited expression seemed to be in complete opposition to the emotions coursing through her system.

In the moment, when she passed her flowers to the girls and faced the man she'd known most of her life, she ignored the fear and forced herself to settle.

The fact that Ryder possessed the forethought to acquire a delicate yet perfectly practical wedding band for her added unexpected guilt to her carousel of emotions. He always thought of everything, while she got by with throwing things into the air and seeing what landed where.

Tears blurred her vision as he slid the pair of dainty bands of diamonds and gold over the worn string she hadn't been able to bring herself to remove. She spoke the words she was meant to speak, all the while reminding herself to breathe.

When it came time to seal their union with a kiss, she found herself trembling as she lifted her face. Ryder's expression radiated a gentle combination of promise and hope and a thread of gratitude she wasn't certain she deserved. The second Ryder lifted his mouth from hers and ended the kiss, she raised her hand to his cheek, blinking as if seeing him for the first time.

He rested his forehead against hers as the applause from their audience broke through their moment. When she turned, she saw Hadley at her side, a cell phone angled up and Olivia Talbot's excited face filling the screen.

"You didn't think I'd let you two get married without watching," Hadley said, chastising them before passing the phone over.

"Oh Daddy! You look so handsome. Hi, Corliss!" Olivia, dressed in what looked like a pretty summer, flowery frock, waved at them through the screen. "Happy wedding!"

"Happy wedding day, Sprout," Ryder said. Corliss rested her head on his shoulder, unable to ignore the tightness in his voice. "We'll see you in a couple of days."

"Will you save me some cake?" Olivia asked.

"Definitely," Corliss promised, as she felt her husband's—*husband's?*—arm slip around her waist. He pressed a kiss to the top of her head and waved good-night to his daughter, and Corliss prayed she hadn't just made the biggest mistake of her life.

RYDER WASN'T ENTIRELY sure what to expect from his wedding day, but one thing he hadn't counted on was his bride going uncharacteristically quiet. The Corliss he knew was rarely, if ever, at a loss for words.

It wasn't that she'd stopped talking completely. She had her happily-ever-after smile firmly in place as she talked with their guests—most of whom were her extended family, but he knew when she wasn't feeling sure of herself. And her unsteadiness had nothing to do with the flowing champagne.

"I believe it's customary for the bride and groom to share at least one dance." Big E nudged a bottle of beer into Ryder's hand, something he appreciated since he didn't particularly care for champagne.

Ryder toasted his uncle-in-law but shook his head. "Corliss and I aren't exactly dancers."

"In my experience," Big E said. "And I've attended my fair share of Blackwell weddings in recent years, these events are all about tradition, not staying in your comfort zone."

Ryder smirked and resisted the urge to run a finger under his collar again.

"No one expects a Fred-and-Ginger performance."

"With the two of us, you'd be lucky to get Lucy and Ricky. That said…" He set his beer on the window ledge and, after a quick stop to discuss things with DJ Ty Blackwell, he strode across the room to claim his bride. She managed to cover the shock quickly, but not so quickly he didn't see it jump into her eyes as he slid his hand down her arm and entwined his fingers with hers. "We should take at least one turn around the dance floor."

"Oh sure. Yeah." She handed her half-filled

champagne glass to Hadley before allowing him to pull her onto the dance floor. How she managed to maneuver in those sky-high, ankle-breaker sandals was beyond him, but he chalked that ability up to one of the many feminine mysteries of life. He drew her into his arms and she wrapped hers up and over his shoulders, and instantly, the tension he suspected she felt radiated beneath his touch.

Rosie, Gen and Abbey were all embracing their inner dancer by flitting and jumping and spinning their way around the floor to the music, which, as soon as Ryder and Corliss came together, slipped into the familiar power ballad that had played once upon a time at their senior prom.

"How do you do that?" Corliss said with a surprising amount of irritation in her voice.

"Do what?"

"Find exactly the right song for the exact right moment. That's the song they played at the prom after John Tunney and Lionel Banks started that shoving match over who was the better football player."

"Was it?" Ryder blinked innocent eyes down at her as she glared up at him. "I just remember it was the first song we ever slow danced to. It's nothing to be upset about, Cor."

"You remember everything." Her brow furrowed as if she couldn't quite grab hold of her thoughts. "You think of everything. It's like…"

"What?" He swayed to the music, trying his best not to stomp all over her feet.

"It's like you've been holding all this in reserve for when it happened. Or, when this happened, or…" He could hear it in her voice, her desperation that he tell her she was wrong, but he couldn't. As of this moment, he had almost everything he'd ever wanted in his life, right here in his arms. Until this moment, he hadn't let himself believe it was possible. "I'm scared, Ryder."

He would have stopped dancing if he hadn't felt Big E and all the rest of the wedding guests' eyes on them.

"What are you scared of?" He drew her closer, tightened his hold and tucked her head under his chin.

"I said we wouldn't let anything change things between us, but it already has, hasn't it?" She held on to him. "I don't want to lose you, Ryder. I don't want to mess this up."

"You couldn't lose me now even if you wanted to." When was she going to accept that? "You're kind of stuck with me. It's official."

"Yeah, well now you're stuck with me, too. At least for the next six months? And what are we supposed to do about—" He could feel the heat rising to her cheeks. "Uh, Ryder, what do we do about the sleeping arrangements?"

It took a lot of effort not to smile. He should have known she'd be worrying this to death. "My bedtime is usually around eleven or so—"

She smacked a gentle hand against his shoulder, only to gasp when he caught her fingers with his. He held her hand against his heart, which was beating irregularly with her this close. "Whatever happens between us from here on is entirely in your control." He lifted her hand to his lips and brushed a kiss over the back of her fingers.

She pushed out a breath so hard he felt her tighten in his hold. "I don't know what to do with that, Ryder. I don't know—"

"It's okay. We'll figure it out." Now he did stop dancing, he stopped moving, and ignoring the couples who had joined them on the dance floor, kept his voice low. "We're both in uncharted territory and we don't have a map or any timeline," he told her. "For the record, I'm exactly where I want to be. And I'm still the Ryder you've always known." That's what this all came down to—the gamble they were taking with their friendship.

"That's why I proposed this crazy plan in the first place," she murmured. "Because I know who you are, deep down. I didn't do this on a lark you know. I didn't see another way for you to get Olivia back without some nasty legal battle with your in-laws."

"Maybe have faith," he said. "I know this was a solution for me to bring Olivia home. I'm not forgetting that, Corliss. But I'm looking forward to being back at the Flying Spur, helping you and your family move forward with the ranch." She pulled back, looked up at him and, appearing to surprise herself, she lifted her mouth to his for a kiss filled with many questions and a lot of promise .

"I know it seems like I jumped into this feetfirst without thinking of the consequences," she murmured against his mouth. "Maybe for a little while we can just…see where things go, once we're back at the Flying Spur?"

Translation: they wouldn't be sharing a marital bed anytime soon. He understood why.

"Speaking of the ranch," he said, wanting to shift the conversation to another topic. "How are you going to break the news to the folks there?"

"I'll call Mason later. Other than that, I bet this will do most of the talking for me." She lifted her hand to examine the twinkling diamond ring and the thin string tucked underneath. "It is very pretty. I can't believe you found time to get one."

"As much as I'd like to claim credit, you have your Big E to thank for that." Ryder twirled her slowly and then put his arm around her again "That ring belonged to Denny's grandmother." Ryder watched a mix of wonder and affection flash across her face. "I wish I had chosen it, but I think, in a way, it chose you." Family, after all, was what made Corliss's, and every Blackwell heart, beat strong and steady.

"You know, there won't be any hiding this when we get home." She took a deep breath, and when she let it out, some of the worry she'd been carrying faded from sight. "And so I'm not even going to try to."

Now, that, Ryder thought with a smile on his lips, sounded like progress.

CHAPTER ELEVEN

CORLISS COVERED YET another yawn after making the final electrical connection on the horse trailer. She stood and stretched, trying to shake the exhaustion away in the cold Montana-morning air. The truck was already packed and pointed in the direction of home.

She blamed her lack of sleep on an overabundance of food and excitement rather than the new batch of butterflies that seemed to have taken up residence in the pit of her stomach. Funny how they seemed to be swarming in time with the thoughts flying around in her head. She hadn't done herself any favors by slogging down multiple cups of coffee before arriving at the stables. She'd be lucky to fall asleep sometime in the next century.

At Skyfire's stall, she reached her hand out in silent request for the horse to approach her. "Takin' you home today, boy. You made an excellent impression. Good job." She clasped the horse's head with one hand and stroked affectionately between his eyes. "As pretty as it is here and as much as you love it, I really hope you don't have to come back."

Skyfire whinnied. Corliss smiled, rested her forehead against his and closed her eyes.

"Getting an early start back, then."

Corliss turned her head at the sound of Big E's words. "Ryder got confirmation from his father-in-law this morning. Olivia's flying in first thing tomorrow. Best we get back and settled before things get out of control." She eyed the old man, debating how cautious she needed to be with what she told him. "You've dragged this out until the last minute, Elias. You ready to stop dancing around my proposed deal and give me a straight answer?"

"I'm sure you learned yesterday my two-step's a bit rusty," Big E said. "I've had Ethan's assistant examine Skyfire and open a file on him." Big E walked over and rested his hand against the horse's neck. "Near as she can tell, your pride and joy is in excellent health and makes for a fine stake for a loan. But I don't make any equine decisions these days without getting Ethan's input. He'll be back in Falcon Creek this week. Once I talk with him, I'll be in touch."

"You're stalling," Corliss accused, not happy with the idea of continuing to spin her wheels. "We both know you're going to say yes. Why are you pretending like you're not? Why the delay?"

"Because I like being in the driver's seat and I'm too set to change my ways now." If he was irritated at her accusations, he didn't show it. If anything, he looked entertained by them. "Get your plans together, Corliss. Find the horses you want to train. Unless Ethan comes back at me with a flat-out no, we'll move ahead with my investment in yours and Nash's plans. But as far as the paperwork? That'll have to wait a bit."

She bit the inside of her cheek. No need to tell him she'd already called Nash and given him the go-ahead to find the horses he wanted. "Why do I get the feeling you've gotten more out of this visit than I have?"

"Oh, I don't think you can say that," Big E teased in a way that had Corliss chuckling. "You're the one heading home with a brand-new husband. Speaking of. Where is Ryder?"

"Getting breakfast to go from Francie in

the kitchen." As discussed, the morning after their marriage hadn't seemed any different than the one before. She'd slept in the bedroom and Ryder had taken the sofa. "As much as I'd love to stay longer, I'm a rip-the-bandage-off kind of person. Better to just get this show on the road. I'm betting Gran's anxious to hear all the details of the trip. And our conversations."

He nodded. "You and yours are always welcome here, Corliss. I hope you understand and accept that." Big E sounded as close to contrite as Corliss believed him capable of being. "As far as I'm concerned, the separation between our families is over."

Corliss inclined her head as a new bundle of nerves developed. "Thanks, but I'm not sure Gran's going to agree with that idea. We'll see what happens. Keep your eye on the news," Corliss said as she unlatched Skyfire's stall and stepped inside to get his bridle and bit strapped on. "Chances are, when she hears what's gone on the last few days, the Wyoming Blackwells will end up as fodder for a headline."

"Everything you've told me about my sister proves she hasn't changed one lick in sixty years." His smile seemed a little sad. "That gives me tremendous peace of mind. I'll go round up your husband."

Husband. Ryder Talbot was her *husband* now. Corliss offered a grateful smile. The doubt that had settled last night now returned, but she batted it back into silence. Circumstances aside, when all was said and done, she and Ryder were still friends. She'd just have to make certain they stayed that way.

She thanked the stable hands for the care they'd given Skyfire before leading the horse out to the trailer. No sooner had she gotten him latched in and closed the trailer than Ryder appeared. Corliss planted a hand on her hip and gaped at the food containers piled in his hands. "What's all that?"

"Breakfast. Along with extra biscuits," Ryder announced with that charming grin of his firmly in place. "And the top layer of our wedding cake to share with Olivia and your family when we're all together."

Behind him, Hadley, and Ty, carrying Aurora, along with Rosie piled in to bid their goodbyes. "That should defuse the bombshell you'll be dropping," Ty said.

"Can I come to Wyoming and play with

your little girl?" Rosie asked Ryder after he stashed the boxes in the back seat of the truck.

"Don't see why not," Ryder said. "We'll have to make sure there are lots of horses for you to ride when you do. Maybe by then, Olivia will have her horse sense." He tickled Rosie's chin and sent her into a fit of giggles. "Thanks for everything. All of you." He headed around the front of the truck.

"Guess he's driving," Corliss muttered and hugged Hadley goodbye. "This has been great. Thanks so much for all you did. I know most of it was unexpected."

"You're family," Hadley assured her with another quick squeeze. "We might have to plan a huge Blackwell family reunion at this point. For multiple branches of the family tree."

"Now, that would be something to talk about," Corliss agreed. She came to a halt in front of Big E, tilted up her head and planted her hands on her hips. "Well. It's been an experience, Uncle."

Big E pulled her in for a hug. "You take care of yourself, Corliss. And I'll be in touch."

"You'd better be." She knew the history between Big E and Denny had yet to resolve itself, but some things, like saving Denny's ranch, were important. She knew he knew that. Though Corliss wasn't so naive to think that her one visit would fix everything between the octogenarian siblings. But maybe she'd started chiseling away at the bad feelings. She climbed into the truck and slammed the door. "Let's go," she said quietly to Ryder, surprised at the regret she felt at leaving her newly acquainted family. "Time to get back to reality."

"You did remember to refill our coffee cups, didn't you?"

"Please." Corliss rolled her eyes and then glanced at him. "I'm well aware of my husband's addictive proclivity for liquid caffeine."

She secured her seat belt and Ryder stepped on the gas and together they waved goodbye to the Blackwells of Falcon Creek.

RYDER WAS USED to tension. During the years he'd spent fighting fires on oil rigs—a job where stress management was a prerequisite—he'd developed a sixth sense about it. Anxiety had a very specific way of filling a space before its almost complete and paralyzing effect captured everyone in sight.

He wasn't in the middle of a fire, at least, not the kind he was trained to fight. But one thing he'd learned in life was that there were all types of infernos.

What he wasn't used to was this level of tension on dry ground. Especially coming from Corliss. "You keep grinding your teeth like that, you won't have any left."

"It's either that or eat another biscuit." She flashed him a smile that didn't come close to reaching her eyes. "I can't afford to outgrow these jeans."

Because she needed him to, he laughed. "Is it telling your family we got married that's got you caught up in knots?"

"By now they know. I called Mason last night and told him."

"I get it." Ryder nodded.

"I didn't want to blindside him," she explained.

"He okay about it?" He'd known the kid forever, but distance had always played a big part of their friendship.

"He says he is. We'll see." Corliss shrugged.

Ryder repressed a frown. "So, if that isn't what's got you worried, it must be…"

"Denny." Corliss said. They sped up the final hill and the Flying Spur came into view. "I'm counting on her affection for you being a buffer for her anger with me."

"Happy to be of service."

He reached over, covered her hand with his and felt her wedding band against his palm. Her hand tensed, as if she wasn't sure what to do. "It'll be okay, Corliss." As he spoke, her fingers relaxed. "Denny loves you and respects you too much to stay angry for long."

"You are such an optimist." Corliss surprised him by turning her hand over and sliding her fingers through his. "For the record, she's still holding a grudge about the Flying Spur getting pushed out of a national sponsorship for the rodeo back in 1987." She smirked, and a flash of the spunky Corliss he knew appeared. She shifted in her seat to look at him. "I guess with Olivia arriving tomorrow, we have a lot to get right."

"There's been so much going on. So much change and upheaval and—"

"You don't owe me an explanation, Corliss.

This is an odd situation to find ourselves in. But we are in it. Together, remember."

"Keep that optimistic attitude in place. And be prepared for a bit of bombardment from my family."

"You can't see it, but I'm actually wearing armor under my shirt," he teased. "What's a family for, if not to give one a hard time? In fact…" He withdrew his hand and, clasping the wheel, leaned over and squinted at the small crowd standing in front of the house. "I think the bombardment might already have started. Unless you're always welcomed home with balloons and banners?"

"For crying out loud," Corliss muttered. Adele, flanked by her twin toddlers, Ivy and Quinn, were dressed in their Sunday best and launched toward them when Corliss pushed open her door. "This is ridiculously over-the-top." But there was a huge smile on her face when she scooped up her nieces for a big Blackwell hug. "You two grew while I was gone. Isla!" She bent down and spoke to Levi's not-so-little, little girl. "I'm so happy to see you."

Ryder emerged from the truck at a slower pace as Nash, Levi and Mason, along with dogs Bow and Arrow, came forward. He could see they each had small bags in their hands, and for a moment, he wondered what was going on. Suddenly, both he and Corliss were doused with handfuls of bread crumbs, which sent Bow and Arrow into a barking, jumping frenzy.

"Last time I got married it was rice," Ryder joked as he brushed off his shirt.

"Maybe you are old," Nash joked. "According to Mason, rice is bad for birds. Since the wonder chef always keeps a stash of bread crumbs in the freezer, we went with that. Can't believe you two kept this relationship of yours a secret." Nash held out his hand and, even as he shook it, slapped Ryder hard on the back. "Welcome to the family, brother. And good luck to you."

"For the record, this was her idea," Ryder told Corliss's brother. He smiled at the sight of Corliss showing off her wedding ring to her sister and nieces. "But I didn't say no. Hey, Levi." He greeted the middle Blackwell sibling. "Good to see you again. How's the back?"

"Well, I'm upright," Levi said with a strained smile. "I'd say welcome to the family, but..." Levi shrugged in that easygoing manner he had. "That's old news. You two come on in. Mason's fixed a Sunday supper fit for a royal couple."

"Has he?" He noticed Mason still standing separately from the rest of the family and took the hint. He approached Corliss's thirteen-year-old son, who for the first time in his life, seemed to eye Ryder warily. "Mason."

He had to give the kid credit. Just like his mama, he didn't flinch. But he also didn't take a step forward. "Before you guys left, I teased Mom about you two." He arched a brow. "For the record, I was joking."

Ryder nodded. "A lot happened while we were in Montana and getting married was one solution." He hesitated. "Me marrying your mom doesn't change anything, Mason. Not between you and me."

"Doesn't it?" Mason didn't look convinced. "I'm getting a stepfather and stepsister in the space of a few days. Seems like a lot of change to me."

"Change doesn't have to be a bad thing. And I never would have agreed to your mom's marriage idea if I didn't think you wouldn't be a great addition to Olivia's life. I realize this is a bit—"

"Weird. The word you're looking for is *weird*," Mason finished for him, but there was a lighter expression on his face as he glanced over at his mother. "She looks happy." His observation appeared to erase the darker doubts he carried.

"I have always cared about you and your mom." Ryder laid a hand on Mason's shoulder. "And you and I have always been friends. I'd like for that to continue."

Mason nodded. "It'll be nice, seeing Mom smile more. I always thought it would be cool to have a little sister or brother. Can't be mad now that I'm getting one, can I?" He eyed Ryder even as Ryder felt the guilt kick in. Until now he'd primarily been worried about Olivia getting too attached. He'd forgotten that Mason's feelings were involved as well. "What's going to happen if we lose the Flying Spur?"

Appreciative of his confidence, Ryder kept his voice steady and sure. "You aren't going to lose the ranch."

"Being thirteen doesn't mean I'm stupid. I've heard Mom and them talking." The quick, thoughtful expression on his face gave away the kind of man he was turning into. "What happens if we can't pay back that loan?"

"We're going to make sure this land remains Blackwell land," Ryder said. "We have a plan, or your mom does, and it's a good one. You have to trust her. Trust me, too, because I'm a part of this now, okay? Your home is going to stay your home." He remembered how important the promise of stability had been to him when his father died; Denny and the Blackwells had given him that.

The least he could do was make the same commitment to Corliss's son.

"All right." Mason gave a jerky nod and seemed to understand. Ivy and Quinn squealed behind them. Ryder stepped back just as Corliss bent down to release her nieces, who scrambled away to play with the dogs.

Corliss slung an arm around Adele's shoulders. "I need to take Skyfire to his stall. I'll meet you all inside in a bit."

"I can help," Ryder offered.

Corliss shook her head. "No, thanks. I've got him."

He recognized that tone; she was feeling the need for some alone time—something she was used to having a lot of. Something he was going to have to remember during this upheaval.

"Skyfire'll have even more company now," Adele announced. "Thanks to Nash's sweet-talking."

"Oh?" Corliss faced her brother.

"I spoke to Preston Merriman the day you left," Nash said. "Convinced him we were worth taking a chance on and that we're open for business again. He brought down three of his horses yesterday for me to train." Guarded optimism shone in his eyes. "I offered him the reduced rate, of course, and it'll be on a probation basis, but it's progress. You make the deal with Big E?"

"We agreed we'd wait for Corliss to tell us what happened," Levi said. He scattered the last of his bread crumbs on the ground.

"I changed my mind," Nash said. "Are we a go?"

"I'll know for sure in a day or so." Corliss shot a look at Ryder. "Elias wants to consult with one of his grandsons on Skyfire before he firmly commits."

"It's a formality," Ryder added, not liking the doubt he saw flashing across Nash's face.

"Big E suggested you start looking into the horses you want to buy. He wouldn't have told us that if he didn't plan to say yes."

"Then, why didn't he?" Adele asked. It was a bit of a mystery.

"Because he and our grandmother are more alike than either of them would be comfortable admitting," Corliss answered. "Speaking of Gran, where is she?"

"In the stable with the new horses." Levi shrugged. "Waiting for you."

Ryder shifted to attention. "You sure you don't want me—"

"No." Corliss shook her head and, as she walked past Mason, pulled her son in for a brief hug. "It'll be okay. Why don't you take your stuff upstairs to my room, then get ready for dinner? Gran and I will join everyone in a little while."

"Gran hasn't evicted you," Nash called after her. "If that makes you feel any better." He grinned at Ryder and retrieved the bags from the truck.

Corliss walked into the trailer to retrieve Skyfire. Levi went inside the ranch house.

"You need me to show you where Corliss's bedroom is?" Nash asked, grinning.

The ribbing had definitely begun. "I think I can find my way, thanks."

"Well, you get lost, give a holler," Nash teased. "You're in the thick of things now, Ryder. You're officially one of us."

"Maybe I should be considering changing my name to Blackwell. Make it legal."

"Now, there's an idea," Nash chuckled. "One thing every member of this family can agree on. There can never be enough Blackwells."

"Took your time with that horse, Little Miss. Something you're worried to tell me?"

Corliss stopped short, just inside the stables, at the sound of Denny's voice. She'd taken her time—too much, probably—unloading Skyfire and leading him around the long way. Denny had called a truce before she'd left, but there was no telling how much thinking she'd been doing in the past few days. "No, ma'am." *Just...testing the water before diving all the way in.*

Denny stepped up and brushed her hand over the nose of one of Nash's new horses, a black beauty that left Corliss breathless. How she'd missed the feel of a full stable.

Skyfire gave a welcoming whinny and drew the other horses to their doors. "Always knew that stubborn Blackwell streak would rear up and bite me one day. Well? What'd he say? You've been gone longer than I thought you'd be."

"He knew who I was from the jump." Corliss led Skyfire into his clean stall and hefted a bucket of feed over the gate for him to enjoy. She rested her hand on the horse's nose, drew in some of his strength and patience. "Said at first he thought I was you and that you'd come back to make peace with him."

Denny harrumphed, but not with nearly as much vehemence as Corliss expected. "I was never as pretty as you are."

"He misses you, Gran." Corliss hesitated. "And he's sorry."

"Sorry for what?" Denny's scoffing question reminded Corliss there was still a very large open wound to heal.

"He's sorry for all of it. He said he made a mistake, not standing up for you against your parents. Also said if you'd married Frank Weston, you'd have run right over him in no time, so to speak."

"Hmm, can't say he's wrong there. What

else is he sorry for?" Denny's lips twitched before her eyes turned steely once again. She ducked her chin, her breath catching in her throat.

"What?" Corliss demanded. "What's wrong?"

"Nothing." Denny reached out and caught Corliss's hand, curled her fingers as she drew her close.

"Oh, that. Yeah. Um." She blinked back an unexpected flood of emotion. "Ryder and I got married."

"That I'd heard." Denny continued to look at the ring. And the string that remained tied around Corliss's finger. "That's my grand-mother's ring. The ring..." Denny's voice caught. "The ring my mother refused to give me when I left with Cal."

Corliss hadn't heard that part of the story. "Gran?"

Denny shook her head as if coming out of a dream. "I didn't think I'd ever..."

"Big E gave it to Ryder before the cere-mony." Corliss was so glad not to have to lie. "He said it always should have been yours and that giving it to me felt like the right thing to do."

"Big E. Can't believe people still call him that after all these years." Denny pinched her lips tight as she touched gentle fingers to the ring. "Guess maybe he's capable of doing the right thing after all."

"Gran—"

"Did he give you what you needed?" Denny sniffed. "What you asked for?"

"Not entirely. Not yet. But he will," she added in a rush at Denny's glare.

"Don't go counting those chickens just yet, Little Miss."

"Yes, ma'am."

"This marriage of yours…" Denny released her hand.

"It's just to get Ryder's daughter back," Corliss explained and nearly bit her tongue. She should have known she couldn't have kept the truth from her grandmother, despite her assurances to Ryder. But Denny would understand. And she'd keep their secret. "He needed—"

"You," Denny told her flat-out. "He needed you and you stepped up. Stepping up is what family does. It's what people who love each other do."

Corliss's stomach jumped. She did love

Ryder. But did she *love* Ryder? If she did...
What did that even mean?

"Don't you hurt that boy," Denny ordered
in that don't-dare-defy-me-again tone of hers.
"You take care with his heart, you hear me?
He's always taken care with yours."

Corliss nodded. "I will."

"Good." Denny gave a sharp nod of her
own and walked away. "Now, come inside
and see what we did for Olivia's room."

CHAPTER TWELVE

"DAD, YOU'RE SQUISHING ME." Olivia's voice rang like splendid church bells in Ryder's ears. Ryder hugged his daughter, her overstuffed backpack and tablet computer one last quick time before setting her on her feet so he could get a good look at her. She let out a big breath and beamed up at him. "That's better. Hi." She blinked those big baby blues at him. He felt joy at the thought of there not being a screen between them. She was here, after more than a year apart. Finally, his little girl was with him again. "Dad, you okay?" She reached out her hands, caught him around the waist. "You aren't going to cry, are you?"

"If I was, there's no better excuse than seeing your perfect little face." He couldn't stop himself from bending down again and bringing her in for another hug. He set her back down and could see Nina in his daughter's eyes, and for the first time, the guilt was no more than a gentle wave. "I am never letting you out of my sight again, so get used to it."

"Aw, man," Olivia whined. "Does that mean you're going to come to school with me and everything?"

"Well, maybe not school." He turned and held out his hand for her to take it. It had taken him a good long time to work the kinks out of his body after spending the night on the sofa. That he hadn't woken Corliss up with the recurring nightmare was a blooming miracle. He really needed to get a handle on that, if for no other reason than to preserve his spine. And their matrimonial charade. "Let's go get your bags."

"I only have one and this." She patted her backpack as they made their way through the nearly empty regional airport. "Grandma said she'd ship everything else once I was settled."

"Oh?" He'd already sent the Whitlocks the Blackwells' Wyoming address. Just another excuse to drag out Olivia's transition and make things more difficult for him. The fact he hadn't received a straight answer to his asking when they might be coming out left him thinking they could arrive at any time. Maybe even the next flight.

"I made sure I brought everything important." Olivia announced. "Like Ernie, of course."

"Of course." Four years after Ryder had sent Olivia a stuffed polar bear from his time in Alaska, she still carried it around with her wherever she went. And that, Ryder thought, as the hot irritation flooded through him, was enough to thaw out any frustration he felt toward his in-laws. "Ernie's going to have a lot to get used to out here."

"Like wearing a hat." She pointed up to his own cowboy hat. "Do I get one of those? You said I could get boots. Cow*girl* boots," she added as if he'd forgotten.

"Of course. In fact, we'll hit up Spurs and Saddles on our way home. They have everything you'll need. But we have a stop to make first. What?" he asked when she kept looking around as if searching for something.

"Where's Corliss?"

"She's busy. Every day's a workday on a ranch."

"Oh. Yeah, I know. I've done a lot of reading the last couple of weeks. I even found the Flying Spur's website. I know all my new uncles' and my aunt's names. And my new grandma. Is she my grandma?"

"That would be Miss Denny to you, and yes, in a way. And don't forget your new cousins." Countless cousins if he included all the Blackwells of Montana.

"Awesome. I've never had cousins before." She skipped alongside him as they headed to his car in the parking lot. "Wow! This truck is huge! So much bigger than Grandpa's SUV. I hope we don't hit a moose on the road. I read where more than six thousand animals are hit by vehicles in Wyoming every year. Is that true? I don't want that to be true." She wiggled out of her backpack and jumped into the passenger seat. Ryder stashed the luggage and walked to the driver's side. "Oh, wow. Look at that! Dad, there's so much sky and space! I don't see hardly any buildings at all. Where do all the people live?"

"Well, Wyoming is different than Florida in one sense, since there aren't nearly as many people here."

"I know that, Dad." Was it possible to *hear* his daughter's eye roll? "I just meant the people who do live here. Oh, I made a list of places I want to go. There's Yellowstone, of course."

"Of course." Ryder hadn't been there in a dinosaur's age. "Where else?"

"All the national parks. Oh, and there's a big garden in Cheyenne and an Old West museum. Hang on, I'll pull up my…" She flipped open her tablet cover only to be distracted by the scenery flying by. "Ohhhhh." She pressed her fingertips against the window. "Dad, it's so pretty." She whipped her head around so fast her long brown hair went flying around her shoulders. "Can we get something to eat? They only had cheese and crackers on the plane, and I didn't want the carrots Grandma gave me." Her nose wrinkled and Ryder made a mental note not to include carrots in her future lunches.

"I have to stop in a town called Cody to see about a couple of horses."

"Horses?" If possible, Olivia's eyes went even bigger.

"The Flying Spur trains horses, remember? So we need horses." He'd been hoping to keep their visit to the Bluefield Ranch a surprise, but, much like his daughter, he couldn't keep a secret. "Is that okay with you?"

"Getting a horse of my own?" She practically squealed. "Oh yes, yes, yes! Wyoming is already amazing!"

"Hang on, because there's more to owning a horse than just fun. They're a lot of responsibility."

"Daaa-ad." The old I-don't-want-a-lecture-already tone kicked in.

"I mean it, Sprout. Horses need a lot of care, even from someone as little as you."

"I'm not so little," Olivia argued. "I grew a whole inch over the summer."

Even more than that over the past eighteen months. "You'll have a chores list, both for your horse and for helping around the ranch. Everyone has to pitch in."

"Dad, I know. Mom told me about you growing up here."

"She did?" Ryder's hand tightened on the wheel. "When?"

"All the time. She found this book for me one time, about a little cowgirl. It was one of my favorites for her to read." And there, for the first time, was a flash of uncertainty. "Is it okay if I talk about Mom?"

"Of course. Why…?" He didn't have to finish the question. He already knew the answer.

"I want you to talk about your mom as much as you want. You loved her, Sprout. I loved her, too. And I miss her."

"You do?" Again, the way she asked had the resentment against his in-laws surging.

"I do. Things weren't perfect between us, but we were always friends." Distant ones at the end, perhaps. He couldn't help but worry that history was going to repeat itself with Corliss. "Plus, she gave me the best gift anyone's ever given me."

"Me, right?" Olivia's grin sprang back to life, then dimmed again. "Mom used to say that, too." A beat passed and her mood shifted again. "I'll start making a list of all chores I'm going to have to do for my horse."

He did not assume for one moment that this conciliatory, agreeable Olivia was going to last long. His daughter was notorious for asking questions and arguing until she absorbed every scintilla of information. "The school year starts next Monday, and we'll meet with your tutor to get you scheduled for additional hours."

"I read that a lot of ranch kids are home-schooled," Olivia stated. "Is that true?"

"I'm sure it is." Not an option he was anxious to entertain. At least, not yet. "Corliss and her brothers and sister all went to school in town. The same one I went to."

"Am I going to the same school as *you*?" The disbelief in her voice had Ryder scowling. "The same building's there?"

"It wasn't made out of twigs and twine, you know?"

"You're funny, Dad." Olivia gave him another cheeky grin. "Now. About that list…"

CORLISS GAVE THE industrial pliers a hard twist and tightened the last line of wire fence that needed repairing.

"It'll be good to have Wyatt home and have another pair of hands." Nash pocketed the wire clippers and pulled off his hide gloves. "With him and Ryder around, we'll get the rest of the place whipped back into shape in no time. Don't know about you, but I'm starting to replace fence wire in my sleep."

"It'll be nice to have Wyatt home, in any case," Corliss said in what she hoped was a warning tone to her brother. It wasn't a secret that Nash didn't approve of their youngest brother's affinity for ranch-hopping and working anywhere other than at the Flying Spur. Despite them not having horses to board or train for such a long while, there was always upkeep and maintenance that needed doing, and as money tightened, repairs seemed to multiply. "Don't go poking at him as soon as he does get home," she added. "He's not a kid, anymore, Nash. He doesn't need our approval or guidance."

Nash eyed her from under his hat. "He doesn't need your protection anymore, either."

Corliss let out a breath as she crimped off the wire end and tugged on the line before stepping back. "Just be patient, okay?"

Corliss's nerves frayed at Nash's disbelieving snort and she gave him the same glare he'd aimed her way. "How's Luke doing? You haven't brought my nephew out to the ranch lately."

"He's been busy," Nash said. He torqued his pliers a little too roughly. "Him and Helen both."

"I did see your ex in town when Ryder and I drove through. She was talking with Phil Mitchell outside Tucker's Ice Cream Shop. What's going on there?"

"No idea."

Clearly, Nash didn't want to talk about the

ex-wife he still carried a torch for. Corliss retrieved the last of the wire and tossed it into the back of the truck. She pulled off her gloves, shoved them into the pocket of her jeans.

"There's been no point in bringing my boy out here if there aren't any horses to ride."

"Yes, it's not like Denny would like to see her great-grandson. Or I'd like to see my nephew."

"All right," Nash said in a way that clearly said he wanted to change the subject.

"Your son's five." Corliss plowed on, despite knowing he didn't need the reminder. "Spending time with his dad is pretty much on the top of his list for things to do. You could start teaching him about the Flying Spur, Nash. This place is his, too. What's the deal?"

"The deal is you need to mind your own business." He snatched up the scattered tools and dropped them into the truck bed.

"Right." Corliss glanced at her watch. She realized she'd definitely hit a raw nerve. "We should probably be heading back. Ryder said he and Olivia would be here before dinner.

What?" she asked when Nash narrowed his eyes at her.

"You and Ryder have been married what, a couple of days, and he's already sleeping on the sofa."

Corliss cringed. "I swear you spend more time in the main house than you do in your own."

"I was out of coffee. What gives?"

"Sometimes, marriages take time to adjust," she admitted, trying not to dwell on the unexpected pang of sadness she'd felt when Ryder waited until all was quiet and, with his pillow, went downstairs to sleep. Had it been a mistake not to...? No. Now that Nash had noticed, however, she and Ryder were going to have to have a conversation about how to keep up pretenses. Especially if, as Ryder believed, Olivia's grandparents could make a surprise visit at any time. If they couldn't convince her family all was well, how would they ever convince the Standishes? "He has bouts of insomnia," she thought suddenly. "It's no big deal."

"If you say so. I'm just saying kids are perceptive."

So, it seemed, were big brothers. Clearly

their ruse hadn't passed muster. "Stop circling your point and land, please."

"Maybe don't give the kid anything else to doubt or be afraid of."

Ah. Relief swept through her. This wasn't about him not believing she was really married, but being concerned about Olivia's perceptions. "Olivia won't have time to be afraid of anything," Corliss argued and jerked her thumb at him to jump in the truck.

"I remember one particular summer when Mason had that same dream about you being lost in that storm. He'd wake up crying because he thought you weren't coming back and that you'd left him alone."

"He was seven," Corliss said even as her heart pinched. "And I came back. Besides, he wouldn't have been alone. He'd have had you and..."

"Olivia's eight," Nash said. "And her mom didn't come back. Her father nearly died fighting a massive oil rig fire. At the very least, you owe her your best effort. This marriage of yours, it came out of the blue and you've spent a good many years making it very clear you were happy being alone."

"Then Ryder came back," Corliss said. "And I changed my mind."

"And I'm happy for you. For both of you. In a world gone mad, I have to admit, seeing you two finally realize there was more to it than friendship, it gives me hope," Nash assured her. "I'm just saying…make room for them, Corliss. Marriage changes people. Don't make the same mistakes I did. Don't push them away because you're too scared to hold on."

"She isn't even here yet," Corliss snapped. "And I don't push—"

"You push, Corliss. So far you've only pushed against people who push back. I guess what I'm saying is maybe Ryder's worth letting in."

First Denny and now Nash had pretty much accused her of setting Ryder up for a massive heartache. As if Ryder didn't know what he'd gotten himself into by marrying her. And, yes okay, now that she stopped long enough to think about it, she had been unnerved being this close to Ryder 24/7. Not because she didn't want him there.

Because she did.

"DO YOU HAVE any questions about Corliss and her family before we get there, Sprout?" He glanced in the rearview mirror and frowned. "What are you doing?"

"Putting on my new boots." Olivia kicked the back of his seat. "Oops, sorry. They're a little...tricky. Got it!" She kicked out her feet and knocked her toes together. "These are so awesome, Dad. Thank you for all my new clothes. Now I won't look like a dork at school. I'll fit right in."

Ryder hoped so. He'd had her school records and test results sent from the academy in Florida she'd been attending, and near as he'd been told, she was going to jump one, if not two grades come next week. One thing he remembered Nina talking about was that Olivia did so much better when she was challenged rather than being bored.

"Is that the ranch, Dad?" She shot up in her seat and looked out the window again, pointed to the house in the distance. "It's so pretty and blue!"

"It is. So there's the main house. That's what you're seeing there. And they've got a large stable for the horses they train—"

"The website said they do cutting horses. That means they're for the rodeo right?"

"Mostly," Ryder told her as he took the final turn onto the main road. "Cutting horses serve a lot of different jobs. Business has been a bit slow lately, but they're getting back in shape. Ranch life's going to be a bit different than what you're used to, Sprout." The list they'd made of things she could do to help out had been a big wake-up call for his daughter. "There's something for everyone to do here. Not all of it's going to be fun, but it's necessary work. Caring for the animals is the primary focus, and that's something I bet you'll like."

"Uh-huh. Oh, look at the dogs!" Olivia practically squealed as Ryder parked next to Corliss's beat-up truck. "Bow and Arrow!" His daughter was already unhooking her belt and shoving open the door.

"Be careful with them. Let them get a good sniff before you try to hug them or anything." He'd spent enough time with the dogs last night, and watched how they were with Adele's twin girls, to know they'd be good with Olivia. By the time he rounded the back of the truck, he found Olivia on the ground and her arms full of dogs.

She giggled and tumbled to the ground just as Corliss emerged.

Ryder's heart beat double-time at the affectionate expression on Corliss's face as she looked at his daughter. If she'd had a long day, it certainly didn't show. The jeans and vintage T-shirt she wore spoke of an early finish out on the fence line he knew she'd been working today. She'd left her hair down, something she did so infrequently that Ryder found himself staring as if looking at a mirage.

Standing there, on the porch of the old ranch house, arms crossed over her chest, she made him feel as if he'd officially come home.

"Been wondering when you two were going to show up." Corliss's pronouncement had Olivia gasping. The dogs barked and shot straight over to Corliss. "Welcome to the Flying Spur, Olivia."

"Oh. Hi!" Olivia tried to scramble to her feet, but her boots were still just a little too big and she almost tripped. Ryder caught her before she face-planted in the dirt.

"Time for tissue in the toes," he told Corliss, who was nodding.

Olivia sprang up and dusted herself off, doing this odd shimmy and wiggle as she patted her hands on her shirt and backside.

"New boots, huh?" Corliss walked over, crouched down and pushed her fingers into the toe of Olivia's boots, the same way he had back in town. "They're a good fit, actually. Practical, too. Not too fancy. You like them?"

"I love them," Olivia confirmed and just like that the ice was broken. "Dad took me to Spurs and Saddles, and they had all kinds of stuff, but he said I needed boots especially."

"Can't live on a ranch without a good pair of boots." Corliss held out her hand. "It's nice to finally meet you in person, Olivia."

Olivia accepted the hand, frowned as she shook it. "Dad said I should call you Miss Corliss."

"That sounds like an excellent suggestion," Corliss agreed without missing a beat. "One thing we don't worry about here on the Flying Spur is asking a wrong question. There's no such thing."

"Okay." Olivia sagged in relief. "That's good, because I made a list."

"She really did," Ryder warned.

"I'll do my best to answer all of your questions. Dinner's just about ready." Corliss stood back up, brushed a hand over Ryder's arm and said, "Welcome home." The smile on her face eased the tension he'd watched increase over the past few days.

Ryder couldn't have formed much of a sentence if he'd tried, but he did have the wherewithal to smile back at her. "Thank you."

Corliss looked back to Olivia and held out a hand. "I've got a few people anxious to meet you, Olivia. There's more family that'll come around later this week."

Olivia grabbed hold of Corliss's hand and hopped up the porch steps. Corliss called to him over her shoulder when he moved to gather up the shopping bags, "We can get those after dinner."

Ryder waited a beat before following.

"Full circle," he told himself as he stepped onto the porch and ushered the dogs in ahead of him.

He prayed this worked, because seeing his daughter so happy in Wyoming meant everything to him.

"How do you like your first Flying Spur dinner, Olivia?" Nash sat back in his chair. Corliss polished off the last of her pot roast and watched the girl's reaction.

"Yummy." Olivia eyed the bowl near Corliss. "May I have more broccoli, please?"

"Of course." Corliss, as enchanted with the in-person Olivia as she'd been with the video-chat one, handed her the bowl and spoon. The little girl was everything she'd expected her to be, complete with Ryder's heart worn squarely on her short green sleeves.

"Grandma says if I want seconds, it should only be veggies." Olivia placed a careful spoonful on her plate and eyed the biscuits near her dad. "It's one of her rules."

"Sweetie, around here," Denny announced from the head of the table, "we burn off most everything we eat, so you have seconds of whatever you want." Denny motioned to Ryder to pass the towel-topped basket of biscuits to Olivia. "Except my shot of whiskey," she added with a surly look at Corliss. "Not complainin' mind you, just sayin'."

Corliss's lips twitched. "Appreciate that, Gran."

"Save room for dessert," Mason said from

his seat between Ryder and his uncle. "I made my last blackberry pie of the season today, so enjoy it."

"Tell me you made jam before you ran out of berries," Corliss pleaded, then looked at Olivia. "He makes amazing jams."

"I'm allergic to kiwi and raw tomatoes," Olivia told them, then cringed. "Sorry. I was supposed to tell you that right away." She gave loyal Bow a quick pat as he sat by her side.

"Your dad already let me know," Mason said. "We don't eat a lot of kiwi, but you can eat tomatoes if they're cooked, right? Like with spaghetti?"

"I love spaghetti!" Olivia declared. "But we don't eat a lot of it in Florida."

Corliss could feel Ryder's anxiety mount with each mention of Olivia's grandparents. The poor kid was stuck on auto repeat of all her grandparents' rules. A few days on the ranch should be enough to take care of that, Corliss thought, and made a mental note to make that a reality.

"Spaghetti and all kinds of pasta are a frequent meal in this house," Nash said. "You haven't lived until Mason's made his superdeluxe lasagna. I see you got new boots. Pretty snazzy, Olivia."

Olivia grinned. "Daddy bought me all kinds of stuff to wear for when I do my chores. We made a list. Wanna see it?"

"No tablets or cell phones at the table," Ryder said when she started to get up. "That's our only dinner rule here."

"Oh. Right." Olivia slumped back into her chair. "Sorry. Me and Dad came up with a whole separate list for taking care of Ambrosia."

"Who's Ambrosia?" Corliss asked Olivia, then glanced to Ryder.

"She's my new horse," Olivia told them. "She's so pretty. She came over to me right away. She's almost three years old and she's brown and has a gold star right here." She poked a finger between her eyes. "Same place as my scar. How cool is that?"

"You bought her a horse?" Corliss asked Ryder, and even she nearly winced at the odd tone in her voice.

"He bought three," Olivia announced as she finished her carrots. "He bought Ambrosia's mama, too, because families should always be together. And then he got a boy horse—"

"Stallion," Ryder corrected her.

"Right. Stallion. I knew that." Olivia looked irritated she'd gotten it wrong. "Foxglove. He looked sad. His last owners weren't so nice to him and he was all alone in the pasture and Dad saw him right away and said he wanted him."

"You bought three horses?" she asked Ryder. "You didn't say you were going to do that. Where did you go to get them?"

"Bluefield Ranch in Cody." Ryder pushed his plate back as Mason got up to clear. Olivia munched on her biscuit. "I gave him a call yesterday to see what he had for purchase."

"Bluefield, huh?" Nash asked and cast a glance at his grandmother. Corliss frowned. "You need help picking them up?"

"I arranged for him to deliver, actually. He sounded curious when I told him the Flying Spur was back up and running, so I figured why not have him come by here." The all-innocence expression he offered the table scraped against Corliss's nerves.

"You're a right sneaky one, Ryder Talbot." Denny waggled a finger at him. "You haven't been gone so long you forgot Justin Bluefield is one of the biggest gossips in three states."

"Seeing as everyone else has a hand in saving this place, made sense to do my part. Dropping a little information with Bluefield seemed an expedient way to get the word out about the Flying Spur being open again," Ryder said. "He should be here sometime tomorrow afternoon."

"Oh, you're good." Nash laughed.

"That's a smart man you married." Denny passed her plate to Nash, who stacked his on top, then passed to Corliss, who did the same and carried the stack over to the counter. "This time next week, I'll bet we have a whole stable full of horses to tend to and train."

Corliss knew what Denny was hinting at. That if they had a full stable of horses, they wouldn't need Big E's loan. But there were still operating and living costs to maintain, and board and training fees wouldn't come close to covering her and Nash's part of the loan repayment.

"Will there be room for Ambrosia and her mama and Foxglove?" Olivia asked.

"Plenty of room," Denny assured her as she

eyed Corliss. "In fact, how about you and I take the dogs for a walk and see which empty stall you like best for her? Ambrosia's a nice name for a horse."

"She likes all kinds of apples," Olivia told them. "I looked up what kinds there are. I almost went with MacIntosh, but Ambrosia sounded prettier. Do you think she'll like it?"

"Her name?" Denny asked. "Can't imagine not. Mason, we'll have our pie in a bit," she told him. Olivia got up and brought her plate over to Mason.

"Thank you for dinner," she said.

"You're welcome, Olivia." Mason bent down and whispered something in her ear that had Olivia nodding excitedly before she went out the back door behind Denny, boots clomping with every step, the dogs racing after her. "I told her I'd teach her to make biscuits in the morning if she wanted."

"Nice," Ryder said. "Thanks."

"You really bought three horses?" Corliss asked him as he got up to help clear. "Why didn't you say anything?"

"Didn't think I needed to." Surprise jumped into his eyes. "We need horses here, right? Why? What's wrong?"

"Nothing. I just…"

"She's probably ticked she didn't think about approaching Justin Bluefield herself," Nash observed and poured himself a cup of coffee from the pot on the counter. "Man can move information faster than high-speed internet."

"That's not true," Corliss protested. "I'm not ticked."

"You look ticked to me," Nash goaded.

"To me, too. Are you telling me I overstepped some invisible line?" Ryder set the bowl and plate down and stared at her in that calm, assessing way he had about him.

"Of course not."

"Even I didn't believe that," Mason muttered. Nash grabbed his coffee, then steered Mason out of the kitchen. Corliss gaped after them, resisting the urge to feel oddly abandoned.

"What's going on, Corliss?" Ryder asked.

"Nothing." She turned, not expecting to find him so close. Suddenly, she couldn't figure out what to do with her hands. "It's nothing, really."

"It has to be something because I can't

think of any reason for your nose to be out
of joint over me buying a couple of horses."

"Three," she corrected. "You bought three
horses. And you didn't tell me."

"I wanted to surprise you." But there was
no humor in his eyes. Only confusion and a
good dose of disappointment. "Corliss, talk
to me. What's this really about? You can't
be mad at me for buying horses Olivia and
I need."

"I know." She pressed her fingers to her
temples. "I know you do. I don't understand
why..." She sighed and resisted when he
caught her hands and brought them away
from her face. "Ryder, don't."

"Don't what?"

"Don't be nice to me. Not when I'm being
a—"

"Pain?" Nash offered when he ducked back
into the kitchen, popped open the fridge to retrieve the cream. "Sorry. Just needed...yeah.
I'm leaving now."

"What he said." Corliss huffed at her brother's retreating back. "I'm just cranky, I guess.
It's been a long day. Let's just forget it."

"No." Ryder looked to be debating whether
to push her for the truth. He must have de-

cided because he took a step closer and slipped his arms around her. "We decided, together, to keep up this ruse. We can't make that work if we can't talk to each other," he whispered. "You're the one who's been worried about things changing between us. Stop letting it. Stop throwing up warning signs that anything else is going on."

"That's not what I'm doing," she said against his chest. Had she ever, in her entire life, found a place more perfect and sublime as being in his arms?

"Then, what are you doing?" he asked. "Picking a fight over something completely trivial? Sabotaging this before we have a chance to succeed."

"You always do that." She lifted her head and pounded a gentle fist against his shoulder. "How do you puzzle out what I'm doing and thinking and feeling before I have a chance to figure it out?"

He cupped her face and kissed her. One of those system-resetting, sparks-down-to-her-toes type of kisses that had her clinging to him despite her knowing she should push him away. When he did lift his head, he smoothed a thumb across her tingling lips.

"I don't think you're in the right frame of mind to hear the answer to that question." She took a step back, but he took a step forward and rested his hands on her shoulders. "If you don't want to talk to me, that's fine. You want to keep picking fights? That's fine, too. I'm not going anywhere. I can't, remember? This was not the best idea but it's too late for regrets or second thoughts." He pressed his lips to her forehead. "Things between us are only going to be as complicated as you and I make them, Corliss." He headed toward the back door.

"Where are you going?"

"I'm going to join Denny and Olivia and see where our horses will be living. Why?"

"No reason." She shrugged and earned an arched brow that, even after two days of marriage, she interpreted as his lie detector. "I—I guess I'll meet you out there later, then." She stopped short of asking what he'd do once the six months was over and they didn't need to be married anymore, but she didn't have the nerve.

"I guess you will." His smile returned before he walked out.

She was still staring at the back door when

Mason returned. "Something you want to say?" she asked at his expectant expression.

"Who, me? No." He slid the blackberry pie out from under its cover and began cutting slices. "I just think it's funny. All this time I've joked about you not dating or being in a relationship and it never occurred to me you were already in one."

"I take it we're back to the 'other'?" She felt as if she were setting herself up for one massive punch line.

"It's okay to care about him, Mom." Mason handed her a plate with a slice of pie along with a sympathetic smile. "I promise. It's okay to love him."

But that was the problem, she thought when he turned back to retrieve the dessert and she picked up a fork.

She wasn't entirely sure it was.

CHAPTER THIRTEEN

THE DREAM HIT with the same intensity as always, only this time, instead of Ryder seeing his friends trapped behind the flames, it was Corliss and Olivia he couldn't get to in time.

His desperation and panic had him pulling out of the nightmare so fast he left his breath behind. He shivered against the cold sweat bathing his skin and stared into the darkness of the bedroom he now shared with Corliss.

He bit back a groan, shifted his legs over the edge of the bed and buried his face in his trembling hands.

"Ryder? Bad dreams?"

Corliss's concerned voice turned his jellied spine to steel. He reached back for his pillow, refusing to look at her. She leaned over to touch his arm. "Sorry. Can't sleep. I'll just—"

"No." She shifted, clicked on the bedside lamp that gave soft light. "No, we aren't doing

this again. This talking thing goes both ways.
If you aren't comfortable in my room—"

"That's not it." Oh, how he wished it was.
He gripped the pillow in his fist. Sleeping beside Corliss had been one thing he'd hoped
would help. Would bring him peace while he
slept. He felt her shift and readjust the blankets that were meant to separate them. He
forced himself to look over his shoulder, but
he couldn't read her expression. "That's not
it, Corliss."

She shrugged. "Okay. What is it, then? Is
it me? Is this whole us not…you know." She
waved a hand between the two of them as if
landing a plane. "It's not that I don't want to
be with you, Ryder. It's more…"

"More what?" For the first time since he'd
come home to Eagle Springs, he felt a defi-
nite crack form in the shell she'd built around
herself. "Tell me, Corliss."

"I don't know if this is mortifying or ridiculous." She smirked at their new favorite
word. "I don't know how to be around someone anymore, Ryder. I'm not sure if you've
noticed, but I have what some might call trust
issues."

"I noticed." Because talking was helping

shove away the fog of panic the dreams always left behind, he faced her. "I'm a little surprised that distrust extends to me." Surprised and disappointed. Trust was the one thing he assumed they didn't have to worry about.

She tucked her knees up and rubbed a hand across her forehead. "Sometimes, I think when Jesse took off, he ran over my heart on his way out of town. What?" She lowered her hand and met his gaze. "What's that look?"

"Nothing. It's just…" It was Ryder's turn to force a laugh. "I always hated that guy."

"Don't I know it," she muttered. "But you know what you never did? You never tried to talk me out of how I was feeling. You just let me…vent and cry on your shoulder and go back for another round. Why didn't you say anything?"

Telling her the truth now couldn't be any worse than the nightmare he'd just awoken from. "Maybe because saying it meant admitting I was feeling something more than friendship and I wasn't ready to admit that. Not until recently."

"Ryder." Tears filled her eyes as she

dropped her hand onto his. "That can't be true."

"Except it is." Well, it was out now, wasn't it? And along with his confession, a lifetime of pent-up pressure released and allowed him to breathe. "Remember my twelfth birthday? Denny and your dad threw me a party here at the ranch, and Denny made me a strawberry cake."

"I still can't wrap my head around the fact I married a man who hates chocolate," Corliss whispered.

"I know." Ryder chuckled. "I make things so difficult. But those candles were burning, and Denny told me to make a wish, and when I looked across the table, there you were, with those beautiful big eyes of yours and your grungy jeans and scuffed boots. Your ponytail was half-loose and there was only one wish to make."

Her brow furrowed, and he could tell she was trying to stop the tears from falling.

"Now, here I am." He lifted her hand to his lips and pressed his mouth against her knuckles. "Took a while, but I'm kind of proud how we came together. The way I couldn't let myself hope for. And it's okay, Corliss, that you don't feel the same. I'm just grateful you were willing to do this whole fake marriage thing for my daughter."

"And for you," she told him. "I did it for you, too, Ryder. And honestly? I don't know how I feel." Her confusion lit a spark of hope in his heart. "I think maybe that's why I was so testy about the horses. I know how to survive the life I've already got. The life I've been leading pretty much on my own. But this thing between us?" She drew in a breath and squeezed her fingers around his. "This scares me down to my bones, Ryder."

"I've been scared, Corliss. I've been down-to-the-bones terrified and had the worst happen." For the first time since the fire that had ended his career, the ghostly plumes of smoke vanished into the past. "I came out the other side. Scarred. More weary, perhaps. More cautious in some ways but more determined in others. The point is, I'm still here. And so are you. Maybe we can be scared together and survive together."

If they'd been in a cartoon, he'd have seen the light bulb flash above her head. "The accident." She shifted forward, tugged her hand free and moved closer to him. "That's what you were dreaming about. That's..." She trailed off, something akin to relief on her face. "Why didn't you tell me you have nightmares about the fire?"

"There's nothing you can do about them, Corliss. There's nothing I can do."

"Is that why you left to sleep on the sofa the other night? Because of the dreams?"

He nodded.

She touched a hand to his face, cupped his cheek. "And here I was thinking it was me that drove you off. I am so sorry I didn't realize sooner. You were right, in the kitchen tonight, when you said this isn't going to work if we don't communicate. We have six months to get through, Ryder and we need to for Olivia's sake." She took a deep breath. "Maybe there's more I didn't consider. Or was too afraid to consider. Maybe we can—"

It was on the tip of his tongue to ask if she was pitying him, but a thud sounded outside her bedroom door. They jumped apart, looked at each other before both shifted their attention to the other side of the room.

"The dogs?" Ryder asked.

"They sleep in Mason's room. Maybe it's Denny?" She scooted back and climbed out of bed, but Ryder beat her to the door. "I can handle bumps in the night, big man."

He had no doubt. "Well, now you don't have to."

"I do...so." She huffed as Ryder pulled open the door and nearly tripped over his daughter. "Olivia?" While Ryder caught his footing, Corliss crouched and touched the little girl's shoulder as she sat up and scrubbed her eyes. "Sweetheart, what are you doing on the floor? Don't you like your room?"

"I got scared," Olivia whispered and curled her legs in under her long flowered nightgown. "I had a bad dream and I couldn't remember where I was and I didn't want to bug you or Daddy."

Ryder's entire body tensed, but one meaningful look from Corliss had him forcing himself to relax. He bent down to meet Olivia's gaze. "You could never bug me, Olivia." He knew it would take time to prove this to her, but sometimes, words were all he could give her.

She looked up at him, chin trembling. "I'm a big girl now. Grandpa said bad dreams build character and that they don't mean anything. But I was scared, Daddy."

She'd come to him yet stopped at the threshold.

Pride and pain struck in equal measure.

"Your grandfather is wrong." It was the first time he'd come right out and said it, and as he did, he held out his arms. His heart seized as Olivia threw herself at him. He clung to her as tightly as he'd wanted to for the past eighteen months. "I don't want you to ever think you can't come to me about anything, Olivia. You understand me? Anytime of the day or night. I will never, ever be upset about that, no matter how big you get."

"You mean it?" Olivia mumbled against his neck as he stood up, still cradling her in his arms.

"I've never meant anything more. You want me to take you back to your room and tuck you in again?"

Olivia shrugged.

"Olivia?" Corliss came up behind her and laid a gentle hand on her back. "Do you want to stay here with me and your dad? We can leave the light on if you want."

Olivia turned her head and sniffled. Ryder could feel her tears on his skin. "Really?"

Ryder turned and looked at Corliss, silently

asking the same question. The idea of keeping Olivia at heart's length was already gone. The only thing to do now was to embrace the relationship she and his daughter were building and handle the fallout when it happened.

Corliss nodded. "Really. Come on. Both of you," she urged them back into the bedroom and, before she closed the door, retrieved the blanket, pillow, along with Ernie, her stuffed polar bear, and the stuffed horse they'd won for her in Montana.

Ryder set Olivia on the mattress and she scrambled like a seasoned pro right into the center of the bed.

"Fair warning," Corliss told her as she handed over the animals and plucked the blankets back. "I'm getting up in just a few hours."

"That's okay. As long as I don't have any more bad dreams, I can sleep through any noises," Olivia announced.

"Good to know." Ryder walked around to his side of the bed and climbed in.

"Closer, please." Olivia grabbed each of their arms and tugged them near.

"Oh, you're a snuggler, then," Corliss teased. "Mason used to do this when he was little. And then I used to tickle him to make him fall asleep."

"I'm not ticklish," Olivia announced as Ryder pressed a kiss to the top of his daughter's head. "Daddy, do bad dreams come back?"

Ryder hesitated and looked over Olivia's head at Corliss as he answered. "Sometimes. But the bad dreams can't hurt you. Not unless you let them."

"How do you let dreams hurt you?" She tilted her chin back until her head rested on Corliss's shoulder.

"By keeping them to ourselves," he told her.

"Bad dreams only have as much power as we give them," Corliss added, looking knowingly at Ryder. "And talking about them gives them someplace else to go. It gives you someone else to fight them with."

"Oh. Okay." Olivia smothered a yawn. "You can turn the light out now, Miss Corliss. I'm not scared anymore."

"Good." Corliss reached back and flipped off the light.

It took a moment for his eyes to adjust, but

when they did, Ryder saw Corliss watching and smiling at him in the dark.

And that was enough to keep the dreams at bay for the rest of the night. Possibly forever.

"I DON'T KNOW about this." Olivia scrunched up her face, planted her hands on her hips and stared at the stirrup she was supposed to slip her foot into. She'd been here for nearly a week and, despite her sudden bout of reticence over riding, Olivia had fallen into ranch life—and its early to rise schedule—fairly easily.

Ryder and Corliss had fallen into a pattern, as well, but it was obvious, at least to Corliss, that their fledgling and somewhat confused union was still finding its footing.

This morning had dawned bright and sunny and, contrary to Olivia's declaration the other night of being able to sleep through any noises, she was up the second she heard Corliss starting the morning coffee. Now, with a couple of days and breakfast behind them, Olivia lifted one booted foot, examined it, then shook her riding-helmet-encased head. "I don't think I bend so good. Uh-uh."

Corliss had wondered when reality would

come into play for the little girl. After Justin Bluefield had delivered Ryder's three horses, Olivia had been chattering nonstop about wanting to learn to ride, but she'd had to wait until both Corliss and Ryder felt she understood enough about horses and their care to take the next step.

Olivia also had obligations to fulfill first: meeting her new teacher on Wednesday morning, followed by another meeting with the private tutor Ryder had hired for Olivia's bonus math, science and chess lessons. Olivia hadn't liked the idea of having homework already, but she'd gotten it out of the way quickly, thanks to her freshly painted desk and bookcase Nash and Mason had arranged in her bedroom. They had dropped into a good schedule that had Olivia alternating between working in the stables with the horses in the morning and helping Mason with breakfast.

The routine—firmly tied around family—put Corliss's plan to prevent Olivia from getting too emotionally attached to the Blackwells in serious jeopardy.

In six months, it was going to be excruciating to say good-bye to her, but she'd meant it when she'd told Ryder she would always be Olivia's friend.

Corliss's mood, however, dipped with each passing day. Between not hearing from Big E and the looming threat of Olivia's grandparents showing up, there was no telling what the hours held. As far as her great-uncle was concerned, he'd promised to let her know this week if the deal was a go. It was Friday and the week was nearly over. Yet she hadn't gotten a call from Big E or confirmation that she and Nash could go ahead with purchasing the new horses Nash would train for sale.

Friday did bring something joyful though. Corliss's promised riding-class time—it was obvious Olivia had come to the conclusion cowgirl-ing was nowhere in her future. "I'm too little," she announced.

Ambrosia, as sweet tempered as her name implied, turned her head and nudged Olivia's arm, as if to say, "Get on with it already!"

"There's no such thing as too little," Corliss told her gently. "I was years younger than you when I was first in the saddle. Besides, it helps being able to ride around here. Wyoming is a big place." She stopped short of saying the Flying Spur as this wasn't going to be Olivia's forever home. "Most everyone rides around here, Olivia. Maybe you should reconsider?" Corliss had suggested to Ryder she might be the better one to teach Olivia how to ride. Now, she wasn't so sure. The more time she spent with the little girl, the deeper Olivia slipped into her heart.

"Pretty soon I bet you'll be able to jump into the saddle without any help. Come on, Olivia." Corliss motioned for the little girl to take hold of the reins and led Ambrosia over to the fenced riding paddock. "Climb up here."

"Climb? Up there?" Olivia shot Corliss an I-don't-think-so look. "What if I fall?"

"Then you'll get up and try again." Coddling and humoring didn't have any place on a ranch. Olivia had to learn the ins and outs of ranch life, be able to take care of herself around horses and animals. "Bumps and bruises and scrapes are all going to happen, Olivia. On or off a ranch." She motioned for Olivia to climb up the fence slats. "Just hold on and pull yourself up. You know how to climb, right?"

"I guess." Olivia still didn't look convinced. She managed, not quite as gracefully as Corliss had expected, but she finally planted her backside on the top rail. "Is that it?"

"Swing your legs over here." Corliss tied off Ambrosia's lead and gave the horse a good, solid, scrubbing pet. Ryder had chosen his horses well and this one in particular seemed to have been made just for Olivia. She positioned Ambrosia right in front of Olivia. "Okay, here's how you're going to get in the saddle. We'll put your foot right here." She settled Olivia's left boot firmly in the stirrup and pointed to the saddle horn. "Grab that with your left hand. And you're going to swing your right leg up and over the saddle, okay?"

"Okay." There was a tremor of fear in her voice, but also a determination Corliss recognized as completely Ryder. "I thought this was going to be fun."

"How about you wait and decide if you've had fun once we're done for the day? Ready?" She stepped back and kept her hands up close to Olivia as the girl followed Corliss's instructions. Once she was sitting up straight in the saddle, something akin to wonder exploded in her eyes. "See? You did that like a pro!"

Corliss patted Olivia's leg. "Can you settle your right foot the way I did your left?"

"Like this?" Olivia scrunched her face again and bent down to adjust her boot.

Corliss untied Ambrosia's lead, walked around the front of the horse and examined Olivia's placement. "Perfect. You're impressing me already. How does the saddle feel?"

"Weird." Olivia squirmed a bit. "But I don't think I'm going to fall off."

"Hey." Corliss reached up and took the little girl's hand. "We all fall off at some point. It's part of learning. And so is getting back up on the horse, yeah?"

Olivia nodded. "Yeah."

"Hey, Mom!" Mason jogged over. "Are Gran and Adele going to be back for dinner?"

"Doubtful," Corliss told him. "Adele mentioned taking Gran to see Harriet at the Cranky Crow after running errands. Why?"

"Gran's tired of chicken but I've got a new recipe I want to try."

"Consider yourself safe from chicken backlash."

"Will there be biscuits?" Olivia said hopefully.

"Of course." Mason scoffed as if there was

any doubt. "If you're done riding in time, you can help me make them."

Corliss looked at her son and thought back to her tough conversation with Ryder in Montana. Lying to her family—to her son—might have been the right thing to do at the start, but now she couldn't help but wonder if Ryder had been correct. Mason had stepped into the big brother role with such enthusiasm, she couldn't help but worry what would happen when she and Ryder went their separate ways.

But what would she change? And how would she change it? Cooking duties aside, Mason had introduced Olivia to various ranch responsibilities and also video games, no doubt so he'd have someone new to challenge him since Nash and Levi had both gotten too good for Mason's Blackwell ego. They'd bonded. Despite her assumption the family fit would be more difficult, they'd exceeded expectations and created complications Ryder, but not Corliss, had foreseen. There was no changing the past. But the future? That had yet to be decided.

"How long do I have to ride?" Olivia asked after Mason had headed inside.

"You just want to get this over with so you

can make more biscuits, don't you?" Corliss teased. "It won't be for long. Just until you feel a little more comfortable up there. I'll lead Ambrosia for a while so you can get the feel of being in the saddle. Hang on to the horn, remember," she said quickly when Olivia wobbled once Ambrosia began to move.

"Are we going to run?" Olivia called, after only a few steps.

"Not today," Corliss told her. "Let's get your walking legs under you first."

"M'kay." The fear was fading from her face, and the white-knuckled hold she had on the horn began to ease. By the time they circled the paddock three times, the excitement Olivia had displayed before today had returned. "This is amazing!" she called, her voice bouncing as she jiggled in the saddle. "I could do this forever!"

And just like that, Corliss thought as she led her around the paddock for the fourth time, a new Blackwell—however temporary— was born.

"I FORGOT HOW you feel a day's work in every muscle and joint." Ryder did his best not to cringe as he dropped out of Nash's truck.

Spending the morning and half the afternoon repairing fence hadn't exactly been on his wish list, but it had felt good to be doing something worthwhile. Helping out the Flying Spur was one reason he was here, but his heart wasn't in ranching. It never had been, which is why he'd accepted a training contract with Roustabouts ten years ago.

"We'll get you back in to ranch life yet," Nash teased as he slammed his door. "You coming inside?"

"Just texting Corliss." He had no sooner sent the message than he got a response. He grinned, shook his head. "Apparently Olivia's a natural on horseback. They're in the—"

"Looks like we've got company." Nash rounded the back of his truck and gestured to the car making its way down the dusty road.

"You expecting someone?" Even as Ryder asked, he took a step forward and frowned. "Who drives a sedan around here?"

"Bankers with bad news," Nash said.

It wasn't a banker. The ka-thudding in Ryder's chest was like an alarm sounding. Time to put his and Corliss's "marriage" to the test. Literally and figuratively.

As the car parked behind Nash's vehicle,

the familiar silver-streaked head that emerged from the driver's side had every ounce of contentment draining out of Ryder's body. The older couple, as usual, looked picture-perfect, without a crease or loose shoelace. "Whitlock. Vivian."

"Your former in-laws?" Nash asked quietly.

"In the flesh." Leaving his brother-in-law to follow, Ryder removed his hat, smoothed his hair and approached Olivia's grandparents. "Welcome to Wyoming."

Vivian Standish seemed surprised at his openness as the guarded uncertainty faded from her Florida-suntanned face. The long silk skirt and blouse she wore had no business on a ranch and were as impractical as the designer heels on her feet. "I hope we aren't intruding," she said, shooting a look at her husband. "We were afraid if we called first—"

"You'd find a way to keep us from seeing our granddaughter," Whitlock finished, clearly ignoring his wife's warning.

About this time was when Ryder normally would have felt those knots of apprehension and stress cinching so tight that he couldn't breathe. But they weren't on Whitlock's turf

now. They were on his. And his relationship with Corliss had shifted over these past
days. Shifted into a real and equal partnership. He was convinced they were making a
go of things.

Now all they had to do was convince his
in-laws.

"As I've told you multiple times, Whitlock," Ryder said carefully. "I have no intention of keeping you from seeing Olivia. So
of course you're welcome."

Nash, after slapping Ryder on the back
as if to tell him not to let the old man goad
him, stepped forward and extended his hand.
"Nash Blackwell. Corliss's brother. Welcome
to the Flying Spur."

After a moment of hesitating, Whitlock accepted the greeting. "Whitlock Standish."

The fact Ryder had to bite back a grin at
Nash turning on his charm calmed the last
of his nerves.

"Whitlock, huh? With a name like that,
no one would guess you're not from around
here," Nash teased. "Ma'am." He walked
around the car and closed Vivian's door for
her before offering her the same greeting.
"It's a long haul from Florida. I bet you could

do with a tall glass of lemonade and a place out of the sun."

Vivian seemed to sag in relief. "Oh well, that would be—"

"We want to see Olivia," Whitlock announced.

"Whitlock, for heaven's sake, they aren't defendants in your courtroom," Vivian snapped in a way that had Ryder blinking in surprise. "Mind your manners."

Whitlock's jaw tensed. Oddly enough, Ryder took that as his version of an apology. Rather than postponing the inevitable and anxious to get the upper hand for a change, Ryder simply said, "Olivia's having her first riding lesson with Corliss. Let's head over there right now and you can see how she's doing."

"She's riding already?" Vivian gasped as Nash continued to escort her. "Isn't that awfully fast?"

"Around here, ma'am, the faster and earlier you get familiar with horses, the better," Nash said. "Corliss is one of the best riders in the county. Olivia couldn't be in better hands."

Ryder wondered what Whitlock and Vivian were thinking as they made their way to the training paddock. The Flying Spur was homey and maybe on the rundown side, nothing at all like the mini-mansion community the Standishes lived in. No doubt they were confirming their long-held suspicions that Ryder had no business being married to their only child.

Ryder's concern for his in-laws vanished at the sight of Olivia on Ambrosia. Girl and horse were walking with confidence around the perimeter of the paddock. Olivia looked as if she'd been doing it since the day she was born. Pride swelled inside of him and he had to bite back a gasp.

"Okay, now ease back a bit on the reins, Olivia," Corliss called from where she stood against the fence. "Slow her down, but gently. You two are a team remember, but you're still the leader."

"Oh my." Vivian's words had Corliss turning around at the unfamiliar voice. "She's—"

Corliss's gaze flicked immediately to Ryder, the question bright in her eyes as he nodded and lifted one shoulder ever so slightly.

"She's almost better than I was at that age." Without missing a beat, Corliss ducked under the fence as they approached. "Mr. and Mrs. Standish. Pleasure to meet you in person. I'm Corliss."

"Hello." Whitlock barely glanced her way before he stepped up to the fence, gripped the top rail in one hand. Vivian, on the other hand, turned to Corliss and offered a smile.

"I apologize for not calling first. We should have, I know."

"I understand," Corliss assured her. "We have to pick our battles sometimes, don't we?" She angled a don't-say-a-word look at Ryder, and he held up his hands in surrender. "Come see how she's doing."

"I don't want to disturb her," Vivian whispered almost in reverence. "Our Nina rode dressage when she was a teenager and she never wanted us to come watch."

Ryder knew it had been that way because they were constantly at Nina. But he kept that observation to himself.

"I used to sneak in, though," Vivian confessed to Corliss with something akin to wonder in her eyes as she watched Olivia trotting around the paddock. "I never told her, but it was the highlight of every week for me. Olivia looks just like her."

"That explains her horse sense." Corliss slipped a comforting arm around Vivian's shoulders. "She was apprehensive at first. You should have seen her looking up at that saddle the first time. Now I can't get her out of it. She's going to be sore tomorrow."

"I'm going to head inside and get that lemonade together." Nash backed away, sending Ryder a look that wished him well.

The four of them stood at the fence. Ryder's pride increasing as he took in the fact Olivia was very focused. Her eyes were narrowed in that way she had whenever she concentrated, with the left corner of her lips caught between her teeth. He saw a hint of pink on her arms, a sign he needed to stock up on some sunscreen. On their next visit to town, he'd make sure they made a special trip to Spurs and Saddles for her very own hat.

"One more time around, Olivia. Then we'll call it a day," Corliss called from her place between Ryder and Vivian.

"Awwww…" It was only then Olivia shifted her gaze to them, and her expression turned to shock.

Ryder saw what happened next as if in slow-motion. Olivia tensed, the surprise and uncertainty mingling on her face as she pulled back on the reins of Ambrosia's bit. The horse skidded to a stop, bucked up and down so fast and hard that Olivia slipped right out of the saddle and landed hard on the ground. He swore he could hear the whoosh of breath escape.

Corliss's hand dropped hard over his and squeezed even as he shifted to jump over the fence.

"Olivia!" Her grandfather was halfway between the rails before Corliss darted in front of him.

"No!" Corliss held up her hands, and Vivian pulled Whitlock back. "She has to learn to fall as much as she needs to learn to ride. We don't need the horse spooked any more than she already is." Corliss hurried over to Olivia and as his daughter sat up, Corliss crouched down.

Ryder struggled to keep his expression and fear in check. It was all he could do not to rush over and check over every inch of his little girl, but showing her any sign of fear would only increase her trepidation when it came to getting back on Ambrosia.

Even from a distance, he could see the tears

on Olivia's cheeks streaking through the dirt and accomplishment of the day. Corliss spoke to her in low, soft tones. Olivia nodded, and together they stood up and, just as Ryder had wanted, Corliss did a quick check of Olivia's arms and legs, just to make sure nothing was broken. After, Olivia did a little dance of brushing the dirt off her new jeans, then turned her face up as Corliss swiped a finger under his daughter's eyes.

It was that action, in that moment, that Ryder embraced the truth. His truth. Six months wasn't going to be enough time to be married to Corliss Blackwell. Six years wouldn't be. Maybe not even sixty. All this time he'd believed it was the Flying Spur that gave him a home, but it was Corliss, not the ranch, that sheltered his heart.

It might take some convincing, it might take moving heaven and earth in tandem, but Ryder was going to do everything he could to show Corliss that their union, their marriage, was meant to be.

When Olivia faced them, she was smiling again. Corliss sent her over, and then she went to retrieve Ambrosia.

"Grandma! Grandpa! Did you see? I was

riding!" Olivia leaped through the fence rails and into her grandfather's arms.

"Are you hurt?" Whitlock demanded as he set her back down but didn't let go, as if he needed reassurance. "Are you—"

"Grandpa," Olivia admonished and rolled her eyes. "That was the third time I fell today. I'm really good at it! Hi, Grandma."

"Hi, baby." Vivian had locked her arms around Olivia and still seemed to be shaking even as she hugged her. "You gave us a right fright out there."

"I'm sorry. I got surprised." Olivia's nose wrinkled. "I'm not supposed to lose focus when I'm on a horse. Corliss says that's rule one. Rule two is always cross in front of her face, not behind her."

"Seems like you've already learned your biggest lessons then, Sprout," Ryder told her and earned one of her heart-stopping grins.

"Daddy, it was so much fun! Not the falling part, but the riding. I can't believe I get to do this every day if I want!"

"Olivia!" Corliss called as she brought Ambrosia back to the fence. "You know rule three."

"I know." Olivia rolled her eyes again and

dropped her head back in true child frustration. She started to climb back through the railings.

"What are you doing?" Whitlock asked.

Ryder stepped forward, but Corliss gave him a look that had him backing off.

"Getting back on the horse," Olivia told him matter-of-factly. "I can't end the day on the ground. Corliss said. I end it in the saddle on my terms. Right, Corliss?"

"Exactly right." Corliss pointedly looked at Whitlock as if she was expecting him to challenge her. "Come on, kiddo. One more quick turn around the paddock, then we'll get cleaned up for dinner. You'll stay, won't you?" she asked the Standishes in a way that made it impossible for them to refuse. "I'm sure Olivia would love to show you her room and around the ranch."

"I don't—" Whitlock frowned.

"We'd love to stay, thank you," Vivian cut off her husband's almost refusal.

"Cool!" Olivia exclaimed. "Watch this! Can we do the foot thing, Corliss?"

"You bet." Corliss bent down, cupped her hands together and hoisted Olivia back into the saddle. Within seconds, she had the reins in her hands and was trotting off on another loop.

"Character building, wouldn't you say?" Ryder couldn't help but direct his words at Whitlock. "There are a lot of life lessons to be learned on a ranch, in a town like Eagle Springs. Folks care about each other, look after each other. And as far as the Blackwells are concerned, there's no one better to help me teach all that to Olivia than Corliss and her family. She's safe here," he said. "I know you want to believe otherwise."

"That's not true," Vivian spoke up, "She's all we have left of Nina. We don't want to lose her, too. And we don't ever want her to forget her mother."

"Why don't we go inside? I have something to show you." He motioned for them to follow, and after Whitlock cast one last look at Olivia, they left the paddock and went around to the front door of the main house.

It was a homey place with broken-in sofa cushions and scattered books and magazines on the table. It was a house people lived in and welcomed others into. It wasn't a show-place necessarily, apart from the pride the Blackwells felt for their family. He walked to the mantel over the stone fireplace, where a myriad of framed photographs sat crammed together.

There were pictures of Corliss and her siblings, their parents, and of course, Denny through the years. One family photo looked recent and he suspected it had been taken last Christmas. He reached in and pulled up the silver frame he and Olivia had chosen in town her first day in Eagle Springs.

"This was Corliss's idea." He handed the picture—one of Olivia and Nina shortly before Nina's death, on the beach, laughing as if they'd had their best day ever—to Vivian. "She and Olivia and I sat on that sofa and went through all the pictures I had on my phone, all the ones Nina sent me over the years. Olivia picked this one for the family collection."

Vivian's eyes teared up and she handed the frame to her husband.

"Neither of us have any intention of erasing Nina from her life. Or from my life," Ryder cleared his throat of the emotion building there. He felt the couple's sadness through to his bones. "I will be forever sorry I couldn't be the man that Nina needed and wanted or deserved. But I can't live in that sea of regret any longer. Not if Olivia is going to thrive and not if she and I are going to move forward. You both are welcome to be part of her life as much as you'd like. That will never change."

Whitlock shook his head, as if he couldn't quite believe what he was hearing. Before he could respond, the back door banged closed and quick footsteps pounded through the kitchen.

"I was afraid you were gone!" Olivia exclaimed as she catapulted herself toward the older couple. "Corliss said she'd take care of Ambrosia's saddle since I can't do it myself. I unbuckled it though, and I got off her bit."

"Good job, Sprout." Ryder affectionately touched the top of Olivia's head. "Now, how about you go jump in the shower because you stink."

She wrinkled her nose and laughed. "I know I do! Isn't it great! I smell like the ranch! Come on, Grandma." She grabbed Vivian's hand and tugged her along. "I'll show you my room. It's so cool! Mason and Uncle Nash and Grandma Denny did it for me. They even made me a study corner and painted my name on a bookcase!"

Whitlock and Ryder stood silently in the living room until Whitlock placed the frame back on the mantel, where it belonged.

"I don't expect we'll ever be friends," Ryder said. "But for Olivia's sake, we need to find a way to get along, Whitlock. She's lost enough. I don't want her growing up without a grandfather."

"Nor do I," Whitlock agreed. After a moment, he gave Ryder a slow nod. "I think maybe I could do with a drink. Don't suppose there's any Scotch?"

"There is." Ryder smiled. "But if you're interested in trying something local, we've got a bottle of something called Mule. Come on into the kitchen and you can tell me what you think."

CHAPTER FOURTEEN

"So how long do you plan to stay in Eagle Springs?" Corliss asked the question she had no doubt Ryder wanted to.

Now that the impending doom of Olivia's grandparents' arrival had happened and the visit, near as she could tell, was going well, the pressure lifted and she felt… Well, she felt almost daring. More than once over Mason's chicken dinner she'd locked gazes with Ryder and shared a secret smile. Under the table, he'd caught hold of her hand and squeezed, causing a twisty dance of excitement to run through her, which she hadn't let herself embrace before now. Add in homemade peanut butter brownies and Olivia's animated descriptions of ranch life, and Corliss pushed their worries aside and let go of the fear.

Not that Corliss hadn't noticed the icy tension between Ryder and Whitlock—at least, at first. She had yet to get a private word with Ryder to find out what had transpired be-

tween the time they'd been outside the house
to the time dinner was served, but she'd bet
big money it had something to do with the
Mule that Ryder and Whitlock had shared.
The judge had actually managed a few smiles
and even cracked a joke at dinner.

"We thought we'd stay in town, at least
until Olivia started school," Vivian said.
Mason poured Whitlock a large cup of coffee. "We have a room at the Barn Door Inn.
Charming little place. It has its own little
bookstore just off the registration desk."

"You should try their café for breakfast,"
Corliss told her. "Best ham and egg biscuits and
red-eye gravy in the county. Present company
excluded," she added quickly when Mason and
Olivia began to object. "Your granddaughter's
turning into quite the baker," she added.

"I was going to help with the biscuits tonight, but I was riding still," Olivia said.
"Mason told me I'm not bad to have around."
She sat up straighter in her chair. "I think that
means I don't annoy him."

"Not yet, anyway," Mason teased. "And
just so you know, Mr. and Mrs. Standish, the
high school is right next door to the gram-
mar school. Olivia gets into any issues or has
problems, I'll be right there."

Corliss leaned in and smiled at her son even as regret resurfaced. "Sometimes, he's too good to be true," she said, chuckling at his blush. "Hard to believe he's incapable of getting his laundry into the hamper."

"Ha, ha, Mom." Mason grimaced.

"We appreciate knowing Olivia has a good support system here," Vivian said. "It'll make going back to Florida a little easier."

Corliss could only imagine how difficult it would be for them to leave Olivia behind. The young girl had certainly managed to make an indelible impression on Corliss just after a few days.

Across the room, Nash's cell phone buzzed for the third time since dinner began. It earned him a wide-eyed challenge from Olivia. "I know, I know," he said before she could chide him for leaving to answer the call. "No cell phones or tablets at the table. I bet you'll grow up to be a sheriff someday."

Corliss got up to refill her coffee, only to stop with the pot in her hand. "Does anyone hear that noise?"

"Sounds like a muffled jet engine," Ryder said.

"Is there an airport nearby?" Whitlock asked. "I thought we flew into the closest one."

"You did," Corliss said. "No, that's a truck or something." She glanced out the window, saw the sun had just about set. "If you all would finish those brownies so I don't come down here at midnight and polish them off, that would be great." She flashed a smile before she headed to the front door, Ryder right on her heels. He clicked on the porch light as she stepped outside. "Someone must have taken a wrong turn."

As the vehicle drew nearer, Ryder muttered, "Oh boy."

"Oh boy, what? Do you know who it is?" Corliss squinted, trying to get a better look at the giant metal circle on the front of the motor home. The one with the branded *BW* displayed for all to see. *"BW?"* Her stomach dropped all the way to her toes. "Ryder, you don't think—"

"Oh, I think, all right." The motor home lurched to a creaky stop right in front of the porch steps. She stared, dumbfounded, as a large figure moved inside the vehicle before emerging from the side door.

"Land's sake but this place is a trek." Elias Blackwell stopped and rolled the kinks out of his shoulders before throwing out his arms. "You two look like you've been caught in a bear trap. I told you I'd be in touch about our deal, Corliss."

"Silly me for assuming you'd call." Even as she moved in to give him a hug, she found herself prepping for how to deal with Denny when she got home. This was not going to go over well. "Why didn't you call?"

"Can't have a certain someone we know trying to skedaddle out of here before I arrived, now, could I?" Big E said in all seriousness. "I hope you have a place for me to park this thing and plug in. I figured it would be a while before I'm let in the front door, so might as well bring my own lodging."

"Denny's not here right now," Ryder told him as he greeted him with a handshake. "Good to see you again, Big E."

"And it's good to be seen. This rig of mine's had better days, but it got me here. Eventually. Cupboards and fridge are bare, though. Hoping I'm not too late to get in on whatever supper your boy's fixing."

It was that Blackwell charm, she thought, that had her smiling and ignoring the mounting panic inside of her. She did not even want to think about what Denny's reaction was going to be upon discovering her long-lost brother had decided to make an appearance at the Flying Spur. "How do you feel about fried chicken?"

"I feel just fine about it." He slung an arm around each of their shoulders. "Looking forward to getting a look at this place first thing in the morning, and I expect a full tour. Oh, but before we do that." He stopped, returned to the motor home and quickly produced a folded up piece of paper. "Let's get this out of the way so it doesn't interfere with other things." He handed it over to Corliss. "Read it first, of course. Don't have to tell you that, I know. The parameters you proposed are right there and Ethan's signed off on Skyfire, well and proper. He was right sorry not to get a look at the fine animal in person. Once you sign off, I'll have the funds transferred to the account of your choice. Now." He slapped his hands together. "Where's this fried chicken?"

Stunned silent for the moment, something she assumed happened often around Big E, Corliss trailed after Ryder and Elias as they headed for the kitchen.

"I see this here's a full house, isn't it?" Big E boomed and had everyone at the table jumping. "I'm your great-great-uncle Elias. You must be Mason."

"Uh, I am. It's nice to meet you." Mason stood up, confusion on his face as Big E slapped him on the back hard enough to have him nearly pitching over. "Mom?" he squeaked.

"Call him Big E." Knowing exactly how her son felt, she smiled in sympathy. "Can you fix him a plate?" She didn't bother to wait for a response. Instead, she skimmed the contract. Her hands trembled as that dread she'd felt for the past few weeks disappeared. She was, in essence, holding the money she and Nash needed to earn their part of the ranch payment. "Nash?" She looked up, searched the kitchen for her brother.

"He had to answer his phone," Olivia announced. "I recognize you from the wedding," she said to Big E, leaning all the way back in her chair to look up at him.

"And what a wedding it was," Big E confirmed. He claimed Nash's empty chair and introduced himself to Vivian and Whitlock. "Sorry for dropping in. I'd hoped to get here earlier today, but sometimes machinery doesn't want to cooperate. What's that you're drinking there, Whitlock?"

"It's called Mule," Whitlock toasted him with his empty glass. "Aptly named, I assure you."

Without looking at her husband, Vivian pushed his empty glass back onto the table. "He's had enough," she warned Ryder, who grabbed the now half-empty bottle.

"There you are," Corliss said when Nash wandered back into the kitchen. "What's wrong?" She didn't like the dazed look in his eyes. "Something's happened? Wyatt? Levi?"

"No, nothing like that. Um." She'd never seen him so confused. "That was the sheriff." He held up his cell as if that explained everything. Nash glanced around the silent room, stopping short when he caught sight of Big E. "You're new."

"Elias Blackwell," Corliss told him.

"Of course, you are." Nash, not missing a beat, gave him a bit of a salute. "Welcome, Uncle. Corliss, we have a problem."

Ryder poured a healthy shot of Mule for Big E, who downed half of it and let out a whoop his cowboy ancestors would have been proud of. "Now, that'll take the wrinkles out of your long johns. Let's have it, nephew. With this group, we should be able to solve any problem you've got."

"Nash?" Corliss asked. "Just spit it out already."

"It's Denny and Adele." His moment's hesitation felt like an eternity. "They've been arrested."

"ARRESTED," CORLISS MUTTERED from the passenger seat of Ryder's truck. "How is that even possible?"

"It's Denny. Anything is possible." Ryder checked in the rearview mirror and noticed Big E had squeezed into the backseat. "Mason fix you enough to eat, Big E?"

"More than," Big E confirmed. "Dinner and a show. You Wyoming Blackwells sure know how to entertain. And here I thought my grandkids were at the top of the family shenanigans pyramid. Corliss, you were absolutely right. Your son is a magician with ingredients. Best chicken I've had in a cow's age, and those biscuits…?"

Ryder turned onto the road that in another eight miles would lead them straight into the heart of Eagle Springs and hit the accelerator.

"I can't believe you two are talking about food," Corliss said as she stared out at the dimming light of the setting sun. "While I appreciate you coming with me, I could have handled this situation myself."

"Consider us useful sidekicks," Ryder suggested.

"I'm perfectly capable of—"

"Posting bail?" Ryder suggested and earned a glare of his own.

"Got ya covered there," Big E assured her. "Don't you worry your—"

"Big E, I swear if the next words out of your mouth are *pretty little head,* I'm going to have Ryder stop this car and you can walk back to the ranch."

"Corliss, leave him alone," Ryder said, his humor beginning to fade. "No one in this car is arguing about your ability to take care of your family."

"No?" she challenged.

"No," Ryder confirmed with a firm look in the rearview mirror at Big E. "We aren't."

"Don't take it personal, son," Big E said, but there was a sharpness in his voice Ryder hadn't heard before. "She's striking out at us, at you, because she's scared and knows it's safe to. You won't abandon her and walk away, even though that snippy attitude of hers certainly gives you cause."

"Great," Corliss muttered under her breath. "Now he's a marriage counselor."

"Maybe we need one," Ryder said before Big E could respond. "We figured out a good reason to get married. Maybe what we need to do is figure out a good reason to stay married?"

Corliss's eyes were wide as saucers as she stared at him. "What did you just say?" she asked.

Ryder hid a smile. He thought that would get her attention, and her mind off Denny and Adele. "You heard me." He also knew her well enough to count on her not to want to continue this conversation with an audience. And they would continue it. Soon. Big E's chuckle broke through the tension. "Something tells me you two are going to be just fine."

Ryder reached out and caught her hand. "At some point you're going to have to accept you are not alone. Not anymore." Not ever again if he had anything to say about it. "Yeah?"

"Yeah." She nodded as if coming out of a

trance. "Yeah, okay. Just do me one favor." Still holding onto Ryder, she looked back at her uncle. "Let me handle things with the sheriff. I've known Grady for years—"

"We both have," Ryder reminded her. "He's a stand-up guy," Ryder told Big E.

"Yeah, well, we don't need Big E bulldozing his way into the station and giving Grady what-for when we're the ones who have to live in this town."

"I only bulldoze on the second Saturday of every month," Big E said far too smoothly. "You are welcome to take the lead."

"And we're hitting town in record time." Ryder eased off the gas. Friday night in Eagle Springs didn't boast a huge amount of social activity these days, save for a multitude of customers outside the Cranky Crow, waiting for tables. With the music pumped and playing on the outdoor speakers, the weekend had officially begun and residents were ready to let loose.

Ryder slid the truck right into one of the two empty spots in front of the sheriff's office. "Corliss, why don't you take a few minutes to cool—" But he was talking to an empty seat. Corliss was already out of the truck and slamming the door.

"Gotta admit," Big E said from behind him. "That niece of mine is a real spitfire. Just like her grandmother. Yes, indeed." Big E was taking his time with opening his door, leaving Ryder to hurry after Corliss.

"It would be easier to wrangle wild Mustangs," Ryder muttered, and as Corliss disappeared through the narrow wood-and-glass door, he heard Big E approaching. "You heard her, Big E. Give her a chance to find out what's going on before you barge in there."

"My baby sister's in jail," Big E said with the seriousness and determination Ryder had expected to hear in the car.

"Your baby sister is eighty years old and can take care of herself." Except when it came to getting bailed out of jail, apparently. "Just…give us ten minutes, okay? Ten minutes, and then you can come in. You're only going to get one shot at this reunion. Don't you want to have the best chance possible with her?"

Big E frowned. "There are times I don't appreciate logic, son."

Ryder shrugged. "It's my superpower. Ten minutes."

"I'll give you five." Big E looked at his watch. "Go."

Ryder went inside and instantly felt nine years old again. From the swinging door that connected to the fire station beside it, to the wood trim wainscoting lining the walls, time had stood still. The only major changes he noticed were the updated computers and reduced number of filing cabinets. The rather impressive coffee station situated against the back wall was testament to Grady's and his deputy's admirable caffeine addiction.

Given the fire station was next door, he'd spent a lot of time here as a boy. Before his father died it had been a second home for him. He waited for the grief to descend. Instead, he was filled with memories that lightened his heart even as a toddler's wail exploded in the room.

The station housed the same two desks, one right inside the main door with a shiny nameplate that read Deputy Kirby Tate. The other sat directly across from the two small cells, both of which were occupied by a glaring Blackwell woman.

"She dragged you out here?" Denny frowned and released her grip on the bars. Adele sat on the corner of her bunk, arms crossed over her chest, as she glared daggers at Sheriff Grady McMillan.

"Trust me, I'm just here as backup," Ryder said with a pointed look at Corliss, who had her hands full with her niece Quinn, whose screams were hitting high decibels. He hoped Corliss got the message that Big E wasn't going to wait much longer.

"Oh, hush now, Quinn. You're okay." Corliss bounced her niece on her hip. "The mean old sheriff's going to let your mama and great-grandma out of their cells in a minute."

"I will not," Grady countered. His own arms were filled with Ivy, who was looking at her twin sister with what Ryder could only describe as admiration. "I've got Adele and Denny for disturbing the peace and attempted assault—"

Denny hollered, "I didn't even touch—"

"Gran, quiet. I don't need you incriminating yourself." Corliss reached into the diaper bag hanging on the back of the double stroller and came out with a juice box. With barely a glance at Ryder, she held it out to him. "Could you open this for her, please? Better yet, never mind. Here." She handed Quinn over and did the box herself. "Uncle Ryder's got you, baby." She brushed a hand down the side of Quinn's tearstained face and offered him a grateful smile that told him she knew exactly what she'd said.

"Hey there, little one." Ryder kept his voice low as he gave her the juice box. Quinn quieted right down. It had been so long since he'd held a little girl this age and size, but it came back to him easily. He didn't miss a beat and took her on a stroll around the station. "What exactly happened, Grady?" When Corliss frowned at him, Ryder shrugged. "He's an intelligent man, Corliss. He doesn't arrest people without a reason."

"Believe me," Grady said and lowered Ivy into her stroller seat. He then followed Corliss's lead and pulled out a juice box for Ivy. "I wouldn't have if the bank manager didn't insist on pressing charges."

"That account specialist tripped over his own two feet trying to get away from me!" Denny exclaimed. "If you don't believe me, ask Adele."

Adele rolled her eyes and remained silent.

"According to Brock Bedford, the bank manager," Grady said with strained patience, "Denny was asking the loan officer for confidential information and not taking no for an answer. He claims you attempted to staple the young man's tie to his desk."

"They're lucky that's all I tried to staple! I have a right to know who the main investors are in my family's bank. We helped start that bank. I'm entitled!"

Ah. That's what she'd been after. The name of the person who had called in the loan on the Flying Spur.

Grady waved Ryder and Corliss over to the back corner of the room and lowered his voice.

"Listen, maybe Stu did trip over his chair trying to get away," the sheriff said. "And if Denny had stopped there, it would have been a funny story to tell, but she didn't. She practically tackled Brock when he dove in to try to save Stu. It took two tellers to get her to step back so they could help him up."

"And how does Adele fit into this?" Corliss asked.

Grady patiently rubbed a hand across the back of his neck. "Seems she and the twins came in to see what was taking Denny so long, saw the tellers holding Denny back and…took exception to anyone manhandling her grandmother. Suffice it to say, chaos ensued, the kids started screaming, and the assistant manager hit the panic button…"

"Okay, I got it." Corliss held up her hands as if she didn't need to hear the rest. "Let them out, Grady. I'll take full responsibility."

"She really will, too," Ryder chimed in. "And FYI, we are just about out of—"

The door swung open and Big E filled the threshold. "Time," he called.

Ryder focused immediately on Denny, who appeared to have become a stone statue as she stared at the brother she hadn't seen in more than sixty years.

There was no expression on her face. No movement in her body to tell them anything about what might be going through her mind. But if that set jaw was any indication, she was neither surprised nor amused at Elias Blackwell's showing up.

"I gave you seven minutes," Big E announced. He acted as if not a day had passed since seeing his sister and strode right up to her cell. "Delaney."

Denny's gaze narrowed and the ice cracked. She looked him up and down, still not moving from her spot behind bars. "You got old."

Big E grinned. "So did you."

"Family reunions are so touching," Ryder said to Grady and earned a significant nudge from Corliss. "Careful." He tightened his hold on Quinn. "I've got the baby."

"Not baby," Quinn said and went back to slurping her juice and resting her head on his shoulder.

"What are you doing here, Elias?" Denny demanded.

"Came up to finalize a deal with your granddaughter there." If Big E was offended by Denny's haughty attitude, he didn't show it. "Imagine my surprise to hear my sister got herself arrested the same night. Fortuitous timing on my part, wouldn't you say?" He faced Grady, who had stepped forward. "What's it going to take to get my sister and great-niece out of here?"

"Same old Elias," Denny muttered.

"Truer words," Elias confirmed. "So, Sheriff? My other great-niece and nephew over there say you're a stand-up guy. You need someone to post bail?"

"I don't want or need his money!" Denny told them. "Don't you dare accept a penny from him, Grady McMillan."

"Look." Grady sighed. He sounded as if he wanted to be anywhere other than where he was. "All I fancied for a Friday evening was a beer, a burger and a ball game on the TV. I'd prefer not to spend the rest of tonight on the receiving end of eye darts from this one." He inclined his chin toward Adele, who arched a brow in his direction. "I'll speak to the county prosecutor in the morning, figure out what sort of deal we can make. Worst case, they'll be required to appear before Judge Harrington in a few days' time. If you can guarantee they'll be there—"

"They will be there," Corliss said. "I'll make sure of it."

"*We'll* make sure of it," Ryder added.

Looking relieved, Grady retrieved the keys from his desk and unlocked the cells. Because Grady was an observant man and because the room was thick with tension, he placed himself between Denny and Big E. "Whatever issues you two have, please take them out of public view and back to the Flying Spur. I don't have the energy for another arrest tonight."

"But you're so good at it," Adele challenged with a smirk that had Ryder checking with Corliss. She shrugged and inclined her head as if she sensed something between the sheriff and her sister as well. "Come here, sweetheart." Adele held out her arms to Quinn, but the toddler clung to Ryder's neck. Adele dropped her hands to her sides and sighed. "Fine. Tag, Ryder, you're it."

Ryder chuckled and earned a grin from his niece. "I like you, Quinn. Two years old and already full of the Blackwell spirit."

She wrinkled her nose and giggled.

The alarm at the fire station next door blared to life, startling everyone. They looked to the connecting swinging door that burst open. Ryder instinctively tried to cover Quinn's ears.

"Grady!" Fire Chief Paxton Bellingham stopped short when he saw the crowd. "Sorry to interrupt." He looked curious and seemed about to ask what was going on, but then decided he didn't have time. The fifty-something man, who Ryder recalled as always being strong and fair, scanned the room.

"We've got a fire out at the Slattery place. Youngest girl just called, said her mom and dad are trying to—"

"Josh Slattery?" Ryder asked and immediately transferred Quinn to her mother's arms. Something inside of him had leaped to life. Something he hadn't felt in a very long time. "Out on Old Oak Road?"

"That'll be him. Get the truck, Paxton." Grady got his hat and keys. "Bad timing for us. Three of our volunteer firefighters are away this weekend. We get so few calls, we never thought it'd be an issue." He eyed Ryder. "How about you? You up for it?"

The offer jump-started his heart. "Absolutely." Ryder tossed Corliss the keys to his truck.

"What? Ryder, no." Corliss squeezed his arm. "You can't. You aren't ready. It's too—"

"I can help," Ryder told her. "It'll be fine. I'll be fine."

"Corliss, it's important. Let him be," Big E said quietly and put a gentle hand on her shoulder. She released Ryder, but as he followed Grady out the door, she caught up with him. "He knows what he's doing."

"Please don't go," Corliss pleaded. "If something happens—"

Ryder peered directly into her eyes. He hated the fear he saw there, but it was time for him to step back into the only life he knew. "This is what I do, Corliss. It's what I'm good at. At some point you have to accept that. I have to go." He pressed his mouth to hers, felt every emotion in her kiss. "Corliss, please, let me go."

She stepped back and Ryder sprinted away.

The single engine had roared to life, Pax behind the wheel. Grady called Ryder over, pointed to the collection of protective gear. Seconds later, suited up, Grady and Ryder jumped in the truck.

And didn't look back as Pax hit the siren and drove out into the night.

CHAPTER FIFTEEN

THE LOGISTICS OF Adele getting back to her car at the bank, then arranging the twins in their car seats had been enough to distract Corliss for a little while. Now all she could hear was the silence as she climbed behind the wheel of Ryder's truck. The fear pulsed anew.

She sat there, watching Adele's taillights disappear, gripping the steering wheel as her mind raced and her heart pounded. What was Ryder thinking, going to fight a fire?

What if he got hurt again? What if the nightmares he'd been having were some kind of warning? What...?

Her breath froze in her chest. What if she lost him for good?

"Ryder will be fine. You'll see." Denny's words of comfort didn't ring anywhere close to true. Until Ryder had gone off with Grady and Pax, she hadn't understood the depths of her feelings over possibly losing him. He'd left ten years ago to chase after fires. Now he was doing the same thing, only here, where she couldn't forget it.

"He told me he was done with it," she whispered. "That he wouldn't go back to being a firefighter."

"Did he say that?" Denny asked. "Or was that what you wanted to hear?"

Corliss squeezed her eyes shut, not wanting to admit Denny was right. "He said he'd be fine helping on the ranch. Why can't he be okay where I know he'll be safe?"

"Doesn't work that way," Big E said. "From what I've heard about him, he has a calling, Corliss. Not many people in this world are willing to run into the fire. Does it scare you that there's a part of Ryder you have no connection to?" He waited until she looked at him. "Maybe it's time you changed that."

Corliss focused on her uncle, then on her grandmother, who, to Corliss's complete surprise, wasn't arguing with her brother. Big E and Denny being in agreement was something to take heed of. "I hope you two can behave yourselves for a while longer." She started the truck and drove slowly out of town but once they were on the open road again, she gunned it.

IF THERE WAS one thing fighting oil rig fires had taught Ryder, it was how to adapt to any situation. Fighting fires in a rural area had its own special kinds of problems, especially if there wasn't a natural water source.

Seeing the voracious flames licking into the night sky was both entrancing and horrifying. Billows of black smoke rose against the stars as they consumed one of the outer buildings on the ranch. Two men were using fire extinguishers on sections of the flames, but they weren't having much affect. Near the house, a woman and three young children stood, eyes wide with terror.

"Stable fire," Grady yelled over the siren. "Josh and his brother Matt just finished building it a few weeks back." He pointed to the east. "Don't want to drain their well, if we can help it. Head for the pond. We may need the extra water."

"I see it," Pax yelled and steered the engine to the pond, located about a hundred feet from the burning stable. "Ryder, you and Grady get the pump primed and the hose set up. I'll check in with Josh and see what we're dealing with. Go!"

It had been a long time since his engine training days, but muscle memory was a funny thing. It all came back. Working as a team, he and Grady managed to get the suction equalized and the water flowing through the pump in the engine. The cool air bathed Ryder's sweaty skin as he hauled his section of the hose over to the fire.

"Start at the east wall!" Pax yelled as he ran toward them. "That's where it started. Douse it good. I'll use the stored water in the truck to help Josh and his brother."

The night crackled with ravenous flames. Smoke grew thicker the closer he and Grady got to the stable. That heat tickling his skin and protective gear felt like an odd return to an embrace, engaging him in a dance he never thought he'd perform again.

It didn't take long for Ryder to realize the fire wasn't going to be beaten. He looked back at Grady, who nodded in silent agreement. As they readjusted their hold on the hose and aimed, out of the corner of his eye, he saw headlights headed in their direction. He also heard Josh's wife scream and, when he looked to the doors of the stable, saw Josh struggling to get inside.

"What does he think he's doing?" Ryder yelled at Grady, who shook his head. With Pax around the other side of the building, he couldn't ask the chief the same question. "You got this?"

Grady waved him off, moving up the hose length to grab hold of the nozzle and adjust the flow of water.

"Josh!" Ryder ran full out, tackled the man to the ground and rolled him out of the way just as a new rush of flames exploded from inside.

The wife and children screamed. Ryder shoved himself up, knelt on the ground, one hand on Josh's back to hold him in place. It was then he heard it. The sound no rancher ever wants to hear.

"How many?" Ryder yelled at Josh, who was coughing so hard he was almost retching. "How many horses are inside?"

"Three," Josh gasped. "They're my kids' horses." He looked at him hard. "Ryder Talbot? That you?"

"It's me." An odd calm came over him even as he heard a car door slam behind him. "To the right or left inside? Josh? Where are the horses?"

"One on the left, two on the right. In the back."

Ryder nodded, started to straighten and saw Corliss standing in the beams of the headlights of his truck. The stable continued to burn, the heat increasing, the flames growing, licking the sky.

"Go to your family, Josh." Ryder hauled him up, shoved him toward the house, and without looking back, dived into the flames. The last thing he heard was Corliss shouting his name.

"DON'T YOU EVEN think about it, Corliss Blackwell!" Denny grabbed hold of Corliss from behind when she'd taken a step forward. "Elias, do some good, will you? Tell her."

"You want to help him, Corliss, you stay right where you are. Don't go making him worry about you, too," Big E growled into her ear. "This ain't about you. It's about him moving forward."

"He almost died last time," Corliss managed to say, her throat already raw from the smoke.

"*Almost* only counts in horseshoes," Denny told her. "Time you had some faith in Ryder and what he's capable of."

"I know what he's capable of," Corliss said. She knew what he could survive, what he had survived. But knowing about it after the fact was far easier than watching it unfold before her eyes. Seeing him disappear into the smoke felt as if she'd watched her entire future, every ounce of potential happiness disappear with the man she loved. *Loved.*

She looked to Gina Slattery, Josh's wife, and the three children she and Josh clung to as the fire raged. Josh's brother Matt stumbled back from the stable, Chief Bellingham guiding him as they abandoned their efforts to save the structure. The chief let out a loud whistle, circled his hand in the air, and the water from the other direction stopped.

"Ryder," Corliss whispered. "Where is he? What is he—" Tears blurred her eyes. She swiped them away only to have more appear.

"There!" Denny pointed into the smoke billowing out of the main door. "He's there."

The scene unfolded as if in slow-motion as Ryder strode out, his hands wrapped with three leads. The young horses behind him had empty feed bags over their heads to stop them from being afraid of the flames so he could move them out of the fire.

Clear of the structure, Ryder dropped to his knees, coughing, hacking in breath as Grady, Matt and Chief Bellingham guided the horses away. Corliss couldn't wait a moment longer and ran to Ryder, dropping to her knees as he began to rise.

"Why would you go in there?" she yelled and dragged his helmet and mask off. "You weren't even wearing your tank!"

"No time." His voice was unrecognizable. "They're okay." He took long, deep breaths. "I got them out this time." Tears formed in his eyes, and in that moment, she understood. The colleagues he couldn't save on the rig— the friends, the family he'd lost that day... It was an open wound that could only now begin to heal. "I got them out," he repeated.

She had no words. She couldn't process the riotous emotions swirling through her. All she could do was throw her arms around him and hold on. When his arms locked around her, she finally, even in the midst of smoke and ash, breathed easier.

IT DIDN'T TAKE long for word of Ryder's heroic rescue of the Slattery horses to hit town. By the time he was discharged from the hospital after being treated for smoke inhalation, he was on the receiving end of congratulations and thanks from countless people he knew and even more that he didn't. It wasn't something he was accustomed to. It wasn't anything he wanted. He'd just done what he could do. What he knew he could do.

What he'd want someone else to do for his family should the need arise.

His family.

Standing at the paddock watching Corliss give Olivia another riding lesson, his heart squeezed. Despite the pounding his body had taken during the fire, he felt more alive now than he had since coming home to Eagle Springs. Alive because what truly filled his heart—was right in front of him.

And yet, not everything was perfect.

He glanced behind him, recognizing the sound of Whitlock's rental car as it pulled up in front of the house. He was alone this time, Ryder noticed, and braced himself for whatever his father-in-law had in mind.

"Vivian's doing some last-minute shopping

in town. Thought I'd come out and maybe pick Olivia up for lunch at the Cranky Crow." Whitlock kept a few steps back from him, looking over Ryder's shoulder to Olivia and her horse.

Ryder shifted, tilted his hat back. "She'd like that."

"We'll head out tomorrow, after seeing Olivia off to school. Thank you for that," Whitlock said.

"Nina told me how you used to take off work so you could take her the first day. Every year," Ryder said, "even in high school."

Whitlock's eyes shifted, as if torn between grief and amusement. "Drove her crazy. Being dropped off like that, but it was like marking off the passage of time. Time I'd do anything to get back."

"I know you would. I would, too."

Whitlock nodded. "I see that now. You and Nina, you didn't work perfectly, but you worked well enough to have Olivia. In the end, she's what matters. Vivian and I, we're talking about maybe buying a place in the area, somewhere to stay when we visit." Uncertainty flashed in eyes that had seen too much over the years. "If that's all right with you."

"I think that's a great idea," Ryder assured him. Whatever happened between him and Corliss from here on, they'd do it out in the open. Honestly. With everyone knowing. "Olivia can't have too much family around. And neither can I." He extended his hand and when Whitlock took it, he felt the last of the hostility and resentment melt away.

"I hope you don't mind me saying, I noticed some tension between you and Corliss."

"There's tension all over this ranch at the moment." Denny had pretty much holed up in her suite of rooms, declaring she had no intention of coming out until that varmint brother of hers was long gone. Whatever temporary truce had been called the other night at the sheriff's station was over. Big E offered no hint he planned to leave anytime soon, so it was a Blackwell stalemate. Personally, Ryder didn't know what was worse. The two of them sniping at each other or the silent treatment.

"She's scared," Ryder said to Whitlock. "Corliss doesn't want me fighting fires, and I don't know if I can be happy not fighting them. I was in the right place at the right time the other night." He sipped the now-cold coffee he'd brought out after breakfast. "I don't want to think what would have happened if I'd let her talk me out of going."

"But you also don't blame her for it."

He shook his head, wishing he could be angry, if only a little. He'd spent the past two days giving her the space he believed she needed. But nothing seemed to be changing. They were stuck in limbo. And he was all out of solutions except one. "How can I, when I know it comes from a place of caring?"

"Love," Whitlock said. "She loves you."

"Yeah, well." Ryder smirked. "Don't tell her that."

"She'll tell you in time. When the fear goes away."

"Grandpa!" Olivia jumped down from the saddle and raced over. Rather than follow, like she normally did, Corliss stood back with Ambrosia, stroking the horse's nose and looking anywhere other than at Ryder. "Did you see? I'm starting to gallop!"

"I did see. How about lunch at the Cranky Crow?"

"Ooooh, cool. Is it okay, Dad?"

"More than," Ryder agreed as Corliss led Ambrosia into the stable. "Go on to the house and clean up first."

"I'll wait for you on the porch, Olivia." Whitlock called and glanced at Corliss's back before he followed Olivia.

Ryder left his mug on the fence railing, walked around to the stable and leaned against the frame, watching as Corliss unsaddled Ambrosia and began to brush her down.

"She's coming along with the lessons," Ryder said.

Corliss nodded. "She's a natural. Like both her parents."

"Corliss, we have to talk."

"Talk about what?"

"Talk about the fact you haven't said three words to me since the fire. You've always said you know who I am, Corliss. This is who I am."

"I know."

"I love you, Corliss." There it was. The words he'd always been afraid would scare her off, and yet now, as he spoke them, he knew there was no greater truth in his heart.

"I want a real future with you. Not a pretend one. A future that makes us both happy. A future where Olivia and Mason tease each other and support one another because they're genuine siblings. I want to always be by your side to deal with Denny and the Flying Spur and the loan and your brothers and sister. I want a partnership with you. I want to laugh and fight and yell and love. I want more than what we've got already. It's the best friendship, but I want a marriage."

She stared at him as he approached, tilted up her chin when he reached her and rested his hands on her shoulders. He pressed his lips to her forehead.

"I want you to please move beyond the fear, to what is possible. But if you can't? I'll understand. Though I need to know that, too. I promised I'd never leave, but I'm not staying if there isn't at least hope for us. Not even for six months. It wouldn't be fair to Olivia…or to me."

It hurt, far more than the scars on his back or the heat of any flame, but he did what he needed to do. What she needed him to do.

He turned around and walked away.

"I CAN HEAR you pouting all the way in my room."

Corliss glanced up from her spot on the sofa. Her grandmother stood in front of her, her ancient blue robe wrapped around her.

"Couldn't sleep?" She sat beside Corliss, looked into the flames roaring in the fireplace. "Oh, my girl." Denny patted her leg. "You've really worked yourself into a pickle over him."

Corliss laughed. Not because she found it funny. But because it was true. "Must run in the family. Is this what you've been doing at night, Gran? Waiting for everyone to go to bed so you can escape your self-imposed prison."

"A woman's got to take a stand. Is *he* still hanging around with you all?"

"*He* is. Gran, Big E cares about you. He wants a relationship with you. He loves you."

"Forgive me if that argument seems ironic coming from you." Denny sighed.

Corliss stewed and plucked at the barely hanging on string around her finger.

"You know, as difficult and frustrating as your granddaddy was, I would give just about anything for even one more day with the man.

You want to talk about a risk-taker? I lived for a long time with my heart in my throat, thinking about him wrangling those horses. What kind of fool puts himself right there in harm's way? But I never said a word. Even as I cried inside, I never said a word. You want to know why?"

Corliss blinked back tears. She already knew why.

"I never said a word because that's the man I fell in love with and the man I wanted to spend my life with. Changing him, pushing him to change, that would have broken both our hearts in the end, and the last thing I'd have wanted was for him to resent me or worse—" she looked at Corliss "—leave me."

"He did leave you. He died."

"He died doing what made him proud, what made him who he was on the inside and out. Being true to himself filled his heart. That's always brought me a bit of peace. Ryder isn't your former fiancé, Jesse, Corliss. He is never going to walk away from you for someone else, because you've always been it for him. But for goodness' sake, girl. If he hasn't earned your trust by now, what more can he possibly do?" She stroked Corliss's hair, just as she'd done when Corliss was little and struggling with something on her mind. "Stop worrying about the what-ifs and start focusing on the what-could-bes. There are worse things than being loved by a good man. And if you reject that? You're a bigger fool than that bank manager at Eagle Treasury."

Now Corliss did laugh. "We still need to talk about that."

"Not tonight, we don't." Denny patted Corliss's knee. "You go on and get some sleep. Tomorrow, you can fix things up with that special man of yours. I'll take care of the fire. Go on now."

"Yes, ma'am." Corliss offered a smile and passed her brother coming out of the kitchen. "Nash? Why are you still up?"

"I was hungry." Nash rubbed his stomach. "Mason stashed leftover ham in the fridge. You want to join me?"

"No, thanks. I'll see you in the morning."

She climbed the stairs, slowly, heart thudding as her feelings whirled.

Instead of turning left and going back to Ryder she went right, and opened the door to the guest room.

DENNY COULD HEAR her grandson Nash's rumbling stomach from the sofa. "We need to do something about Corliss, Gran." He sat on the arm of the couch and looked to her. "I don't think I can take this silent wallowing anymore."

"I know." Denny shook her head. "Thought for sure she'd have pulled out of this by now and realize what she has. I guess you and I are going to have to find a way to show her, aren't we?"

"Let me guess." Nash crossed his arms over his chest. "You have something in mind."

"I do indeed." She nodded and stood up. "Come on into the kitchen. I'll fix you a ham sandwich and tell you all about it."

CORLISS LOATHED GROCERY shopping with every fiber of her being. She couldn't blame Mason for not calling in the order, not when she'd absconded with his list in progress and headed into town after dropping him off at school.

She'd bid an early farewell to Olivia, who was excited for her first day at school. Ryder was driving her to Vivian and Whitlock, so they could all see the little girl off together.

She chose the empty silence instead of

meeting up with them, but it left her with too much time to think.

She wasn't in any rush to get back to the ranch, so she didn't hurry with the groceries. She took a long while to choose the fruits and vegetables, using extra care to make sure they were fresh. Nash was keeping busy with bidding on the new horses he planned to buy with the loan from Big E. Big E was holed up in his motor home doing whatever it was he did when he wasn't lumbering around the ranch or joining them for meals.

The man had the patience of ten saints, as far as Corliss could tell. He wasn't budging from the Flying Spur until Denny and he sat down and talked. Something had to give and give soon, she thought, as she drove home.

Corliss muttered to herself as she began gathering the shopping bags. "Some people you just have to push a little. When they're stubborn it means— Oh, Nash. Hey. Here." She shoved the bags into her brother's arms. One look at his face, however, had her frowning. "What now? Please don't tell me someone else has been arrested? Levi? Let me guess. The twins."

"Ryder's gone."

"Yeah, he took Olivia to school this morning. Said he had things to do in town—"

"No, Corliss. He's gone." Nash's brow furrowed. "I don't think he's coming back."

"What?" Corliss snorted. "No, he's not. That's just wrong." But fear slid through her veins. "What makes you think—"

"His things are gone."

"You went into our room?" Abandoning the groceries, she stalked upstairs and opened her bedroom door. Sure enough, his duffel bag wasn't in the closet. Gone also was his cell phone charger he kept on the nightstand, along with a small picture of Olivia. "I don't understand." He said he'd give her time. Had she taken too much? Had she let fear of what might happen destroy what she had already? "What about Olivia?"

"What about her?" Nash said from the hall.

"Her room. Did you check her room?" Corliss pushed past her brother and raced down the stairs. She sobbed at the sight of Olivia's nearly empty room. Her books were gone. Her closet was empty. And Ernie the polar bear and the horse from Montana were nowhere to be seen. She ducked down, searching for her backpack and suitcase. "She has her backpack with her," she reminded herself. But the suitcase was nowhere to be found. "He wouldn't have done this," she announced when Nash poked his head into the room. "He wouldn't have just left without at least saying goodbye." Without giving her another chance to come around, unless she didn't have any chances left. She pressed her palms against her forehead. "I can't believe I let this happen."

"Near as I can tell, he's been half in love with you most of his life," Nash said. "Maybe he got tired of waiting for you to feel the same."

"But I do feel the same! How could I not...? Where would he go?" She paced back and forth. "Did he mention what his appointments were?"

"He said something about meeting with Edna Thornton at the travel agency." He shrugged. "Maybe he's planning to—"

"I don't care what he's planning. He's not going anywhere. Neither of them are."

Nash stared at her, then grimaced when she didn't move. "Are you going to will them to stay here with the power of your mind?"

She scrunched her face, slugged him in

the shoulder when she ran past him, then bolted to her truck that blessedly roared to life. Leaving the rest of the groceries for Nash to deal with, she hit the gas and raced back into town.

"APPRECIATE YOU TAKING the time to meet with me, Chief." Ryder rose from the seat across from Paxton Bellingham's desk. "And I'm grateful you and the town council think enough of me to offer me the position."

"Can't think of anyone better qualified," Pax said. "We'll figure out a way to work around your living arrangements. I understand your concerns, being at the Flying Spur, but I'm sure there's a solution that'll work for everyone."

"I'm sure there is, too." He glanced at his watch. "Sorry to keep this brief, but I need to get going. Olivia's almost out from her first day of school. I'm taking her to the Cranky Crow for a celebratory milkshake."

When Ryder stepped onto the sidewalk, that peace that had been hovering around him finally settled over him. He had a solid plan, starting with a job, or at least, he would have a job in about two months when Pax retired. Until then, he'd split his time between the ranch and town. He looked up at the polished wooden sign of the Eagle Springs Fire Department. The same sign that had swung there when his father was chief. "Full circle," he said to himself as he walked in the direction of the school.

He could already hear the cheers and cries of children having finished their first day. He picked up his tempo, hurrying so he could see Olivia exit the doors, hopefully with a smile on her face. He was late for that, but he wasn't too late to see his daughter racing around the swing set with two other little girls, laughing and squealing and looking as joyous as he'd ever seen her.

"Dad!" she cried when she caught sight of him. Olivia waved goodbye to her friends and retrieved her backpack from a nearby bench. "You're late," she said.

"I had a meeting with the fire chief."

"Yeah?" Olivia took hold of his hand and beamed up at him. "Everyone's calling you a hero, did you know that? You saved those horses. That was Emily and Claire Slattery I was just playing with. They want to be my friends. I've got friends already and it's only the first day of school."

"I expected nothing less. You ready for your milkshake?"

"Yes! I want strawberry, for sure." She considered. "Maybe not. Chocolate cookie dough sounds good, too."

"You can have whatever you want. Tell me something?"

"What?"

"Does my being a firefighter scare you?"

"Yes." Olivia shrugged. "But Mama always said it was okay to be scared. We can't not do things because they scare us. Are you still going to be a fireman?"

"Looks like it."

"Corliss doesn't want you to be one though, does she?"

"She's scared, too," Ryder said and wished he could feel the barriers between him and Corliss crumbling. But the truth was, he was beginning to believe they never would. "She doesn't communicate very well when she's scared."

"Maybe we should com…communicate with her," Olivia said. "I can teach her how to be scared but not too scared and still do stuff. Like how she taught me how to ride a horse."

Eight-year-old logic, Ryder thought. Was there anything better?

They'd no sooner hit the main thoroughfare of Eagle Springs when he spotted Corliss's truck racing down the street toward them. He stopped in front of the Cranky Crow as she screeched crookedly into one of the last spaces in front of the restaurant. The engine had barely stopped before she was out and running for them.

"You're not gone!" She threw her arms around his neck as he tried to grab hold of her. "I thought maybe—"

"Gone where?" Ryder looked over Corliss's head to his daughter, who shrugged. "I'm not going anywhere, Corliss."

"No, you're not, because I'm not letting you. Either of you." She stepped back, reached for Olivia and drew her close. "You were right. I was being stupid and selfish—"

"You're not stupid, and we don't use that word," Ryder told her.

"It's worse than a swear word," Olivia confirmed.

Corliss looked up at him, all the fear, all the

worry, gone from her eyes. "When I saw your things were no longer there, I thought for sure you'd given up on me. Come back. Please. Come back to the ranch. We'll make this work. For real this time. I'm ready, Ryder." She took a deep breath. "I love you. I think... I think maybe I always have."

"Do you now?" He touched a finger to her cheek as the last missing piece of his life puzzle slipped into place. He was grateful. "I'm not entirely sure what nonsense you're spouting about our things, but Olivia and I figured you'd come around. Just one thing you should know."

"What?"

"I've been offered the fire chief position. I just had a meeting with Pax. The job's mine if I want it. Do I?"

She frowned, but Olivia took hold of her hand and squeezed. "It's okay, Corliss," she said. "We can be scared together. I'll teach you."

Corliss nodded, laughing even as she stepped back into his arms.

"We're having first-day-of-school milk-shakes," Ryder told her as he hugged her close. "It's a new family tradition. Care to join us?"

"I would love to," Corliss said and planted a kiss on his lips. "Lead the way."

EPILOGUE

SOUNDS OF A HAPPY, united family echoed from the open back door of the house she'd lived in for more than half a century, and Delaney Blackwell was pleased. So pleased that she took a deep breath and, steeling herself, knocked on the rickety motor home's door.

In the near distance, Bow and Arrow woofed at a little girl's laughter.

It took a moment, long enough for her to wonder if Elias had gone somewhere on the property, but then the door clicked and was pushed out toward her. She stood there, arms straight at her sides, and stared hard at her brother.

"Corliss came around," she told him. "Took tricking her into thinking Ryder and Olivia were leaving, but it's the right result." She took another deep breath and continued. "Given that, I felt it was time I gave a little, too. Not saying I forgive you or anything, but... You going to invite me in or leave me standing out here in the cold?"

Elias arched a brow. "If this is cold, your blood's gone thin." But he stood back and allowed her to enter.

The space was comfortable she thought, as she took a quick glance around, noticed the laptop computer open on the table, the semimade bed in the back. His trash was filled with paper plates from leftovers he'd no doubt been pilfering when he wasn't mooching meals.

"So, Corliss and Ryder are finally making a real go of their marriage? You want a drink?"

Denny almost said yes, then frowned and shook her head. "Dinner's about ready and it's fixin' to be a feast. To be honest, I'm not happy you're still here."

"I'm sorry to hear that." He motioned for her to sit, and he did the same across from her. "Whether I'm in Eagle Springs or back home in Falcon Creek, I'm back in your life, Delaney."

"Denny," she corrected. "I haven't been Delaney Blackwell for a very long time. The money you've loaned Corliss, you didn't have to do that. I didn't ask her to do that."

"I know. She told me in no uncertain terms you did not approve." He glanced out the window. "But it seemed the best way to try to make amends for the mistake I made all those years ago. I was wrong not supporting you when you wanted to marry Cal. It was a betrayal, and one I'd give anything to do over. We lost a lifetime. Two lifetimes," he said. "And we can't get them back."

"Yes, well." Denny sniffed and shoved her hands under her thighs. "If things had gone different, I wouldn't have what I have now and I wouldn't give my family up for the world." And that, when all was said and done, was what she needed to focus on.

Elias nodded. "Seeing as I've had some time on my hands, I've been looking into the affairs of Eagle Treasury. Had a meeting with the manager, Brock Bedford, actually."

Denny sat up at attention. "I knew it!" She pointed a finger at Elias. "I knew when Corliss told me they were dropping the charges it was too easy. You did something."

"I had a meeting," Big E said casually. "Suffice it to say that Mr. Bedford has been made aware you and your big brother are no longer estranged."

Denny's mouth twisted. "Great. Now everyone'll think I can't fight my own battles."

"Not true, dear sister. Oh, you weren't able to cajole a name out of that loan officer, were you?" Big E asked.

"It wasn't for want of trying," Denny told him. "I did think he got awfully nervous when I asked about it, though. That might have been what set me off."

"I thought the same thing when I met with Bedford. I can't put my finger on it, but there's something off with the entire business of your loan," Big E said. "Is there any reason this would be personal for someone? Is someone out there holding a grudge over you or the Flying Spur? Anyone come after you or your home before?"

"What? No. Not that I know of. But that doesn't mean there isn't someone harboring feelings against me. Been doing business in these parts for a lot of years. No doubt I've put many noses out of joint." Something niggled in the back of her mind. Nothing clear or thought out, but just enough to have her frowning. "You really think something else is going on? Something targeting me and mine?"

"I do," Big E said. "The question is, what are we going to do about it?"

* * * * *

Don't miss A Wyoming Secret Proposal, *the second installment of*
The Blackwells of Eagle Springs miniseries,
coming next month from
celebrated author Amy Vastine and
Harlequin Heartwarming!

Get 4 FREE REWARDS!

We'll send you 2 FREE Books plus 2 FREE Mystery Gifts.

FREE
Value Over
$20

Both the **Love Inspired®** and **Love Inspired® Suspense** series feature compelling novels filled with inspirational romance, faith, forgiveness, and hope.

YES! Please send me 2 FREE novels from the Love Inspired or Love Inspired Suspense series and my 2 FREE gifts (gifts are worth about $10 retail). After receiving them, if I don't wish to receive any more books, I can return the shipping statement marked "cancel." If I don't cancel, I will receive 6 brand-new Love Inspired Larger-Print books or Love Inspired Suspense Larger-Print books every month and be billed just $5.99 each in the U.S. or $6.24 each in Canada. That is a savings of at least 17% off the cover price. It's quite a bargain! Shipping and handling is just 50¢ per book in the U.S. and $1.25 per book in Canada.* I understand that accepting the 2 free books and gifts places me under no obligation to buy anything. I can always return a shipment and cancel at any time. The free books and gifts are mine to keep no matter what I decide.

Choose one: ☐ **Love Inspired**
Larger-Print
(122/322 IDN GNWC)

☐ **Love Inspired Suspense**
Larger-Print
(107/307 IDN GNWN)

Name (please print)

Address   Apt. #

City   State/Province   Zip/Postal Code

Email: Please check this box ☐ if you would like to receive newsletters and promotional emails from Harlequin Enterprises ULC and its affiliates. You can unsubscribe anytime.

Mail to the **Harlequin Reader Service:**
IN U.S.A.: P.O. Box 1341, Buffalo, NY 14240-8531
IN CANADA: P.O. Box 603, Fort Erie, Ontario L2A 5X3

Want to try 2 free books from another series! Call 1-800-873-8635 or visit www.ReaderService.com.

*Terms and prices subject to change without notice. Prices do not include sales taxes, which will be charged (if applicable) based on your state or country of residence. Canadian residents will be charged applicable taxes. Offer not valid in Quebec. This offer is limited to one order per household. Books received may not be as shown. Not valid for current subscribers to the Love Inspired or Love Inspired Suspense series. All orders subject to approval. Credit or debit balances in a customer's account(s) may be offset by any other outstanding balance owed by or to the customer. Please allow 4 to 6 weeks for delivery. Offer available while quantities last.

Your Privacy—Your information is being collected by Harlequin Enterprises ULC, operating as Harlequin Reader Service. For a complete summary of the information we collect, how we use this information and to whom it is disclosed, please visit our privacy notice located at corporate.harlequin.com/privacy-notice. From time to time we may also exchange your personal information with reputable third parties. If you wish to opt out of this sharing of your personal information, please visit readerservice.com/consumerschoice or call 1-800-873-8635. **Notice to California Residents**—Under California law, you have specific rights to control and access your data. For more information on these rights and how to exercise them, visit corporate.harlequin.com/california-privacy.

LIRLIS22

Get 4 FREE REWARDS!

We'll send you 2 FREE Books plus 2 FREE Mystery Gifts.

FREE Value Over **$20**

Both the **Harlequin® Special Edition** and **Harlequin® Heartwarming™** series feature compelling novels filled with stories of love and strength where the bonds of friendship, family and community unite.

YES! Please send me 2 FREE novels from the Harlequin Special Edition or Harlequin Heartwarming series and my 2 FREE gifts (gifts are worth about $10 retail). After receiving them, if I don't wish to receive any more books, I can return the shipping statement marked "cancel." If I don't cancel, I will receive 6 brand-new Harlequin Special Edition books every month and be billed just $4.99 each in the U.S or $5.74 each in Canada, a savings of at least 17% off the cover price or 4 brand-new Harlequin Heartwarming Larger-Print books every month and be billed just $5.74 each in the U.S. or $6.24 each in Canada, a savings of at least 21% off the cover price. It's quite a bargain! Shipping and handling is just 50¢ per book in the U.S. and $1.25 per book in Canada.* I understand that accepting the 2 free books and gifts places me under no obligation to buy anything. I can always return a shipment and cancel at any time. The free books and gifts are mine to keep no matter what I decide.

Choose one: ☐ **Harlequin Special Edition**
(235/335 HDN GNMP)
☐ **Harlequin Heartwarming**
Larger-Print
(161/361 HDN GNPZ)

Name (please print)

Address   Apt. #

City   State/Province   Zip/Postal Code

Email: Please check this box ☐ if you would like to receive newsletters and promotional emails from Harlequin Enterprises ULC and its affiliates. You can unsubscribe anytime.

Mail to the **Harlequin Reader Service:**
IN U.S.A.: P.O. Box 1341, Buffalo, NY 14240-8531
IN CANADA: P.O. Box 603, Fort Erie, Ontario L2A 5X3

Want to try 2 free books from another series! Call 1-800-873-8635 or visit www.ReaderService.com.

*Terms and prices subject to change without notice. Prices do not include sales taxes, which will be charged (if applicable) based on your state or country of residence. Canadian residents will be charged applicable taxes. Offer not valid in Quebec. This offer is limited to one order per household. Books received may not be as shown. Not valid for current subscribers to the Harlequin Special Edition or Harlequin Heartwarming series. All orders subject to approval. Credit or debit balances in a customer's account(s) may be offset by any other outstanding balance owed by or to the customer. Please allow 4 to 6 weeks for delivery. Offer available while quantities last.

Your Privacy—Your information is being collected by Harlequin Enterprises ULC, operating as Harlequin Reader Service. For a complete summary of the information we collect, how we use this information and to whom it is disclosed, please visit our privacy notice located at corporate.harlequin.com/privacy-notice. From time to time we may also exchange your personal information with reputable third parties. If you wish to opt out of this sharing of your personal information, please visit readerservice.com/consumerschoice or call 1-800-873-8635. **Notice to California Residents**—Under California law, you have specific rights to control and access your data. For more information on these rights and how to exercise them, visit corporate.harlequin.com/california-privacy.

HSEHW22

COUNTRY LEGACY COLLECTION

19 FREE BOOKS IN ALL!

Cowboys, adventure and romance await you in this new collection! Enjoy superb reading all year long with books by bestselling authors like Diana Palmer, Sasha Summers and Marie Ferrarella!

YES! Please send me the **Country Legacy Collection**! This collection begins with 3 FREE books and 2 FREE gifts in the first shipment. Along with my 3 free books, I'll also get 3 more books from the **Country Legacy Collection**, which I may either return and owe nothing or keep for the low price of $24.60 U.S./$28.12 CDN each plus $2.99 U.S./$7.49 CDN for shipping and handling per shipment*. If I decide to continue, about once a month for 8 months, I will get 6 or 7 more books but will only pay for 4. That means 2 or 3 books in every shipment will be FREE! If I decide to keep the entire collection, I'll have paid for only 32 books because 19 are FREE! I understand that accepting the 3 free books and gifts places me under no obligation to buy anything. I can always return a shipment and cancel at any time. My free books and gifts are mine to keep no matter what I decide.

☐ 275 HCK 1939 ☐ 475 HCK 1939

Name (please print)

Address   Apt. #

City   State/Province   Zip/Postal Code

Mail to the **Harlequin Reader Service:**
IN U.S.A.: P.O. Box 1341, Buffalo, NY 14240-8571
IN CANADA: P.O. Box 603, Fort Erie, Ontario L2A 5X3

*Terms and prices subject to change without notice. Prices do not include sales taxes, which will be charged (if applicable) based on your state or country of residence. Canadian residents will be charged applicable taxes. Offer not valid in Quebec. All orders subject to approval. Credit or debit balances in a customer's account(s) may be offset by any other outstanding balance owed by or to the customer. Please allow 3 to 4 weeks for delivery. Offer available while quantities last. © 2021 Harlequin Enterprises ULC. ® and ™ are trademarks owned by Harlequin Enterprises ULC.

Your Privacy—Your information is being collected by Harlequin Enterprises ULC, operating as Harlequin Reader Service. To see how we collect and use this information visit https://corporate.harlequin.com/privacy-notice. From time to time we may also exchange your personal information with reputable third parties. If you wish to opt out of this sharing of your personal information, please visit readerservice.com/consumerschoice or call 1-800-873-8635. Notice to California Residents—Under California law, you have specific rights to control and access your data. For more information visit https://corporate.harlequin.com/california-privacy.

50BOOKCL22

Get 4 FREE REWARDS!

We'll send you 2 FREE Books plus 2 FREE Mystery Gifts.

JENNIFER SNOW
Alaska Reunion

LORI FOSTER
STRONGER THAN YOU KNOW

FREE Value Over **$20**

NOT A SOUND
HEATHER GUDENKAUF

B.J. DANIELS
Crossroads

Both the **Romance** and **Suspense** collections feature compelling novels written by many of today's bestselling authors.

YES! Please send me 2 FREE novels from the Essential Romance or Essential Suspense Collection and my 2 FREE gifts (gifts are worth about $10 retail). After receiving them, if I don't wish to receive any more books, I can return the shipping statement marked "cancel." If I don't cancel, I will receive 4 brand-new novels every month and be billed just $7.24 each in the U.S. or $7.49 each in Canada. That's a savings of up to 28% off the cover price. It's quite a bargain! Shipping and handling is just 50¢ per book in the U.S. and $1.25 per book in Canada.* I understand that accepting the 2 free books and gifts places me under no obligation to buy anything. I can always return a shipment and cancel at any time. The free books and gifts are mine to keep no matter what I decide.

Choose one: ☐ **Essential Romance**   ☐ **Essential Suspense**
                  (194/394 MDN GQ6M)   (191/391 MDN GQ6M)

Name (please print)

Address   Apt. #

City   State/Province   Zip/Postal Code

Email: Please check this box ☐ if you would like to receive newsletters and promotional emails from Harlequin Enterprises ULC and its affiliates. You can unsubscribe anytime.

Mail to the **Harlequin Reader Service:**
IN U.S.A.: P.O. Box 1341, Buffalo, NY 14240-8531
IN CANADA: P.O. Box 603, Fort Erie, Ontario L2A 5X3

Want to try 2 free books from another series! Call 1-800-873-8635 or visit www.ReaderService.com.

*Terms and prices subject to change without notice. Prices do not include sales taxes, which will be charged (if applicable) based on your state or country of residence. Canadian residents will be charged applicable taxes. Offer not valid in Quebec. This offer is limited to one order per household. Books received may not be as shown. Not valid for current subscribers to the Essential Romance or Essential Suspense Collection. All orders subject to approval. Credit or debit balances in a customer's account(s) may be offset by any other outstanding balance owed by or to the customer. Please allow 4 to 6 weeks for delivery. Offer available while quantities last.

Your Privacy—Your information is being collected by Harlequin Enterprises ULC, operating as Harlequin Reader Service. For a complete summary of the information we collect, how we use this information and to whom it is disclosed, please visit our privacy notice located at corporate.harlequin.com/privacy-notice. From time to time we may also exchange your personal information with reputable third parties. If you wish to opt out of this sharing of your personal information, please visit readerservice.com/consumerschoice or call 1-800-873-8635. **Notice to California Residents**—Under California law, you have specific rights to control and access your data. For more information on these rights and how to exercise them, visit corporate.harlequin.com/california-privacy.

STRS22